tenderfoot
toni jordan

hachette
AUSTRALIA

Published in Australia and New Zealand in 2025
by Hachette Australia
(an imprint of Hachette Australia Pty Limited)
Gadigal Country, Level 17, 207 Kent Street, Sydney, NSW 2000
www.hachette.com.au

The authorised representative
in the EEA is
Hachette Ireland
8 Castlecourt Centre
Dublin 15, D15 XTP3, Ireland
(email: info@hbgi.ie)

Hachette Australia acknowledges and pays our respects to the past and present Traditional Owners and Custodians of Country throughout Australia, and recognises the continuation of cultural, spiritual and educational practices of Aboriginal and Torres Strait Islander peoples. Our head office is located on the lands of the Gadigal people of the Eora Nation.

This is a work of fiction. Names, characters, places and incidents either are the product of the author's imagination or are used fictitiously. Any resemblance to actual persons, living or dead, events, or locales is entirely coincidental.

Copyright © Toni Jordan 2025

This book is copyright. Apart from any fair dealing for the purposes of private study, research, criticism or review permitted under the *Copyright Act 1968*, no part may be stored or reproduced by any process without prior written permission. Enquiries should be made to the publisher.

Lines from Kenneth Slessor's poem 'Country Towns' reproduced on page 76 first published in Kenneth Slessor, *One Hundred Poems: 1919–1939*, Angus and Robertson, Sydney, 1944, p 81. Reproduced by permission of HarperCollins Publishers Australia Pty Limited.

A catalogue record for this book is available from the National Library of Australia

ISBN: 978 0 7336 5182 3 (paperback)

Cover art and design by Alex Ross Creative
Cover photography (colour overlay) courtesy of Shutterstock
Author photograph by Tania Jovanovic
Typeset in 10.75/15.8 pt Sabon LT Pro by Bookhouse, Sydney
Printed and bound in Great Britain by Clays Ltd, Elcograf S.p.A.

**Praise for the novels of Toni Jordan,
including Nine Days and Addition, soon to be a major
feature film**

'Funny, warm, delightful!' LIANE MORIARTY

'A tonic and a delight' PIP WILLIAMS

'Brilliantly observed and highly entertaining' JOANNA NELL

'Just delightful . . . with Toni's trademark warmth, sensitivity and tenderness' KATE FORSYTH

'Jordan combines pace and humour with a razor intelligence and a deft, illuminating touch on darker subjects and themes . . . Sharp-eyed, engaging, endearing and ultimately optimistic' *Sydney Morning Herald*

'Told with Toni's signature observational humour and wit on ordinary life' *Woman's Day*

'One of this country's most exceptional writers' Better Reading

'No one does smart-funny quite as well as Toni Jordan' ArtsHub

'Fabulous' *Who Weekly*

'A magic mix of domestic drama, self-doubt, self-discovery' *Adelaide Advertiser*

'Such a clever book' Living Arts Canberra

'A charmer of a book' *Daily Telegraph*

'Terrific . . . warm and quintessentially Australian' Sydney Arts Guide

ALSO BY TONI JORDAN

Addition
Fall Girl
Nine Days
Our Tiny, Useless Hearts
The Fragments
Dinner with the Schnabels
Prettier if She Smiled More

For Lee Hartzenberg

Wait for the boxes to open . . .

. . . wait for the race to begin.

Wait, and your greyhound will cease to be the dog you know and become an entirely different kind of animal.

You can see it happen, if you look. For some, it happens at the beginning of a race, as soon as they jump. The instant the doors to the boxes lift and they are released from their whining, pawing anticipation, these dogs transform.

For others, it takes longer. It might happen on the back straight when the field has settled in. For dogs like that, the beginning is a lark. They love running, and their friends around them are all running, so they join in. They have no more motivation than that. Until, all at once, the race becomes something else. They become something else, something unrecognisable that no longer notices the barracking of the crowd or the other dogs beside them.

They have one thought. They want to catch the bunny, and kill it.

The thought of killing consumes them. They want to hold that bunny between their teeth and tear its chest with their claws; they would give their life for that moment of fresh blood. They can already taste the blood; they can smell it. They are driven, obsessive. They have no fear.

Once I knew a dog that dislocated his hind leg by bolting at speed through the slender gaps in a paling fence to reach a cat on the other side. In that sickening moment, he felt no pain. His own safety meant nothing compared with his longing to pull out the cat's entrails and yank tufts of its fur with his teeth and bury his snout inside the viscous warm cavities of its body.

During a race, the dogs never catch the bunny because it's not real. Old-timers call it a 'tin hare', this lure covered in fur on a steel cable pulled by an electric motor around a track or up a straight. It's a trick played by humans to deceive the dogs into running. There is no heart within that metal body, no blood, but the dog doesn't know that. It looks like a bunny, it bolts like a bunny. That's enough for the dog.

Even now I have memories of standing on the fence in front of the betting ring among all the other punters gripping their form guides, craning their necks. I can still feel the cold metal rail in my hands. And I remember all of our dogs and their sweet faces, their habits and their temperaments. Some were fawn, some were black and some were brindle. Each of them had doe eyes and powerful haunches and a few had the softest ears. They brought me so much joy as they ran for our amusement and profit, chasing the bunny until it seemed their chests would burst.

This is what I learned from all those years of watching: racing greyhounds are the gentlest, most loving of animals. They are lazy on the whole, usually patient, almost always calm. Yet I also learned that it's possible to start off lighthearted and uncommitted to a task, but midway become possessed by desperate wants. Only when it's too late do you discover that the thing you would have died for was made of tin, without a heart. It was not worthy of your sacrifice.

Chapter 1

When I was twelve and we lived in Morningside on the top of the hill, there were three of us upstairs – my father, my mother and me – and four quiet souls living downstairs, underneath the house. My parents' cars no longer fit down there, what with the four kennels and the raised bench for treatments, the second-hand ultrasound with its clicking dials, and all the tins and barrels and buckets, some empty and others filled with different kibbles and powders next to the perfectly good desk that my father had found at Tingalpa tip on which he mixed the dogs' special meals. There were two sets of smaller scales for the food and big scales for the dogs, the double-walking machine with the broken belt on one side that my father hadn't got around to fixing, and filing cabinets where he kept the certificates, breeding sheets, application forms and ledgers with times and distances for all the dogs we'd ever had and many more he took an interest in. There were always hessian sugar bags, some soaking in buckets of bleach and others piled in a corner, washed and dried but still blotchy with dark, creepy stains deep in the fibres and a bristled texture that made them awful to touch. On the wall were hooks for leads and muzzles and collars, and a rack for coats, and between everything were murky crevices and cobwebs and, if you looked carefully enough, the twitching antenna that gave away a lurking cockroach. And most of all, that warm, clean smell of dog, and the menthol of liniment.

It was cool and dark under there, even in subtropical humidity. That's what most people remark upon when they find out I grew up in Brisbane in the 1970s. 'I couldn't take it,' they say. They imagine sweating and flushing and their hair frizzing, and days spent under the aircon, dreaming of ice.

But in my memories it is always cold. I remember the electric blanket on my bed and my flannelette pyjamas folded in front of the three-bar heater in the lounge room and Campbell's Tomato Soup in a mug burning my tongue. I remember shivering through swimming classes and afterwards sitting in my mother's car in my clammy togs, wrapped in a damp towel, skin puckered into goosebumps. Wishing the car would go faster because at home, a hot bath was waiting. I have never again felt the relief of inching into that steaming tub, watching the waterline creep up my legs as I lowered them, the submerged flesh turning first white then crimson, the delicious almost-frozen heat of it.

In my memory, that Tuesday afternoon in late August was cold, or what we thought of as cold when I was a child.

It was the day two things happened, one after the other. It was bad luck. I can't help but think that things might have turned out differently if a few weeks or even days had separated them. In my more clear-sighted times, though, I know that these thoughts are me preparing a defence for a judgement that's yet to come. There is no escaping it – I was the one responsible for the way things unfolded over the months ahead. I was the cause of it all.

Still, it's my story. I can tell it however I choose.

The first thing happened like this: towards the end of big lunch, Trudy and Rowena and I were squatting on our haunches playing knuckles in the patch of dirt between the cyclone fence of the tennis court and the row of houses that backed onto the school.

Then Nitsy, who was lookout, yelled, 'Tammy's coming.'

I squinted. Sure enough, the blurry shape crossing the grassy slope beyond the bike racks at the bottom of the playground began resolving into Tammy. She was heading straight for us. There was no other destination possible – everyone knew this narrow dug-out space was our spot. After school the boys came here to smoke but not even Darryl Gould dared to sit in Mrs Murphy's class reeking, so it was ours at little lunch and big lunch. We'd brushed it clear of twigs and edged it with pebbles, but it was ringed by high grass dotted with cigarette butts and scrunched-up paper bags that once held cream buns, and in one corner were two split SunnyBoy cartons, still vaguely pyramidal and sticky with Orange Explosion, teeming with ants. Here, we were hidden from prying eyes. Not even the groundsman came this far.

As Tammy neared, Nitsy joined us and we huddled in a circle with our arms around each other's shoulders, our breath hot and close and our hair falling down like curtains between our faces.

'Maybe they want a truce,' said Trudy.

They did not want a truce, of that I was sure. Every big lunch, they sat in the corner underneath our old Grade 5 classroom. Larissa bagsed it by bolting down the stairs from her desk nearest to the door as soon as Mrs Murphy let us out. It had a solid brick wall at one end which the boys sometimes used for handball, but other than that the advantages were clear: it had a bench on either side so they could sit closer together, and the ground was cement, ideal for elastics and all kinds of games. That's how we ended up here, so far away, squished between the houses and the tennis court, surrounded by litter.

When Tammy reached the edge of the grass, she stopped and called out to us.

Why our primary school had a tennis court, no one knew. The gravel parade ground at the top of the school was where we girls played netball but only on Friday afternoons, when the teachers handed out balls and bibs and walked from game to game in pairs, chatting and smoking, blowing the whistle at seemingly random moments. The boys had sport on Fridays too, but if I ever knew what they played, I can't recall it now. If it rained, we stayed undercover and practised the Nutbush.

No one played tennis, that was clear. We had no racquets, no balls, no net. Few of us wore school uniforms. Most of the boys didn't wear shoes.

Tammy's shoes were shiny black patent with a strap across the top. She wore white ankle socks with a lace trim, and a pink corduroy pinafore with a collared shirt underneath. Tammy was the New Girl. We had never had a New Girl before. Mrs Murphy had told us where Tammy was from on her first day a few months ago, but it meant nothing to us. Was it . . . England? Was it . . . Sydney? Somewhere far away, we were sure of that. And it wasn't only Tammy's shiny shoes that everyone noticed. Sometimes her mother picked her up from school, in their car. This was unusual enough – we walked or rode our bikes – but sometimes her father was the one waiting for her in the turning circle near Mr Swan's office. Her father was a policeman, Tammy told us, which we thought funny because Tammy was the best shoplifter of us all, expert at slipping lip glosses and earrings into her pockets at Kmart, her skill and daring the secret to her seemingly instant popularity. The first time Tammy's father picked her up, the rest of us stood gaping, hoping to see a gun, and if he looked like Detective Sergeant Frank Banner from *Division 4*. He didn't.

I told my father when I got home. 'A copper, hey?' he said. He was sitting at the dining room table, reading the form guide with a pen in his hand. There was beer in a glass in front of him. He didn't look at me as he spoke but made a doodle in the margin of the newspaper: a stick figure with his hands in the air, surrendering. 'Always remember, Andie. Cops and crooks are two sides of the same coin. Steer clear of them both.'

I knew this already. My parents sometimes talked about the cops bashing people and the unfair convictions of unlucky acquaintances, the brute power of cops to do anything they wanted. Other things I knew: *The country's going to the dogs now that Whitlam the commo's in charge* and *National Service'd fix these useless teenagers on the news, complaining about everything, quick smart.*

Tammy's gang and ours had not always been at war. We were the girls of Grade 7, after all, and for years before Tammy came along, our loyalties were fluid, groups forming and splitting, undying friendship one day and sworn hostility the next. I cannot recall what this particular fight was about. All I remember is the fury I felt, the disproportionate size of it in my mind. There had never been anything so important.

When Tammy called out, I looked at Rowena, who looked at Trudy, who looked at Nitsy.

'I'm going to see what she wants,' I said.

'Be careful,' whispered Rowena.

I crossed from where my gang waited, fingers hooked through the tennis court fence, towards Tammy, scanning for any sudden movements in the distance, because Rowena was right; this could be a trap. Larissa and Deb could be hiding at the back of the toilet block with water balloons or slingshots. And as for Simone: she didn't wear shoes, like the boys, and could swoop in from anywhere. She was the fastest runner in the whole school, and the best at tee-ball, and at Land, which was a complicated game that involved dividing the ground by the number of players, then throwing sticks at each other for the right to take over chunks of someone else's territory. Simone wasn't as good at our other favourite game, Songs, a kind of race where the questioner faced in one direction and called out the name of a song, the race only beginning when one of the challengers, facing towards her, called out the correct artist. She continually mixed up AC/DC and ABBA, and The Sweet and Status Quo. I've never heard of either of these games since. They belonged only to us. We, or one of our forebears at the school, must have invented them.

'Andie,' said Tammy, when I stood before her. One hand shielded her eyes because the smallest glance at the sky left ghosts in your vision when you blinked.

In the middle distance, the bell rang. I hated being late to class, but walking away now was a sign of weakness. Just as I was beginning to waver, Tammy spoke.

'D'ya wanna walk home with me and Larissa this afternoon?' Her voice was airy, as though it meant nothing to her either way.

At first I didn't know what to think. Yes, wars had resolved quickly before, over the past seven years of shifting allegiances between whichever groups we were in at the time. But this time there had been no trigger: no party invitation to secure, no chess tournament underway. And, yes, sometimes a lone defector, motivated by boredom or desire for greener grass, changed sides, only to be loathed and spat at by their former friends for days. After all, we all worked to demonstrate our group's superiority by laughing conspiratorially at nothing and whispering nonsense sounds lightheartedly, while checking for an audience out of the corners of our eyes.

This was not just Tammy alone, asking to walk home with me. She was also offering Larissa. Larissa, who until this latest fight had been my best friend almost constantly since we first sat together in Grade 1.

Larissa and I were sometimes mistaken for each other by Mr Swan, the headmaster, because we were both small and thin with shining blonde hair. Since hostilities had broken out, I no longer went to her house after school. It had been weeks since we'd spoken.

'Yes,' I said to Tammy. And in case I'd been too quick to reply, I added, 'If you want.'

'What did she say?' Nitsy asked, when I went back to pick up my lunchbox and knuckles.

I mumbled, 'I'll tell you later,' and we hurried up the hill, crossed under the classrooms then up the stairs to put our things in our ports, each one smelling of overripe bananas, in the racks outside the classrooms.

The reason I didn't report Tammy's offer was this: I wasn't sure if it included all of us. Perhaps it was only me being sounded out to change sides. I imagined for a moment me and Larissa, together again, waging glorious battle against Nitsy and Rowena and Trudy. Best to say nothing for now, until the situation clarified itself.

The Grade 7 classroom was fibro with banks of glass louvres on opposite walls. It was the best room – upstairs and at the end of one wing to catch what little breeze was available – due to our seniority. This year there was only one Grade 7 class, with almost thirty of us. That hadn't always been the case. A lack of kids or teachers sometimes forced two grades together; Mrs Murphy had taken a composite 6/7 last year. I liked composite classes. I liked sitting near the aisle with one ear on what the older kids were learning, or imagining myself the teacher of the younger kids when we did activities together. Both these things made the day go faster.

That afternoon crawled by. We sprawled across our desks, watching the clock on the wall next to the portrait of the young queen. From my seat in the front row, I watched Mrs Murphy writing something on the blackboard in her small, neat hand. The chalk squeaked as she finished.

'Can anyone answer that?' She turned around to face us and tapped the board with her chalk.

No one made a sound.

'Come on. Someone must know. Where does the legislation go after it's passed through the senate?'

I put up my hand.

'Anyone?' Mrs Murphy said.

I waved my hand from side to side in an arc.

'Anyone else? Other than Andie.'

Mrs Murphy, the eternal optimist, was a rangy middle-aged woman in a tweed skirt and a white cotton blouse who pulsed with restless energy and was a better teacher than any of us deserved. I didn't need to turn around to know that behind me Darryl Gould would be asleep, and Ross Larkin would be ripping small pieces from his exercise book and chewing them to add to the collection of smelly beige stalactites hanging under his desk. Simone likely teetered on the back legs of her chair, searching for the sweet spot where she could balance with only the smallest shifts in weight, a feat she was determined to master.

The school year was half over and then, after the glorious, endless summer holidays, next year, we would leave all this behind and become Grade 8s at Balmoral High. After big lunch on days like these, only a handful of us girls and Alan paid the smallest attention to anything, and no one cared about the passage of legislation, not ever, but especially not now.

I didn't care myself. I didn't care about geometry either, or the route of Blaxland, Wentworth and Lawson or conjugating verbs, not specifically. But I did like to know things, no matter what they were. Knowing things seemed a way of expanding my world theoretically, since the idea of expanding it geographically was beyond my imagining. Besides, things tended to stick in my head even if I'd only heard them once, or seen them on the ABC news, or read them in the morning's *Courier-Mail* or the evening's *Telegraph* or in a library book. Nothing I learned in school would be useful in my life once I left, which was now only three short years away. I knew that. I had my own plan for my future and school played no part in it.

'Anyone at all?' Mrs Murphy said. 'Just take a guess, absolutely free.'

After another silent moment, she resigned herself.

'All right,' she said. 'Go ahead, Andie.'

I dropped my hand. 'Back to the house of representatives.'

'The legislation goes back to the house of representatives.' Mrs Murphy walked to the board and underlined something in chalk. 'And where does it go then?'

I put up my hand again. Mrs Murphy sighed, theatrically.

And so the afternoon progressed. After the bell, I was the last to leave because I liked to order my pencils and felt pens in the same direction in my pencil case, which was powder blue with *ANDIE* in cut-out letters in individual plastic sleeves, and arrange my books in the yellow tub underneath the desk. As I reached the door, Mrs Murphy called out behind me. 'Will your father be at parent–teacher night, Andie?' she said.

Apart from my birthday and Christmas and Easter, parent–teacher night was my favourite time of the year. It was held in the empty classroom used as a library with the stacks of books pushed to the side and replaced with stations of desks and chairs, one per teacher. Mine was always the only father in a room of mothers. My father would start these meetings chatty and charming. He was the most handsome father I knew, and everyone liked him, but the more complimentary the teachers were about me and my grades, the graver he looked. I tried my best also not to smile. I wasn't sure why but smiling when someone says something nice about you was wrong. At the end, my father would ruffle my hair and say, grimly, 'I don't know where she gets it from.' He may well have given the same response to a doctor had I been diagnosed with some disease. It was only the way he touched my head that revealed he was pleased.

On parent–teacher nights, I was allowed to stay up and wait for my mother to finish her shift. She would bring a bottle of asti spumante from the Colmslie, the pub where she worked, and pop the cork like champagne in a movie, and I was allowed to pour it into her glass and then she toasted me, and I would have a sip. The bottle was greenish glass, cold and heavy. The bubbles floated to the surface like tiny crystal pearls. It should be delicious. Certainly my mother thought it was delicious. For me though, every sip, every year, was like a test to see if I was grown-up yet, one I always failed. It was sour and vinegary, a bit like vomit and nothing like lemonade. My mother laughed when I screwed up my face. Perhaps this year, my last at primary school, I would finally love asti spumante as much as she did.

Drinking champagne and hearing my mother laugh were wondrous to me, but that wasn't the reason my report card was important. For as long as I could remember, everything I did was to make my father proud. The feel of his hand on my forehead, the tousling of my hair . . . It's hard to explain how much it meant.

'He will definitely be here,' I told Mrs Murphy.

'Good,' she said. 'Because there's something I've been meaning to talk to him about.'

The decades that have passed since that day have taught me differently, but back then I had no sense of foreboding, much less dread. I assumed it would be something good, something I'd be proud for my father to hear. Some conclusion about my character or intelligence can probably be drawn from that. Overconfidence, perhaps, or a lack of imagination that would have seen a more perceptive child on guard.

But the reality was this: so far, the world had been kind to me, and predictable and small. My world was the walk from home to school, from school to home. Add in Gran's house, Larissa's house, the pub and, on school holidays, the dog tracks at Capalaba on Fridays, at Lawnton on Tuesdays, at Beenleigh on Mondays and at the Gabba on Thursdays, and you have the universe. Nothing ever happened that hadn't happened before.

Tammy and Larissa were waiting for me near the port racks. Nitsy and Rowena and Trudy were also waiting for me further up the path, expecting nothing extraordinary.

A decision needed to be made.

Larissa nodded at me and drew a figure eight with the Chupa Chup stick in her mouth. I see now that she was an odd child with an iron will who could spend all day with a lolly in her pocket and not eat it until the walk home. She could resist Fantales and snakes in a white paper bag, even once a

Curly Wurly, half-melted and folded into thirds. And for weeks, Larissa had doggedly ignored me. This nod was a thrilling step. I nodded back, and then I fell into step with them.

As we walked off, cutting across the grass to avoid Nitsy and Rowena and Trudy, I could imagine them staring at my back, mouths open at my betrayal. It was a terrible thing to do, I see that now, but I told myself that this was not a desertion. We should be one gang, that was obvious. I was acting as emissary. I planned to argue with Tammy and Larissa for the inclusion of the others. We should be united and focused on our natural enemy: the boys.

Whether I would have done that, I will never know.

We poured out of the gate like a creek of kids, dishevelled and stained, ports in our hands. Our school had almost no truancy. Even those kids who failed every test, even the boys who were sent to Mr Swan's office for the cuts showed up every day. What else would you do? Go to the Plaza by yourself? All your friends were here, and most kids lived for little lunch and big lunch, when we played in the dirt and made mud and threw things at each other and constructed complex, multi-day games involving sticks and rocks and hiding. Sitting in class snoozing was a small price to pay for such adventures.

It was Tammy who noticed something was different about my house as we reached the top of the hill.

'There's a strange car in your driveway,' she said, squinting. 'A blue car.'

Our school was on the top of one hill and our house was on the top of the next. Every house in our street was fibro with matching grey besser-block foundations and a low front fence except for ours, which was proper timber and proper brick. I didn't need to see the banana patch or the mulberry tree or the mango tree that me and Larissa climbed, or the chook run with a dozen bantams and two cranky ducks. Even Tammy couldn't see the cement path that led to the incinerator, but she could see the top of the Hills hoist and the white back wall of the house, the one with my window in it. She couldn't see inside my room, the green-blue carpet, my Barbies on the floor. She couldn't see the gravel of the driveway but she could see a strange car that was parked there.

My parents had friends, of course: other trainers and punters at the dog tracks and the other barmaids at the Colmslie. But at home, we never had visitors.

I didn't have time to wonder whose car it was. The road leading down the hill had houses on either side but was a dead end, finishing at the creek in a narrow valley with a wooden walking bridge leading to the other side, the next hill, with our house on the top. There was rarely traffic so we always walked down the middle of the road. The three of us continued a little further to the flat part near the Howells' driveway. Tammy and Larissa stopped and turned to face me. My port, a yellow canvas backpack that I'd decorated with nail-polish stars and hearts, grew heavier on my shoulders, as though it knew what was coming and was urging me to turn back the way I'd come.

At once I knew what was happening. What happened here, historically. This was the running-away spot.

A rough circle formed around us, mostly younger kids who'd guessed something was underway. Larissa took the Chupa Chup from her mouth and pointed it at me.

'We're not walking home with you, Andie,' Larissa said.

'Yeah,' said Tammy.

Larissa's eyes were a soft brown, I remember. She had a thin white line across the middle of her nose. She was the first of all of us to have her ears pierced, and she wore tiny gold sleepers that were shinier than mine.

'We hate you, Andie,' Larissa said.

'We all hate you.' Tammy smiled, showing her perfect white teeth.

I felt my legs begin to buckle.

'You're a show-off, and you're bossy,' said Larissa. 'We hate the way you sit in the front row with your stupid hand in the stupid air.'

'We hate the way you suck up to Mrs Murphy,' said Tammy.

'Oh, and by the way, Tammy's my best friend now,' said Larissa.

The younger kids around us seemed to blur together in a laughing, jeering cloud. There was a buzzing near my ear. Something hot and sour filled my mouth. I swallowed it.

Larissa put one hand on her hip. 'The thing is, Andie,' she said, 'you're up yourself.'

This was, of course, the worst insult of all.

I had no defence. It had not occurred to me that I would ever need one. Everything they said was true — I did sit in the front row, I did raise my hand, I loved all my teachers and knew that I was their favourite. That was who I was, who I'd always been. Our performance in class was irrelevant, as meaningful as the colour of your lunchbox. I would go to the same high school as everyone else. The only repercussion of my grades was the champagne from my mother and my father tousling my hair, and no one knew about that.

Larissa and Tammy gave me the forks in an exaggerated way, with their arms bent at the elbows and their wrists flicking wildly, then they turned and ran the rest of the way down the hill together, holding hands and laughing.

I was left standing, frozen, watching them turn hazy in the distance.

My pulse pounded in my ears. I thought that I might actually die, that my heart would give one final shudder and stop pumping altogether and the blood would gurgle to a stop in my veins and whatever it was that kept my body vertical would fail. Larissa had a piano in her room, and a white glossy seat that opened to reveal a hidden treasure of music and other precious things, like a program from *Swan Lake*, which she'd seen with her grandparents. She could play 'Annie's Song' by John Denver. Larissa took ballet classes on Saturdays and had a white leotard and tights, and satin shoes of the softest pink with long ribbons. I would never be invited there again.

That day on the hill, no other kids approached me, although I knew that they were there, Nitsy and Trudy and Rowena somewhere among them, shapes in the periphery of my vision.

The jeering stopped, and the snickering. Instead a stillness filled the air like a gas. Tomorrow though, the whispering would begin.

I had the strongest desire to drop to the ground and stay there with my legs splayed until the streetlights came on.

Tammy and Larissa would be at Larissa's house soon, I supposed, let in with the key on the chain around her neck. They would be playing canasta on the lounge and drinking cold Tang from the jug in Larissa's fridge and dangling a feather on a string in front of Larissa's Persian cat, Macavity, and tickling his soft white belly.

If I could only make it home to the dogs. The dogs were the keepers of my secrets, the balm for all my worries. They made everything better. They were courageous, unstoppable; they always finished every race, even when they were sore, even when they were injured. Together, the dogs and I would come up with a plan to get Larissa back, to restore everything to the way it should be.

My legs began moving. I gripped the straps of my port and looked straight ahead. By the time I made it home, the strange car that Tammy had seen was gone.

Chapter 2

A kid in Morningside in the 1970s at home on a school day – due to tonsillitis perhaps, or the occasional horror that was the dentist – might glance out the window and see one of our neighbourhood dogs going about their business with surprising intent, as though late for an appointment. Some dogs met by prior arrangement in the bush below the oval in the morning before heading home in the afternoon for frisbee catch in the backyard and tea of scraps or Pal. Others were like extensions of parents: Ross Larkin's labrador, Sandy, walked him to school and home again. A rare few dogs never left their yard. Trudy had a fluffy Pekingese called Cleopatra that slept in a doll's bed next to hers.

And instead of dogs, some kids, like Larissa, had cats. They were cute enough, and cuddly, but were sly, unreliable creatures, according to my father. You feed cats, and water them, yet in a blink they run away to find a better family and you never see them again. Every time we saw a notice on the board at the corner shop that said *Missing: Socks* or *Blackie* or *Coco*, which was a frequent occurrence where we lived, he'd shake his head at the folly of people who trusted cats.

Our dogs were better than cats and better than pet dogs. You couldn't throw a ball with our dogs or tug on a rope – although they liked being read to and being told stories – because they were athletes. They were never allowed outside without a lead and a muzzle and when we walked them, we sometimes passed men who'd say, 'Don't you feed 'em?' My father would smile, but when they passed he'd wink at me and say, 'Never heard that one before.'

It was funny because we *did* feed them, a special mix of roo and kibble and powders which my father weighed then mixed up in a plastic tub.

When I was little, I worried about the dogs under the house in the dark in their single kennels most of the day and all of the night among the cockroaches and spiders, and maybe worse.

'It's normal to them, sport,' my father said, when I asked him. 'Dogs are like people in that respect. They don't know any different.'

The afternoon that I was left on the hill by Larissa and Tammy, I was still shaky and gasping as I let myself in through the gate in the fence then through the back door into that gloomy space. At once I knew something was different. Four animals of that size come to well over a hundred kilos. There's a heat that comes off them. A density of life.

I fumbled for the light switch. Three of the kennels were empty.

Tippy was still there, panting when she saw me, but Shep and Crumbs and Sally were gone. The air still smelled of them, clean and warm, but their blankets were missing from the floors of their kennels and the doors were open and swinging. The hooks that held their leads and muzzles were bare.

I knew at once that something terrible had happened. When I was a child, I felt older than I feel now. It seemed that me and my mother and father had lived together in our house with the dogs for centuries and that the unvarying rhythm of our days was as constant as the sun. My mother worked six days a week, usually finishing late except on Thursdays when she finished at 6 pm, but most Tuesdays she didn't start until four. My father took the dogs for their long walk in the morning, then went to the track, then walked them again at 5 pm before tea. I went with him but was never allowed to walk even one, no matter how much I pleaded.

'You're a girl, and you're five stone soaking wet, love. You couldn't hold it back if it saw a cat,' he'd say. 'You'd be dragged behind like a water-skier at Sea World.'

My father's car wasn't in the driveway, so he couldn't be out walking them. Besides, he always waited for me. Tippy whined and dropped her head to her front feet with her bottom high in the air. I sat on the floor and put my fingers between the wire of her door for her to lick. I wanted to tell her about Larissa and Tammy, but I was too worried about the others. Our dogs were better at running than any normal dog, I knew.

If they ran away, my father wouldn't be able to catch them. They could be miles away by now.

At the top of the stairs, the door was unlocked. I was supposed to get myself a bowl of BBQ Shapes and a strawberry Quik and sit on a stool at the laminate divider that separated the kitchen from the dining room and not bother my mother, but instead, I headed up the hall.

My bedroom and my mother's sewing room were at the far end, and halfway down was a shorter hall that led to the bathroom and toilet, across from the door to my parents' bedroom. Their room reminded me of Jeannie's bottle because of the purple and green shag pile carpet and the gold brocade bedspread. The shiny veneer top of my mother's bedside table was speckled with tiny circular burns, as was the bedhead and the white padded long side of the base. All of her sheets and even her pillowslips were dotted with perfectly round holes, delicate, like lace. I loved to poke my pinky through them. It was only years later I realised how lucky we were not to have burned to death in our sleep.

The door was always closed to keep the aircon in. She should be getting ready for work by now but in case she was asleep, I opened the door just a crack. Smoke billowed out.

She wasn't asleep, or getting ready for work. She was lying sideways across the bed, propped up on her pillows, in her chenille dressing-gown and pantyhose, with a bottle of nail polish in one hand. The state of a woman's fingernails, my mother always said, told you a lot about them and I confess even now to sneaking a glance when I meet someone.

My mother's were hard enough to perform minor home repairs, and flawless – as soon as the polish chipped, she removed it and repainted them a fresh colour. Even later, during the weeks we were hiding and it might be expected she had other priorities, her nails were perfect. She was convinced they played a part in the outcome because, despite the facts of the matter, she appeared like a woman with standards and discipline and control.

'Light us a fag, darl.' She waved her wet nails at the new pack of Benson & Hedges and a disposable plastic lighter on the bed beside the ashtray, already piled with lipstick-tipped butts.

There's an art to lighting a cigarette for someone else. First, purse your lips around it tight, like you're about to suck a thick milkshake through a thin straw. Next, flick the lighter with your thumb, then take one sharp suck the instant you dip the end into the flame. Then wait. If you've done it right, you won't need to inhale again. The end of the cigarette will glow like a living thing. Finally, hand it over quick. I didn't smoke. I had kissed two boys by then: Darryl Gould, who I considered my almost-boyfriend, and Steven Gray, and they tasted the same as the boys I would kiss later at high school dances. It would be years until I kissed a non-smoker and realised I had been tasting cigarettes.

'Where are the dogs?' I said, as I passed it to her.

She took it from me and took a long, deep pull, then she held the cigarette between the tips of her fingers, like a movie star. She was the most beautiful mother in the whole school, the youngest, the most fun. Most of the other mothers couldn't even drive, and mine sailed along in her own little car, swapping her cigarette between her hand on the gear stick and the hand on the wheel. She didn't dress with any particular care, or wear much jewellery. She was skinny like me, with the same green eyes. Her teeth were perfect but of course they were false. My grandparents had paid to have her real ones pulled as an engagement present, which was a thing done then to spare the happy couple unexpected dental bills. At night, her teeth lived in a glass of water beside her bed, gummy pink and bright white, grinning at nothing.

'Hi, Mum.' She sat up to look at herself in the mirror as though I wasn't there, and ran the side of her pinky down one corner of her mouth. 'You look pretty. How was your day?'

'"Hi Mum, you look pretty,"' I said. '"How was your day?"'

'That wasn't so hard, was it?' She met my gaze now, pointedly. 'Fine, thank you for asking.'

'Where are the dogs?'

'The dogs?' She looked at her wet nails, waving them through the air and blowing on them. 'What dogs?'

'Only Tippy's there.'

'Oh, right.' She inspected the end of her cigarette, then bent her wrist and moved it to the crook between her first two fingers. 'Your father sent them to a breeder. They're going to be brood bitches, and Shep's going to stud.'

I could not have been more shocked. We had owned other dogs before these – I could not remember a time when those kennels were empty – but the ones we had now were our family, my own real gang. I knew that Crumbs sneezed three times in a row first thing in the morning and that the little kink in the end of Sally's tail was from when Dad caught it in the station wagon door and that Shep liked it when I rubbed the outside of his ear. I thought they would live with us forever. The idea that they would ever be too old to race had not entered my mind.

'Where? Why? Do they have enough wins? Because you always said that if they aren't champions, there's no point breeding from them.'

She took a long drag, then exhaled in a slow stream. 'Out the back of Laidley. Belongs to a breeder I know from the TAB. And yes, usually breeders are a hell of a lot better runners than our lot but this bloke has a system. Besides, he knows half the fault belongs to the trainer, not the dog. You can't blame those poor bitches for being stuck with your father. It's like a retirement home out there. Half their luck.'

'Can I visit them?'

She laughed. 'I don't work my guts out to spend Sunday driving for hours so you can see the bloody dogs.'

I could feel my face tingling and my nose itching. I bit down on my bottom lip. 'But I didn't get a chance to say goodbye.'

She wriggled off the bed and rested her cigarette in the ashtray on her bedside table and then went to sit on the round velvet stool in front of her dresser which, together with the drawers beneath it, belonged to her. My father's folded clothes were in the drawers in the small dresser between their two wardrobes on the other side of the room. Everything about my mother was glamorous – not only her, but her sparkling crystal tray, ring holder and little bowl, and the shining silver brush, comb and hand mirror, and the soft pink of her Oil of Ulan. She spread her hands wide and, using only the pads of her fingers, picked up a gold lipstick. She removed the cap and twisted the tube until the deep ruby wax emerged.

'Well, that's a very nice response, isn't it, Andie,' she said. 'The dogs are having the time of their lives having gorgeous babies and you can only think of yourself.' She stretched her top lip over her teeth and, concentrating, slicked the lipstick from one corner of her mouth to the other. Then she did the same to the bottom lip and smacked them together. Her voice was cold and crisp. 'I'm disappointed in you.'

Of all the things in the world I hated to hear, this was the worst.

'We've always treated you like a grown-up, your father and me,' she went on. 'But if you're going to behave like a spoilt rotten little kid, then we'll have to treat you like one.'

I felt sick. My mother worked hard, on her feet pulling beers and mixing drinks, and long hours. And here I was, causing her more problems. My eyes stung. I blinked a few times, quickly. 'I'm sorry.'

'I was going to offer to drop you at Gran's tonight for tea and a sleepover. But I'm not sure you've been good enough,' she said.

When I was little, before I started school, my father dropped me at Gran's every morning and picked me up every afternoon because my mother was at work. I still stayed over sometimes but usually on a Thursday because that was my mother's night off and they both went to the dogs at the Gabba and weren't home until late.

I was about to apologise again when I noticed my father's wardrobe door wasn't closed properly. Inside, I could see a nest of wire coathangers on the floor, a wide brown tie and a single white sock. There were no clothes hanging there except for a t-shirt with the logo of a hardware store on the front and the blue striped shirt with the ink stain on the front pocket.

'Where are Dad's clothes?' I said.

She slipped her gown off her shoulders. 'Oh for god's sake.'

I could feel myself swallow. 'Where is he?'

She reached for her mascara bottle and unscrewed the wand. 'I might have known you'd make a fuss. You always were a daddy's girl.'

I felt a pain in my stomach, down low. I wanted to ask again but I didn't want her to be angry so instead I looked down at the carpet, following the swirls of purple as they threaded through the green.

For a long time she said nothing. After the mascara, she traced her thin brows with a sharp brown pencil, she dotted her face with foundation and smoothed it with her fingertips. When she finally spoke, she sounded like Mrs Murphy: exhausted by the insistence of children to act against their own best interests and driven by despair to let them.

'Your father, in his wisdom,' she said, 'has decided that we girls are a burden that he can't live with. Good luck to him, I reckon. If that's the way he's going to be, he can get stuffed.' She tossed her head as though she wore a long ponytail, but her hair was short and meant to be curled with hot rollers. Then she looked at me. 'Don't make that face. What if the wind changes and that's the face you're stuck with? We'll be fine, believe me.'

I felt myself breathing harder and I tried to order my thinking. 'Is he coming back?'

'Well, I won't be walking Tippy,' she said.

'I mean, is he coming back to live?'

She picked up her hand mirror to check the back of her hair, then opened her gold compact and rubbed the thin silk pad into the powder. Her eyes were small and hard, like dark pebbles. 'You never know your luck in a big city,' she said, as she dabbed the pad onto her cheek.

I often failed to understand my mother but never more so than that afternoon. I felt better straight away. There was no need to worry because anything that required luck would come out in our favour. We were people who understood luck. My parents were gamblers, and my grandparents, and all my ancestors back to the convicts. Greyhound training was my father's job, but his *hobby* – the hobby of everyone I knew – was gambling. No one watched television or went to the movies or played sport. They didn't listen to music or read books. Instead, everyone went to the greyhound races and spent all day Saturday and on weeknights glued to the trannie, following their chosen dog or horse, either galloper or trotter. Gambling was our religion and the TAB was our church. Yes, some people punted with the SP bookies and yes, the vig was sometimes more reasonable than the tote or TAB but they were shady blokes involved with all kinds of other crimes, and with serious people. 'Not worth getting mixed up with that lot,' my father always said. 'Before you know it, you're on the tick, and they are not the kind of people you want to owe money to.'

But of course, that wasn't what my mother meant by luck at all. Children don't really know their parents, not as people.

I'm not sure that parents know the character of their child either. When I think back to all the things my mother would call me in the months to come – scheming, cold, wilful – my first impulse is to argue. That's not how I like to think about myself.

Yet in that moment, I did not cry. I did not feel lost or sad, the way a better, more sensitive child would be feeling. I thought my father's absence a temporary condition. I knew there were such things as deserted wives – there had been an article in my mother's *Women's Weekly* – but at the same time, I knew my father would never leave me. It wasn't possible. He and I belonged together. He was the best person in the world, the one who made me breakfast and lunch, the first face I saw in the morning and the last at night when he tucked me in. The house smelled of his Brylcreem, which he applied with a round plastic brush. He didn't say much. He rarely touched me. But he was my hero, and there was not the smallest part of me that doubted his love. I didn't worry about the missing dogs either. The last thing I wanted was for my mother to think me selfish. I would be happy for them, I decided. Besides, Tippy had always been my favourite and she was still here.

Instead, my focus returned to Larissa, to my likely reception tomorrow at school. There would be an escalation, I was sure. I could not go through these last terms of primary school and start at high school as an object of everyone's derision – of that, there was no question. My life would be ruined. Nothing had ever been so important. The sick feeling I'd had since that moment on the hill consolidated into a kind of aching, gnawing desperation to avoid the destiny that awaited me. I didn't know how, not yet. But I was full of confidence.

Chapter 3

My father had not always been a greyhound trainer. At fifteen, he started at the chicken factory at Murarrie where he expected to spend his life slaughtering fowls and gutting them and plucking them bare. He was good-looking and gentle, with a fine frame and small delicate hands. He was steady and he was calm. He didn't talk much, but just being with him – walking the dogs in the evening, or sitting beside him with a library book while he read the form guide with the trannie on – made me feel warm. He knew everything in the world but would only talk in response to a question, and sparingly even then, as though words were valuable and shouldn't be wasted. In the past he'd trained dogs belonging to other people, not just our own like now, and he was tender with all of them, and with me. I don't ever recall him raising his voice.

The chicken factory was where he met my mother. She was a superior sort of girl, a typist in the office, barely five feet tall though no one who knew her noticed, such was the force of her personality. My father, patient and softly spoken, and her, vivacious, irrepressible. They seemed the most unlikely of couples, except for one moment that changed my father's life. One magical, mystical Saturday when he was barely twenty-one, he won a treble. A long-shot treble, on which he'd punted more than he could afford to lose.

My father was young enough to think this win good luck. He didn't yet know that easy, early money curses gamblers, condemns them to a life chasing that heady, opiate rush. With his windfall came a second-hand green Holden EK, the confidence to ask my mother to the pictures and then for her hand, and a piece of land on the top of the hill where they built their dream. They were young and shiny and mostly happy – although looking back, it seems my parents were actors on a stage and I was their only audience. Perhaps all parents are like that: too young and unknowing, performing what they imagined to be married life as gleaned from their own family and people they knew. Perhaps it was obvious that things would end the way they did. I know their marriage wasn't always smooth. The louder she became, the quieter he was. When she drove home from work late, drunk – unremarkable back then – and put a record on the turntable to dance to it – Elvis, that was all we had in the expensive and heavy timber stereo unit – he seemed to physically shrink. He didn't want to go anywhere; she never wanted to stay home. She had the capacity to embarrass him even when they were alone. My mother went to bed late and slept late; my father was unable to lie still from the instant his eyes opened. Sometimes, half asleep, I heard the kennel doors squeal well before sunrise, a sound that travelled up through the floor.

And yes, they talked through me sometimes. 'Your father doesn't want to go out with us girls, Andie,' she would say, while he was trying to concentrate on a race on his trannie, which was old even then – tarnished silver in a black leather case with a long telescopic antenna that needed perfect alignment for the call to be clear.

But to the best of my recollection – and it's close to fifty years ago – my mother rarely said a bad word about him before he left. Yes, she would occasionally stop in the middle of cooking tea, something she did resentfully and with bad grace, hold me by the shoulders and say, 'Promise me one thing, Andie. Never, ever get married' or 'Make sure your husband loves you more than you love him', or her favourite piece of advice, 'Whatever you do, never have children'.

Were they unhappy? I try, but that's a memory I cannot salvage. I am sure of this – the only time I witnessed them fighting was when we'd pick a new pup.

It would seem obvious, from my mother's character and my father's, how those fights would play out – yet my mother would be the one talking to the breeder about pedigree and poring over newspaper clippings of the bloodline. She would press the tiny puppies – six weeks old, some of them – to standing, and splay their wobbly legs to check their conformation and the length of their back, and feel the depth of their chest under their baby fat, and peer into their eyes and inspect their feet and prod their poo with a stick, looking for worms. She liked pups that were big for their age, almost always bitches which she thought more tractable, with a dam that was a proven stayer, preferably invitation-class, and a champion sire, possibly imported. When all this was done, she'd take a piece of old fur and attach it to a rope. Then she'd run around the breeder's yard dragging it, watching the litter and noticing the pups that teetered after it and followed it with their eyes.

'They're either keen or they're not, Andie,' she'd say. 'You can't train it into them.'

My father, who was the professional trainer with his name on the documents and his livelihood at stake, and the alleged breadwinner with an altogether more ordered mind under other circumstances, would lie on the ground with me in a puddle of puppies, playing and being climbed upon, laughing and wrestling. Then he would say, 'That one's pretty.'

This infuriated my mother. She would recite objections: his choice was cow-hocked or too small or too shivery, keeping itself apart from its siblings. Its eyes were close-set and its tail thick and unresponsive. When sensible arguments failed, she took to threats. She would no longer help walk them. She would no longer spend her wages subsidising this ridiculous folly if he refused to behave in a businesslike manner. She cursed him. She called him every name under the sun.

My father didn't care. He was the trainer and she was the wife, and he would have his way in this, if in nothing else. His pup was the one we bought. Sometimes the sweet little things went straight to a rearing kennel, but most often my father would manage it himself. It was an uncomfortable ride home – him at his most chatty and conciliatory; my mother, sitting flush against the door on the long vinyl bench that was the front seat, ignoring both of us as she smoked furiously; and me, talking with forced jocularity, bouncing unrestrained across the back seat with the squirming puppy. My father suggesting silly names for it and warning me to hold it close when he was about to turn a corner and my mother saying it could starve to death for all she cared.

Still, she always seemed to get over it soon enough, at least on the surface. As for the inner workings of her heart – that had always been a mystery to me, and I'm sure to my father also. Perhaps even to herself.

Tucked in my grandmother's spare bed that night, a thousand schemes for how to make up with Larissa rolled around my head. First, I tried to think of some way to improve my social standing so that my friendship would be valued. I couldn't.

Sporty kids could get away with anything but I was the slowest runner in the whole school and the last picked for any team. I was clumsy and ungainly, with bruises on my hips and thighs and arms from the furniture and doors and railings I regularly walked into. There were permanent mercurochrome stains on my elbows and forearms and the heel of my hand, from which my father regularly picked gravel with tweezers, and both my knees were in a constant cycle of bandaids from grazes that healed into raised soft pink scars before opening again the next time I tripped over my own feet. My only skill was climbing. Thinning, high branches held no fear because I was the smallest. Well, me and Larissa. I had won the school chess tournament – it was only much later that I realised how unusual it was for a school like ours to be so obsessed with chess – but that was months ago and, in any case, chess wasn't half as prestigious as sport.

I considered bribery. There was nothing I owned that anyone would want but my mother sometimes brought home cardboard coasters with the pub's logo on the front. The back was blank and perfect for drawing on, and there was something pleasing about holding a stack of them in your hands and shuffling them like a deck. Perhaps she would give me one for every kid in my class. Or I could invite everyone home to watch our television – colour, which no one else had. That would be a start.

When I arrived at school from Gran's the next morning though, I had no solid plan. At assembly, it was obvious that I was out of both groups: there was whispering behind hands and kids jostled each other so they didn't have to stand next to me as we sang 'God Save the Queen' and, hand on heart, pledged our loyalty to country, flag and school. In class, no one spoke to me, not even when I talked directly to them. I was a ghost. Once Mrs Murphy looked at me sharply as though she knew something had changed. This was all disconcerting, but to be honest, I had expected worse. It would have been much worse had Larissa been organising against me.

But she was preoccupied with more important matters. Sometime over the past week, Macavity had gone missing.

At first, her family had barely noticed. It wasn't unheard of for Macavity to stay out overnight, or even several nights. By that morning though, her parents had realised he was gone and had sat her down and explained the odds of him returning were poor. Cats were hit by cars; they vanished in any number of mysterious ways. Larissa turned up late for school with red eyes, not caring about anything else, especially not me. She spent the breaks surrounded by Tammy and Simone and the other girls, who were ostentatiously sharing their Vegemite sandwiches and patting her back.

By the end of the day, I had devised my plan. I was going to find Macavity and return him to Larissa.

I wasn't sure how, not yet. It never occurred to me that Macavity was lost forever, in the same way I didn't consider my father lost. Cats sometimes found a new family and had to be reminded that they had a previous one, or so he'd told me, and I was sure that this is what had happened. It would simply be a matter of finding this new family, wherever they were, and bringing Macavity back to Larissa. If only my father was here. He knew everything about animals – not just dogs, but horses too, and ferrets. Sometimes I thought he could read their minds. If he decided to, I was sure he could find Macavity in no time. I could see events unfolding as clearly as if they'd already happened: my father and me together, tracking Macavity to his new house, and then me, standing in front of Larissa with Macavity in my arms while she, overcome with joy, declared me to be her best friend forever.

As for life without my father – for the first few days I stayed over at Gran's because my mother was working late, which was unusual. After I got home, I was the one feeding Tippy scoops of kibble morning and night, and filling up her water and letting her out for a wee, and I brushed her all over and checked her feet for cuts the way my father did. Like any athlete, she loved to move. I knew she'd be tense and unhappy without my father and without a run, so I spent as much time talking to her as I could.

After a few days of walking Tippy herself, my mother made several phone calls. I listened, squatting just inside the doorway of my room. I heard her say, 'He should have thought of that before' and 'I'm not running a boarding kennel' and 'Good luck to her, she'll bloody well need it'.

My father still didn't show. My mother, grumbling, let Tippy loose in the backyard to empty out. Tippy hated this. She'd forgotten how to walk without a lead, although she was fascinated by the scent of the chickens, sensibly hiding in their hutch. I hated it too, because it meant I had to follow her around with a dustpan and hand broom missing half its bristles, scooping up her poo and adding it to the disgusting pile in the back corner behind the clutch of banana plants. When our dogs emptied out on the street, it never occurred to us to pick it up. It's likely, I think now, that the substantial amount of poo generated by four large animals left steaming on footpaths played some role in my parents being generally ignored by the neighbours.

Without my father to tuck me in, I began to sleep poorly – that was the other change. He'd never read to me, though after a few beers he'd sometimes tell me stories about the daring larks that were the early days of greyhound racing. There were tunnels, he told me, found beneath the starting boxes when the track at White City – which was a long way away, not in Queensland – was developed into factories. He told me about the monkey jockeys, which were banned before I was born, but which I wanted more than anything to see. Without him tucking me in, I felt that I was doing everything wrong – I was wearing the wrong pyjamas, lying in bed wrong, somehow. I tried to read my library book but at the end of every page I'd look back over all the words and it was as if I hadn't read them at all. In the morning I'd wake before the alarm, worried I'd sleep through; I'd leave for school and find myself turning back to check the front door was locked. Without my father at the beginning and end of my day, I had the constant feeling of having forgotten something.

The other practical difference was that no one made my lunch and instead my mother gave me whatever change was in her purse without counting it, sometimes as much as fifty cents. At the tuckshop, a sausage roll was fifteen cents and a Wagon Wheel was eight, so this made me a millionaire. I imagined that my father had taken the dogs to a meeting far away – the Tweed perhaps, or even as far as Casino – and that he'd be home soon, a winner.

These were all small, surface adjustments. What I know first-hand about the upheavals that were roiling inside my mother came one afternoon the following week, when I found her waiting by the port racks when school finished.

She had picked me up from school only twice before – once when Tippy won her maiden and my mother was too excited to wait until I walked home to tell me, and last year when my other grandmother died and we had to get the house ready for visitors in a hurry. Even if being picked up had been usual, though, I'd still have sensed that afternoon was not. I had a vigilance around my mother, a sensitivity to anything out of the ordinary: a different rhythm of her heels tapping on the verandah, or the strap of her handbag pulled taut, compared with its usual relaxed slouch.

The other kids gave me an even wider berth when they saw her.

'Get a move on, bugalugs,' my mother said to me. She was at her most beautiful, smiling with her pearly teeth, her lips red and glossy. 'We're going shopping.'

We went to the butcher and supermarket twice a week, the fruiterer and the fisho came to the house with their vans, and soft drink was delivered in clanking wooden trays. There was no need to pick me up from school to go shopping.

I grabbed my port and ran behind her as she sashayed through the playground, skipping occasionally. She was in the kind of mood that made me feel light and proud to be seen with her, hopeful that all the kids noticed, and the teachers. She had parked on the driveway in a line of cars filled with mothers waiting for children, though certainly fewer compared with these days. I sat beside her in the front seat.

'Ready for an adventure?' she said.

I nodded. Inside the car was hot and smoky. She sat, hands on the wheel, waiting for the car in front of us to move. It didn't.

'God, the world is filled with morons,' she said.

There was a woman in the car in front. She was talking to three smaller children in the back seat and hadn't noticed my mother behind her.

My mother started the engine, then she tooted and raised her hands in a mimed question. The woman in the car in front saw us now, in her rear-view mirror. She started her own car.

'An automatic, I bet,' my mother muttered to me. 'Imagine being so lazy and stupid you can't change gears.'

The car in front still hadn't moved, so my mother wound down her window and leaned out. 'Come on, come on,' she yelled at the mother in front. 'Put your foot on the accelerator!'

Everyone was looking at us now – not just kids, but teachers too, and the few mothers who'd arrived on foot. They had never seen someone as beautiful as my mother, with her fire and verve. The only person not looking at us was the mother in the car in front. She had her head down.

My mother wound the window up again. 'Unbelievable,' she muttered. 'I don't have all day for this shit.' She turned the wheel hard, revved the engine and reversed. We lurched, then one tyre jumped up on the footpath, shaking me in my seat. Then she changed gears and we were off.

But when we finally made it to the end of Darcy Road, my mother turned left. I asked where we were going.

'Wouldn't you like to know,' she said.

We ended up at Myer Coorparoo. I still remember the thrill of the steep ramp to the carpark on the roof. There was a play area there, but I'd never been in because that was for children who were badly brought up and couldn't be trusted to behave. We parked, and I followed my mother though the glass doors and down the escalators, past mannequins and shiny displays.

'Hands behind your back,' she said, but my hands were there already, so I wouldn't be tempted to touch anything – and just as well. Everything was glossy and beautiful, and smelled wonderful. Myer was white and clean and magical.

My mother laughed. 'If your eyes open any wider, your eyeballs will pop out.'

We ended up in a changing room in the lingerie department, among all that silk and lace the colour of cream and caramel and ebony, the lush richness of being a woman. I sat on a pink velour stool in the corner while my mother tried on bras, helped by a stocky, dark-haired older woman with a tape measure around her neck.

'We have some lovely styles on sale, if madam is interested,' the Myer lady said.

'Do I look like I need a bargain?' my mother said. 'I'll try the fanciest ones you've got, with lace, thanks all the same.'

'And does the young lady need fitting also?' the Myer lady said as she measured my mother.

'She's flat as a tack still, thank Christ,' my mother said, nodding at me. 'It can't last. She'll be carrying around udders like the rest of us before too long.'

The Myer lady lowered her voice. 'Sleeping in a bra helps keep them under control,' she said, glancing at me. 'Only take them out in the shower.'

'I sleep in the raw, thanks all the same,' my mother said. 'I'd feel I was being strangled in the night. You're right, though. Listen to her, Andie.'

The Myer lady slipped my mother's arms into a beautiful white satin bra with lace at the top of the cups. 'I also tell my girls to stop running around and don't move too quickly. And don't let men play with them,' she said.

'You're right about that as well,' my mother said. She leaned forward to redistribute the cups, and then said to me, 'Enjoy it while you can, Andie. Boobs ruin your life.'

After she chose her bra, we went to the ladies department. This was not at all like buying things in Kmart, or from the men who came over to our house at night with clothes they'd wheeled out of department stores. While my mother and I stayed in the change rooms, a different Myer lady found sizes and made suggestions, and nodded whenever my mother said something. Every outfit my mother tried made her more beautiful, young and vital – everything I hoped and doubted I would grow up to become. As well as the bra and a silk slip, she bought a polka-dot dress with a wide white collar and belt, a sky-blue blouse that tied in a bow at the neck, a long tan skirt, and a chunky necklace of beads carved in the shape of roses. Then I followed her, hands still behind my back, to the make-up department, where she bought a new lipstick ('Chocolate Kiss'), an eyeshadow palette of three shades of green side by side and a huge tub of face powder with a fluffy powder puff.

After what seemed like hours, she said, 'Now you.'

This was the most exciting thing I could remember happening. In the children's department, I also tried on outfit after outfit. In the mirror, I looked like a teenager. My mother was making suggestions and touching my sleeve and pulling up hems. Once she put her hands around my waist to make a point about a tighter fit and I felt a rush of joy so dizzying and wild that I thought flames would flare from my fingers. Who cared what the girls at school thought? I was here, with my beautiful mother, and she was my best friend. We chose a yellow poncho with a gorgeous knotted trim, a purple party dress with an elastic bodice and thin straps that tied on the tops of my shoulders, a new denim miniskirt with tiny flowers embroidered on the front pockets, two tie-dye t-shirts and a pair of shiny blue patent shoes.

Being looked at by my mother and the shop lady, asked to turn this way and that in front of the mirror – it was heaven to me. I had no idea, though, why we were here. It wasn't my birthday. I had plenty of normal clothes and I hardly grew at all. When she went to pay, the bill was so high that the sales lady phoned the bank before clanking my mother's credit card through the machine and handing her the carbon copy. I thanked my mother, several times. I'm positive I did. I had very good manners.

'Imagine sleeping in a bra like that dumb bint,' my mother said in the car on the way home.

I laughed. 'Imagine.'

'So la-di-da,' she said. '"Does madam require me to wipe her bum?"'

I laughed again, louder this time, in case she hadn't heard me. 'Wait until Dad sees me in my new clothes,' I said.

A dense quiet descended inside the car, different from my mother's thinking-quiet, or driving-quiet. Inside seemed darker than before. I gripped the edges of the seat.

'That's all you can bloody say, after I spent all that money?' She yelled so loudly and at such a pitch, it was as though we were on opposite sides of the street instead of sitting side-by-side. 'That's so bloody typical. Spoilt rotten you are, but I can only blame myself. I never had new clothes when I was your age. I've a good mind to give them to a kid who can feel a bit of gratitude.'

I shut my eyes and felt the door press against my side. It was involuntary, the way my body moved away from her. She raised her hand and reached towards me and I thought for a moment she was going to open the door so I would plunge to the road, but she dropped it to the gear stick and changed into fourth viciously, slamming the clutch. The car made a grinding noise.

'That's the last bloody time I ever do anything nice for you, mark my words. I'm bloody sick of it. You've ruined my whole day, you selfish little cow.'

We drove on for a little while. I could feel her steaming, the energy coming from her. She kept swearing, kept yelling, a stream of everything I was lacking, everything she wished I was, everything I would never be. On and on she went.

'Why do I bloody well put up with you?' she said. 'Why the bloody hell did I ever have a kid, answer me that?'

Her hands shook when she lit a cigarette at the lights at Bennetts Road. She had a few deep drags, and the car behind had to toot when the lights turned green.

'All right, I bloody heard you, dickhead!' she yelled, and she gave him the forks in the rear-view mirror. 'And you,' she said to me, 'take a picture, it'll last longer.'

She must have thought my carefully blank expression was a lack of understanding.

'Do you know what that means, Miss Smartypants? It means stop bloody looking at me. Every time I turn around, there you are, staring like an idiot. Cut it out.'

I turned towards the window. All around us were cars filled with people going places, people heading home after hard days in offices and factories, people picking up children and visiting friends and going to the shops, all with their own lives, none of them known to me. I wondered what they were thinking about, what was important to them, who they wanted to see, and who they didn't.

In less than fifteen minutes, the storm passed. I heard my mother sigh.

'One day, Andie, you're going to work out who your friends are. And let me give you a tip – your bloody useless father isn't one.'

She didn't say anything else for the rest of the drive home.

Chapter 4

It's not that bad things never befell children back then. They did. We knew about the Beaumont children, and no doubt there were others. But the news reports were different – less sensationalist, calmer. And less ubiquitous. To discover what was happening in the world required the effort of going somewhere to buy a newspaper, or delving through your delivered copy, or deliberately switching on the television at a precise time to catch the news. Most parents thought nothing of kids staying home for a few hours by themselves. On full days though, I went to Gran's, who had an entirely different perspective on supervision.

That's why one Saturday morning when my mother was dressing for work, I told her I'd be spending the day at Larissa's. She nodded vaguely and gave me five dollars, enough for two tickets to the movies, and popcorn, from her new tan leather purse, even though I hadn't asked.

'Shout your little friend a Coke and some chips,' she said. 'Or keep it for yourself, I don't give a shit.'

By now, my life at school had settled into a new phase. I'm not sure if it had ever been discussed in some class meeting I'd missed or the idea had spread organically, but no one spoke to me or touched me or even looked at me. It was unnerving, but strangely freeing. After the first few days, it seemed as though I really was invisible, that I could move among them with no danger of being noticed. I didn't test it, but I felt I could do anything – steal someone else's lunch, untie someone's shoelaces and tie them together – without them reacting. Which seemed fair. If my existence was becoming tentative, at least I should have some advantages.

Of course I had no intention of going to Larissa's. I left on my bike at the same time as my mother, but turned back when her car was out of sight and let myself back in with my key. This would be the first day of my plan to find Macavity.

Larissa and her parents would have driven the streets on our side of the creek, I guessed, but what if Macavity had crossed the bridge? Again I wished my father was around: he knew a bloke who was a printer at Cannon Hill who made invitations and banners and forms for offices. Instead I spent the morning writing notices on the back of old menus from the pub and decorating them with my hand-drawn version of Macavity, or as close to him as I could remember. For contact details, I put my own name and phone number, and at the bottom I printed *Reward Offered* in large purple letters.

This was important. Macavity had a bright pink collar with a shiny red tag engraved with his name and Larissa's phone number. No one had rung until now, I thought, because they lacked sufficient motivation. I had twelve dollars left from my birthday, plus the five dollars my mother had just given me, plus what I was saving from lunch. If my father was here, he could have driven me. Instead I loaded my basket with the posters, a role of masking tape and a box of BBQ Shapes from the kitchen, and headed off on my bike.

By midafternoon, I'd stuck posters on telegraph poles on a dozen blocks to the east, far enough away that none of the kids from our school would see them, so as not to ruin my surprise of being the one to find Macavity. I was thirsty, my calves were streaked with black from the chain and my thighs ached from pedalling up the hills. When I turned into our driveway, my mother's car was there. And beside it, a car I'd never seen before. A blue car.

Inside, sitting on the lounge next to her, was a strange man. My mother had the form guide from the paper and a pen on the smoky glass coffee table in front of her; he had a booklet on his lap, one of the proper ones from the races. The two of them were concentrating and he was making little marks on the booklet. The trannie was on; it being a Saturday in spring, likely Eagle Farm, Rosehill or Flemington.

'Shhh,' she said, and lifted her hand to a stop sign.

'And they're off!' the caller said.

Race-calling is one keen-eyed man armed only with binoculars telling the story of the actions and movements of anywhere from eight to twenty-something animals and perhaps their jockeys, and also conveying the atmosphere of the contest and the crowd and the weather in around four minutes, with such skill and accuracy that keen listeners can picture it unfolding before them. Callers don't have time to look at the cheat sheet in front of them when the field is moving at around seventy kilometres an hour, so they memorise the colours of every jockey and the name of every horse or dog for every meet – perhaps two hundred different animals, if you assume ten races with twenty competitors. It's miraculous.

Visualising the race from the call also requires concentration, to understand the specifics of each animal's run, their skills and weaknesses, their good luck and bad from this rapid-fire blast of information. That's why, when a race was on, neither of my parents would tolerate a sound, or even a distracting movement. I would stop mid-story, sometimes mid-sentence. If I had something to tell them about school or a movie I'd seen or a book I'd read, I'd speak as quickly as I could, managing only a few words in the gaps between races, trying to remember where I'd stopped and hoping they did also. When I was younger I'd make a game of it, freezing at the jump, a gambler's game of Statues. That was irritating and childish, I learned, so now I stood with my hands behind my back.

What a blessing this skill proved to be, considering the way my life turned out. As an adult, I am patient and unfazed by pauses that give me time to go over and over what I planned to say. I am never bored. I can entertain myself just by thinking. Failure was when my parents forgot what I'd said before the race, so when I continued at the end they frowned and said I was talking nonsense. Success meant that, when correct weight was declared, they would turn the sound down and say, 'And, Andie?' Something I learned was this: my parents were more likely to listen across a series of interruptions when I turned information into an anecdote. When I gave stories a beginning, middle and end, when I made them intriguing or suspenseful, when I exaggerated, when I mocked other people and made my parents laugh – that's when they remembered what I'd said in the last break between races.

Above all, I learned that attention is the foundation of all human interactions and nothing else – not love, or hate, or anger – can exist without first noticing someone, without seeing them and registering their specific existence at the particular moment somewhere in your mind. This is rarer and more difficult than you might think.

'Here she is, my big girl,' my mother said, when correct weight had been declared. 'Did you have a good day, love?'

There was something odd about her voice. It was too soft and too smooth, and she smiled as though she was consciously pulling down her chin and stretching her cheeks. My mother and the strange man were drinking beer from tall glasses, and two empty longnecks were on the coffee table. My mother wasn't wearing the brown dress from this morning. Now she was in pink pedal pushers and a pretty white lace top, neither of which I'd seen before. She wasn't smoking, though there were plenty of butts in the ashtray on the lounge beside her. The man wore shorts, but not like my father's, which were brown scoops with an orange trim, the kind with the zip in one pocket for change. This man's shorts were tailored, with a belt. He wore a white singlet. Black hairs poked out around the neckline and longer ones flowed from his armpits. His forearms too were covered in dark hair like a pelt and his eyebrows were heavy. They both had bare feet: my mother's, dainty with her painted toes, and his, oversized and spread wide on the floorboards as though half-melted.

'This must be Andie,' he said.

Even sitting he was a tall man, and broad, with extra weight carried evenly around his hips in a way that's more typical for women. His hands made the beer glass look tiny and my mother, next to him, seemed like a child. I'd never seen anyone his size before in this house of small and neat people – it would be years until my mother broadened and thickened, when her lust for all life's good things finally beat her metabolism into submission – and his mere presence was rude, diminishing even the memory of my father with his bulk. He seemed to spill out over the lounge, a tan vinyl mid-century style that was out of fashion by then and would take another forty years to be fashionable again. He seemed younger than my parents. He wasn't handsome like my father. His face was smooth and fleshy, and he had brown crinkly eyes and was smiling at me now.

'Don't stand there gawking,' said my mother. 'This is Steve. Say hello.'

'Hello,' I said.

'I've got a girl about your age. Her name's Tracey,' Steve said.

'Andie's twelve,' my mother said.

'Twelve, hey?' Steve said. 'Don't you fertilise her?'

'You're supposed to be at work, but,' I said to my mother.

'I beg your pardon,' she said. 'One of the other girls took my shift, not that it's any business of yours.'

My mother never handed off her shifts, especially not Saturdays, when regulars gave her both kinds of tips: money, and winners for the races. Her long hours were something she and my father talked about often, like when he was out of clean clothes. 'Any time you'd like to earn more, I'll cut back, no worries,' she'd say to him. 'Six days a week, fifty-two weeks a year. You do it, be my bloody guest.'

'It takes a while to get on your feet,' my father would reply. 'Paul Cauchi, Vic Whatshisname down the coast. None of the famous trainers had many winners at the beginning.'

I heard a clinking noise. Steve was tapping the beer glass with a wide gold ring he wore on his right hand. I'd never seen a man with a ring before. If he had a daughter, he must have a wife somewhere. I wondered where this Tracey lived, and whether he lived with her. Then I noticed that the finger next to the one with the ring, the little finger on his left hand, was missing entirely. I quickly looked somewhere else.

Steve cleared his throat. 'Out riding your bike?' he said, gesturing to the grease mark on my leg.

I nodded.

'Manners,' said my mother. 'You know better than that.'

Manners included standing on two feet with my hands behind my back, looking people in the eye when I spoke, and also the ability to conduct a sensible conversation with adults. 'It's a skill like any other, Andie, and takes practice,' she often said. 'Make an effort.'

'Yes,' I said to Steve now. 'I've been all over Camp Hill. Thanks for asking.'

Too late, I remembered I'd told my mother I'd be spending the day at Larissa's but she made no sign of recalling. She lit another cigarette and took a long drag. 'Steve's going to be staying with us for a while,' she said.

'I make a mean spaghetti,' Steve said.

'You won't see him much on Saturdays. Today's a special occasion. He works hard, unlike some people I could name,' she said.

All at once, Steve looked uncomfortable, as though he was trying to lift his weight off the lounge in case it snapped under him. I didn't know what he did for a living that kept him busy on Saturdays, not at that stage. That would come later. I'd never heard of a man cooking before. My father made my breakfast of Weet-Bix with milk and sliced banana, and my lunch of Vegemite SAOs (preferable, for the worms) or sandwiches with some Iced VoVos and an apple, but I'd never seen him turn on the gas. Spaghetti was foreign muck, according to him, that I'd only eaten at Larissa's. My mother made macaroni and cheese sometimes and roast chicken for our birthdays, but otherwise we had steak or sausages or chops and mashed potatoes and beans with Worcestershire sauce every night. Perhaps this Steve was the cook at the pub, I thought. Perhaps he makes the counter lunches.

'As well as Tracey, Steve has two little boys,' my mother said. 'You'll meet them.'

I opened my mouth to answer, but she raised her hand again and pointed to the trannie. 'Shhh,' she said.

Another race was beginning. My mother and Steve both turned to face the trannie. I tried not to look at them while they listened but it was all I could do to not stare at the space where Steve's little finger should have been.

If I close my eyes, I can still see our lounge room: the long narrow window above the lounge and its armchairs, the coffee table and matching side tables, the television and stereo. After my father left, things that could only be called *objets d'art* began appearing: paintings of gum-treed landscapes with drovers or cattle or swaggies in heavy gilt frames, a pottery ashtray that was glossy where the cigarettes go and rough like bark on the outside, and china figurines of old-fashioned shepherdesses. I can still hear the continuous background noise of the trannie.

The tempo and the rising pitch of the caller's voice revealed this race was exciting, and important. Towards the end, my mother and Steve both started talking to the radio.

Then my mother stood, yelling, 'Come on, you little shit!'

Then Steve was happily yelling at my mother rather than the radio. 'Didn't I tell you? What did I tell you? Solid gold, Val.' His voice was deep and booming.

When the race finished, they collapsed back on the lounge, gazing at each other, laughing and congratulating, exhausted as though they had run the race themselves.

'Are you clearing out the sewing room?' I said.

At the end of the hall, next to my bedroom, was where my mother kept her sewing machine and knitting machine and boxes of material and wool and half-finished projects like the blanket she was crocheting for my bed. I'd never seen her in there, though she told me she made all my clothes when I was little.

'What?' said my mother, still gasping and smiling from the race.

'The sewing room. For Steve to sleep in.'

At first it seemed she hadn't heard me. She straightened and pulled down her blouse and ran her hand through her hair, and only when she'd gathered herself did her lips tighten and harden. 'Are you being a smart arse?' she said in her softest voice, which was a bad sign.

I swallowed and shook my head.

'Whose house is it?' she said. 'Who pays the bloody mortgage? You?'

'She's curious, that's all,' said Steve. 'Lots of changes in a short amount of time.'

My mother took a breath and sat a little further back on the lounge. 'Eventually, for the boys. Tracey will share with you. But get this through your skull – Steve will be in my room.' She narrowed her eyes at me. 'Do you have anything to say about that?'

I shook my head.

'Now, now, Val.' Steve put his big hand on her knee, the one with all the fingers. 'I'm sure that Andie and I will soon be the best of friends.'

Since the day I first met Steve, I've lived a dozen lives, each one luckier than the last. I was married myself for a time: I stood at the altar and promised to love a good man until my death and, in a blink, I signed papers that divorced us. Nothing before or since has ever stunned me as much as the realisation I had at that moment.

My mother was making plans for a future without my father in it. In her mind, he was not coming back. I was shocked at her, at my own stupidity, at the way my life had become something unrecognisable without my noticing. Steve was here instead of my father. He would be sleeping in my mother's bed, cooking in our kitchen.

But at the same time, I felt certain that all was not lost. If only my father would come home, my mother wouldn't need this Steve. As for my troubles at school – my father would be able to find Macavity, I had no doubt. My future happiness, the life I'd envisaged having when I grew up, relied upon him coming home. Besides, my parents loved each other. Back then, I thought that love was simple and forever, and that it needed to be saved at all costs, even though whatever had existed between my parents seemed to have evaporated without leaving a trace.

I spent the rest of the day cross-legged on my bed, playing chess against myself with the set that had been my father's when he was a boy. He was quite good in his day, he told me once, but we never played together. I still own that set. It was perfect for me because the board was some kind of metal and each piece had a tiny magnet under a pad of green felt, so they stayed in placed as I twirled the board to change sides. I was accustomed to formulating one strategy for black and another for white, trying to compartmentalise what I knew about my imaginary opponent each time I made a move. Against myself, I always won and I always lost, which is as good a metaphor for life as I can imagine.

That afternoon though, the games felt especially important, like a test. It felt good to twirl the board, to leave my own perspective behind and understand the objectives of everyone around me.

My father would know how to fix everything. But first, I had to find him.

Chapter 5

Greyhounds reared without littermates can become what is called field-shy: unaccustomed to the smells and sounds of other dogs in close proximity, unused to being bumped or jostled. Unlike horses, racing dogs have no jockey to steer and no whip to motivate. In a race, field-shy greyhounds can't concentrate on the bunny and are sometimes so frightened they abandon the field altogether and run off sideways into the crowd searching for a familiar face. They have forgotten they are dogs perhaps, and that their only job is to chase. They think they're human. For this reason, my father, like many trainers, believed it was better to rear two or three puppies together.

It's an incongruous philosophy for the father of an only child. Before I was born, my mother miscarried late into a pregnancy, and there was another when I was a toddler. I stayed at my grandmother's for the best part of a week. My mother spoke of these missing babies often, always as sons. The loss of boys made it more tragic somehow. She remembered their anniversaries: 1 May and 6 August. She was on the pill now, I knew. She told me once she couldn't stand to lose another.

Had I a brother or a sister, perhaps I would have grown to be more adaptable. Not so field-shy. If I were an older sister, the arrival of another person into our household would not have been unprecedented, and if I were the younger, I myself would have been the disruption. I would have learned to shrug off a little bumping or jostling. Either way, a change to our family circumstances wouldn't have been so unthinkable that I would devote so much energy to opposing it, and risk so much.

From the moment I met Steve, I felt the forces of change pressing, as though I was that small Dutch boy with his finger in the dyke. The next morning I was woken early by a ute backing into our driveway. I looked out my window to see two big, rough-looking men unload a set of weights and triangular stand, a bar, sets of loose dumbbells, a vinyl-covered bench and a huge punching bag they could barely lift, and carry them under the house into the garage. Then they manoeuvred a black leather recliner across the yard and through the front door. The recliner was large enough to fit both my parents and me. It sat in the middle of the lounge like an island. Later, Steve arrived in his blue Ford Falcon with three hard-shell suitcases and a white bag.

I would learn in the years to come that this was typical of the way boyfriends of mothers arrive. In our circles at least, women stayed in the house with their children and, after one introductory meeting, boyfriends moved in with minimal possessions at the start of a relationship and left with the same stuff – worn now, more scuffed, more faded – at the end, sometimes narrowly avoiding the next boyfriend with a new random set of belongings. I hated Steve's heavy, ugly fitness equipment that I had to scramble over to reach Tippy's kennel, and the recliner, bossy and rude, made all our furniture seem insignificant. None of it belonged here. The sight of it made me feel bad, like a sore spot in my mind.

One of Steve's effects especially captured my attention: the white bag. It was a boxy duffle-shape, bigger than a doctor's bag, made of glossy leather that reminded me of Larissa's white piano seat, the one that hid all her treasures. It opened at the top with buckles and a brass clasp and had a small handle in the middle and a long thick strap. A man's name was printed across one side in gold letters. It wasn't Steve's name.

I knew exactly what kind of bag it was. I'd seen them many times, at the track. The name on the bag was that of a bookie.

'Whose is that?' I asked my mother that first night when Steve was in the shower and the white bag was on the dining table, although of course I knew.

'Steve's,' she said. 'From when he was a penciller.'

'Is that his job?' I said to my mother. 'Is he a penciller?'

'Do your ears need cleaning? He used to be a penciller, I said.' She peeled the plastic film off her packet of Benson & Hedges and crumpled it, then she flicked open the lid with her thumb, then closed it again.

My mother would have been an excellent penciller, had it been a job for women. She had that same gift with numbers – at the pub, she kept a running total of the longest drinks orders in her head, and gave perfect change, and her drawer was never out by a fraction. She had a gift with people also – not goodwill exactly, because she mostly thought ill of people, and not intimacy, because she was usually aloof. It was more a kind of desirability, as though her friendship was something to aspire to, something hard-earned. At the track, all the pencillers knew my mother. They knew my father too but whenever we went to the track together, he didn't stay with us. His punting was a serious thing. We would only distract him.

'How did he lose his finger?' I said. 'And what does he do now?'

'Neither of those are any concern of yours,' my mother said. 'Oh, that bag of Steve's? Under no circumstances are you to touch it.'

She took no more precautions than that. Long experience with me had taught her. Our house had no front fence to separate it from the road when I was growing up, and my mother often told the story of me as a toddler following her as she traced a line on the grass with her finger. 'You are not allowed to cross this line,' she told me, and to her pride, I never did. I was as well-trained as any puppy.

At any rate, Steve and the white bag were seldom parted. When he left for work it went with him, and when he was home it sat beside him, or was tucked away in my mother's bedroom.

Steve was home often, although I rarely saw him. My mother began taking fewer shifts at the pub and the two of them were still in bed by the time I left for school. I was never allowed to touch anything that wasn't mine, so the way my mother singled out the white bag was suspicious. A seed of curiosity was planted.

On the Saturday of that week, I woke up sweaty. The sun was already sharp and bright around the edges of the blind in my room. If I raised it, I knew what I would see – the same fluffy clouds above the houses of Morningside that I saw every morning, in the same perfect sky.

I came out to the lounge to watch cartoons, and from the hall I saw my mother still in her dressing-gown sitting on the kitchen divider, where I was absolutely never allowed to sit. Steve was in shorts and a singlet, and he was standing in front of her, between her legs, and he was kissing her neck. Her head was thrown back. When she saw me, she tapped him on the shoulder and he stepped away from her.

'Good morning!' he said, too cheerily. 'We're having breakfast!'

He slept with her now, I knew that much, but I hadn't seen them like this before. I'd never seen my parents so much as hold hands. Also, my mother never had breakfast.

'I can't hear you, Andie,' my mother said.

'Good morning,' I said. 'How did you sleep?'

Steve laughed as though I'd made a joke. 'I slept very well, thank you for asking.'

My mother opened the bottom cupboard and took out a bowl, and proceeded to put two Weet-Bix in it. She sliced a banana on top, put two teaspoons of sugar on top of that, and then sloshed cold milk all over everything. While she was doing this, Steve was making himself toast and spreading it with butter and Vegemite. Even with his nine fingers, he worked with more dexterity than my mother did. It was only when she put the bowl on the divider with a spoon next to it that I realised it was for me. I didn't like that much milk, or that much sugar. My father knew that, but she didn't. I knew better than to say anything. I sat and began to eat.

'Your mother and I have been thinking about taking a little holiday,' Steve said.

'That's a great idea.' I was used to eating by myself with a book in front of me. It was weird to eat with my mother and Steve there.

'Steve wants to take me to Sydney,' my mother said.

'You could use a break,' Steve said. 'You work too hard, darl.'

'Imagine it, Andie,' my mother said. 'Wentworth Park and Harold Park. Maybe Casino on the way back. We could do it in five days. Stay in motels.'

My mother had always wanted to go to Sydney. It was a stupid idea, my father said. Gone were the days when you had to travel to see champions; now even the best dogs raced here because Queensland offered spectacular prize money. My father had seen He's Some Boy win the National Distance Championship at the Gabba the year before last, and he was New South Wales Greyhound of the Year. Not Victorian dogs, though. One day of driving is hard enough for a dog, so my father had to watch the once-in-a-generation Lizrene and his other favourite, Half Your Luck, run at Sandown Park on television.

'You'll be right as rain in the back seat,' Steve said. 'Bring some of your books.'

Of course I wanted to see those famous tracks in real life, but who would look after Tippy while I was gone? In the weeks to come, the value of telling the truth, or rather the lack of value, would solidify in my mind. But feelings are not as simple as whether or not something is true. I wanted to see those tracks, and I did not want to spend five days in Steve's car with him and my mother. Both of those things could be true at the same time.

'Andie. What do you say?' my mother said.

'Thank you,' I said.

Not long after that, two Telecom technicians came to install a new phone line in my mother's bedroom, which she told me I was never to answer, not even if I was home alone. I didn't know anyone with two phones. Some kids at school didn't even have one. Phone lines were expensive, and there was a waiting list. It made me wonder how long my mother had known that Steve was moving in. Perhaps she had been planning it for months.

She hadn't, of course. Now I understand that Steve was the kind of man for whom waiting lists meant nothing.

Back then, I didn't realise that the rules that most people lived by were optional in Queensland for Steve, and for people like him.

A few days later, when I went downstairs to feed Tippy and let her out, I found her already fed and watered. She was panting, and her skin was sheeny from sweat.

Upstairs, the door to my mother's bedroom was still closed. Steve was a late riser, like she was. I was desperate to ask if my father had been, but even the thought of knocking on the door where she and Steve were sleeping was impossible. Instead I lurked outside their door, waiting. When my mother appeared, bleary-eyed in her dressing-gown, she was alarmed.

'What is it?' she said. 'What's happened? Is someone here?'

'Has Dad been?' I said.

She looked up at the ceiling, one hand clutching her gown closed. Her nails were a glittering metallic bronze. 'For fuck's sake,' she whispered, closing the door softly. 'You will be the death of me.'

'Tippy's already been walked,' I said. 'Was it Dad?'

'It bloody well better have been. Not one more day is that bitch shitting in my backyard. Not one more day, I told him.'

'He didn't come upstairs to see me. He could've made me breakfast, like he used to.'

My mother had a look that she saved for checkout girls who were slow at keying the prices of groceries on their machine, and for my grandmother sometimes, when she asked a question, as though they were the scourge of her existence and put on earth for the sole reason of making her life as difficult as possible.

'Breakfast? Your father dumps two Weet-Bix in a bowl and tips milk on it when he's making his own, whoop-de-bloody-do.'

'He tucks me in and makes me lunch.'

'He spends all of twenty seconds turning your light off, and he puts Vegemite and a slice of cheese on bread and throws it in a paper bag with an apple. Open your bloody eyes, none of that makes him father of the bloody year. Who do you think mops and vacuums and washes your clothes and irons them and cooks your dinner?'

It's not that children are by nature ungrateful. I'm sure I wasn't. Now it's obvious that hers was unnoticed and unvalued work but when you're small, the world comes into focus like a polaroid: smudged and indistinct, taking years to resolve to clarity.

'Jesus, wake up, Andie,' my mother went on. 'I've told him and I'm telling you: he can look after Tippy but he sure as shit isn't coming upstairs.'

'But when will I see him? This afternoon?'

She put one hand to her forehead as though her head ached. 'He'll probably walk her again when you're at school. The last thing he needs right now is you rabbiting on.'

'But I want to see him.'

I wasn't hearing her words. I was preoccupied by the fact that I had missed my father by a matter of hours, or maybe minutes. He had been so close, just down the stairs. I didn't understand how I'd slept through his visit. His presence should have woken me, the way the dogs could sense a possum in a tree overhead before anyone could see it.

'Jesus H Christ.' My mother looked into my eyes and spoke very clearly, not flippantly like she usually did, and slower. 'The sooner you learn there's nothing a bloke can do that you can't do better yourself, the easier your life will be. For your own good, stop thinking about him.'

'I can't.'

She sighed. 'He doesn't have a phone, Andie. It's not easy to get in touch with him.'

I couldn't reply. There must have been something in my face though, because after a while she said, 'If you're going to be a baby about it, I'll try and get a message to him. What if he picks you up after school on Friday. Will that do?'

I nodded and thanked her, then I rushed off to get ready before she changed her mind. For the first time in my life, I was going to be late for school.

The reason I had been reluctant to knock on my mother's door had nothing to do with sex. I took it for granted that she and Steve were lovers. She had always been entirely straightforward about the mechanics of the act, and entirely unromantic about the necessity of it. Sex was a bodily function, she believed, like eating and going to the toilet. I'd seen dogs at it since I was very young; for the human specifics, she'd handed me a copy of *Where Did I Come From?* My mother was that way about everything that other people considered beyond children. She never led me to believe in Santa Claus, even when I was tiny.

'Most parents lie their pants off and then act all surprised when their kids don't trust them,' she said. But she also warned me not to let the truth about Santa slip to my friends. 'It's human nature to get shitty at someone who tells you something you don't want to hear,' she told me. 'Those stupid babies can get stuffed. Let them find out the hard way.'

No, it was the very fact of Steve's presence that disturbed me. It was the size of him, the smell – so different from my father – and all that hair. He made me feel embarrassed. I'd have spent more time in my room avoiding him, but this proved unnecessary. He worked long hours – at what, I still didn't know – and after pouring himself a beer, went straight to their bedroom with his white bag. He was always polite, asking me about my day or commenting on the weather, but he didn't linger. I waited until he was out or likely to be asleep to use the toilet or shower – the idea of running into him entering or exiting was excruciating. My room was next to theirs so I preferred to stay in the lounge, lying on the floor in front of the television in my usual position, on my stomach with my elbows bent and my chin resting in my hands, with the sound low. I liked reaching out and feeling the curve of the screen and the velvet static, and seeing the repeating pattern of those three minuscule circles, red, green and blue, that made up the image. So tiny, yet able to show me the world.

—

For the rest of that week, I was counting the minutes until I would finally see my father. When Friday came, I could barely keep my seat. During the afternoon when the whole class stood to recite Kenneth Slessor's 'Country Towns' by heart, I missed the third stanza altogether and went straight from 'Than from a wish to seem polite' to 'Country towns with your schooner bees', and the rest of the class followed.

Mrs Murphy stopped us and said to me, 'What's the matter, Miss Tanner? Did you forget to take your brain pills this morning?'

Because Mrs Murphy spoke directly to me, the rest of the class could see me. Everyone laughed, Clayton Peck so histrionically that he fell to the floor, thrashing. For this, Mrs Murphy put him outside the classroom where he spent the next ten minutes pushing his face against the closed louvres, his nose flattened, opening and closing his mouth like a fish.

I didn't care about any of that. I was shaking inside. Had any other child at my school been speaking to me, I would have been unable to resist saying that my father was picking me up, that I was finally seeing him.

As soon as the bell rang, I grabbed my port and bolted down the stairs and rushed to the turning circle. As usual, everyone parted as I passed by, turning their backs or their heads, unfocusing their gazes. Down in the driveway, none of my class were there but a dozen or so cars were already parked, mostly for the little kids, and a few more came as I waited.

This is one of the occasions where my memory fails me. It was almost certainly warm and sunny that late September afternoon, because it almost always was, but that day remains forever cold to me. I feel certain it was raining too, because I remember standing under the covered walkway that led from the administration block to our classrooms, listening to water gurgling down the gutters and splashing into the drains. An empty school is a desolate thing. Without children and their sounds, it is a brutal and sad space of hard surfaces: bitumen and cement, iron and steel. The only bright thing in the world was an empty packet of Twisties whipped by the wind across the driveway.

When Mr Swan finally came out of his office, he walked past me on the way to his car. He would be locking the school gate behind him, he said. Pick-up had long finished. No one else would be coming now. It was time for me to go home.

Chapter 6

Whenever I travel back to Brisbane now – for work most often, or a wedding or a funeral – I book a window seat on the left-hand side of the plane. A window seat on the left-hand side of the plane, numbered something-A. I take care to avoid the wing. You can't see anything from the wing. For the whole flight, I read my book, waiting for the flight attendant to announce the descent. One moment we're above the puffy clouds and the next below them, watching their shadows dance across the patchwork earth. The cream and beige of buildings that were scattered islands join up and become dense, and the green that seemed endless is reduced to pockets.

Sometimes the plane loops east over the bay and banks to approach the runway from the water. Other times, though, the plane tracks low over the south-eastern suburbs, almost directly above what used to be my primary school. Now, instead of scrubby bush, below the oval is a housing development.

The whole side of the hill and all of our cubbies and secret tracks are flattened. The creek has been concreted and smoothed, and the rocks and rivulets and mud puddles where we caught tadpoles in jars and raced miniature rafts made of twigs and chewing gum, kids lined up on either side cheering – these are gone. Despite this, from the air, the streetscape is greener. There are more trees in yards and on footpaths. Solar panels glint on roofs. Then I see our house. There's a high timber fence around it now, and in the backyard, a shimmering pool surrounded by rocks and palms, as though it were a Daintree swimming hole.

It becomes clear in those moments that childhood is as much a place as it is a time.

As I look down, I sometimes have in mind that my parents found their way back to that house, and to each other, all those years ago. I can almost see them, younger than I am now, turning their smooth faces and talking about the odds on a horse or the treatment for muscle soreness in a dog. In the background, the sound of a race call hums. They are both still alive. They are waiting for me to come home.

Air travel was, for me, more than a decade in the future. When I was twelve, I didn't know anyone who'd been on a plane. Neither of my parents ever held a passport. 'Why would you ever want to go anywhere else? Best country in the world,' they would say – but by 'country', they meant Queensland, which had been the home of our family forever, rather than

Australia, which was full of 'Cockroaches', which meant New South Welshmen, and people who lived even further away like Victorians, about whom I knew nothing except that they spent their holidays here and swam in the ocean in the middle of winter.

The idea that I might ever find the rigmarole of flight as tiresome as I do now – first, the expense of the Uber, then the jostling at the self-service kiosk, then sending luggage down the chute of chaos, then the bovine tedium of the security screening – was unthinkable. In years yet to come, I would cry in front of the Taj Mahal and marvel at the Terracotta Army, I would tour the Colosseum and eat kushiyaki in a darkened izakaya. When I was a child, my parents sometimes drove me places, but my world was mostly bordered by the distance I could cycle or, more often, walk.

As I walked home from waiting for my father that Friday, I wondered how I'd managed to get the day wrong. Was he coming on Monday? Or was it next week? For a sickening moment I wondered if my father had parked at the other entrance on the top of the hill. The idea of him waiting there, scanning each kid as they passed, none of them me, thinking I was avoiding him on purpose – it gave me a bad feeling that I had often in those days, like a tender bruise inside my brain. The only remedy when these sore spots appeared was to read a book or plan my future or watch television so that my mind didn't wander back there.

No, it was more likely that something had gone wrong with the message. My father didn't have a phone, my mother had said. Perhaps she'd left word for him at the wrong place. Or perhaps she hadn't contacted him at all. If I wanted to see him, it would have to be up to me.

Those were my thoughts, at the time. If I seem nonchalant about becoming invisible at school, I guess I was. My mother would have said this was evidence of my heartlessness but even at that age I was methodical, I was focused and determined. I was, in some ways, accustomed to not being noticed. Besides, I would soon find Macavity and make Larissa so happy that my problems at school would fix themselves. Everything would be all right, I was sure, if I tried hard enough and worked hard enough. This was good practice for adulthood, I told myself, which was nothing but problem after bloody problem until you die, or so my mother said.

By the time my mother and Steve arrived home around 10 pm, I'd finished my homework, heated my foil-covered tea in the oven and eaten it cross-legged on the floor, a foot from the television. They were tipsy and cheerful. Steve wore his white bag with the strap across his chest. My mother didn't ask if I'd seen my father, but I didn't expect her to – it was my business, not hers. My parents and I had an unspoken deal: I would never give them any cause for concern, and they treated me the same way they treated each other – politely uncurious, for the most part. At the time, I mistook this for respect.

That night, my mother and Steve each greeted me kindly enough, then almost straight away went to bed. I could hear them moving around for a little while: shoes scuffing on the floor, voices echoing through the wall. It seemed to me that they were strangers – hotel guests sleeping in their room perhaps, and I was a clerk or receptionist going about my business. The house was a strange place at night, with me alone and all the lights out and the flickering television throwing shadows on the floorboards. I began watching an old movie then I woke around 1.30 am, still lying on the floor in front of the television with my head in my folded arms, the test pattern humming.

Staying awake would be harder than I'd expected, so I took a pillow and blanket from my room and headed downstairs. Tippy woke briefly to sniff me, then settled. It was very dark down there, and the cement was so cold it was almost damp. I moved the pile of clean sugar bags in front of the kennels to lie on, blocking Tippy's door so my father couldn't avoid me when he let her out. As I lay my head on the pillow, I could hear a rustling sound under the front of the house where the floor was bare earth and the beams that supported the lounge room upstairs were visible, and was struck with a sudden terror of cockroaches or spiders nibbling my toes. This was a terrible idea. I would never be able to sleep down here, I remember thinking.

The next thing I knew, my father's hand was shaking my shoulder.

'Andie. What the hell are you doing?'

I struggled to sit up, blinking and groggy. Tippy's nose was pushing through the wire, snuffling my hair, loud in my ear. For a moment, I couldn't understand where I was, what day it was. Outside was still dark; I could tell by the windows above the kennels.

'This is bloody ridiculous,' he said. 'You have a perfectly good bed.'

I felt a rush of relief, a pure and clear rinsing out of all the bad, sticky feelings, as though I'd been riding my bike for a long way in the heat and waiting for me was a tall glass of lemonade with ice and a straw. As my eyes adjusted, I saw the details of his face as it exists now in my memory: his strong jaw and fine nose and pale blue eyes, the dimples on his cheeks, his dark hair perfect even at this hour, kept in place with the plastic comb he kept in his pocket.

This was not what I was expecting. These last weeks had been the most difficult of my life, and I'd imagined that his had been the same. I thought he'd look like a derro.

I knew about derros. I'd seen them. Every Christmas morning, I went with my father when he picked up my grandfather from his scary boarding house in South Brisbane. He would be all dressed up, with a present for me – a tin of Quality Street usually, but one year, a trannie of my very own, in the shape of a Coke can – and beside him on the front stairs were men in stained trousers without belts and shirts with torn collars. They had drooping faces and dark eyes, and as my grandfather got in our car, they called after him, teasing him and yelling names and swearing. I could smell them from metres away. They were good blokes, my grandfather said, just jealous they didn't have a family at Christmas, but they frightened me. I had imagined my father would now look like these men – older and greyer, like he'd been through an ordeal. Surely he needed rescuing as much as I did?

But my father was unchanged, as though he hadn't missed me at all. His hair was trimmed; his face was smooth and soft. How could he be shaving when the world had collapsed around us? He hadn't even lost weight. He wore a short-sleeved shirt with a collar and navy tailored shorts I'd never seen before. Where was he living? Who was ironing his clothes and making his tea?

'I wanted to see you,' I said.

'Well, you have. Now get upstairs.' He stood and turned his back to me, then he took down Tippy's lead and muzzle. 'All this carry-on,' he muttered. 'It's been a few weeks, that's all.'

'Someone's moved in,' I said. 'A man. His name's Steve.'

He stopped then and turned to look at me. 'Is that so?' he said. 'Big fella? Dark hair, and lots of it? Missing a finger?'

I nodded.

He shook his head. 'Jesus, she shouldn't have done that. Not with a bloke like him.'

'What are you going to do?'

I watched him take a deep breath and then jerk his chin at me. I knew what he meant, and scrambled out of the way so he could open the door to Tippy's kennel. He knelt and reached forward, and I watched him run his graceful hands across the top of Tippy's head and scratch under her soft ears and cup her face, caressing the underside of her chin and the sides of her mouth where the skin puckered, and then smoothing her eyelids with his thumbs the way she liked. She raised her face to him as though he were the sun; she rolled her eyes back in a kind of ecstasy. Then he fixed her collar around her beautiful neck.

'Absolutely nothing to be done,' he said as he stepped Tippy out of the kennel. 'Your mother's a grown woman and I wish her all the best.'

Whatever I'd imagined him saying, it wasn't this. He mustn't be understanding me. I mustn't be explaining it right. 'But he's sleeping in her bed.'

He shut his eyes then, and hid his face in his hands for a moment. 'Andie,' he said. 'Sometimes things work out, other times it's best to call it a day. Life is short. You only get one chance to make a name for yourself. Nothing good comes from forcing people do things against their will on account of a bit of paper, believe me. That is a recipe for all kinds of suffering.'

I was already suffering, I wanted to tell him. I wanted to say that, in my mind, my parents' marriage was more than a bit of paper, that I missed him, that I loved him, but we never spoke that way in our family. We could say we loved the dogs, we could lavish all kinds of affection upon them. In the end, I said the only thing that I thought sounded reasonable, that he would understand.

'I need you to find Macavity,' I said.

He frowned, as though his head ached. 'What's that when it's at home?'

'It's Larissa's cat. Named after a poem, she said.'

'A poem, hey. Some people have too much time on their hands. And who's this Larissa?'

'My friend from school. My best friend.'

He squatted on his haunches on the floor beside me. 'Is that what's behind this all this carry-on? A bloody cat? Just get the girl another one. People drown sackfuls of kittens every day.'

'But you could, couldn't you? You could find any animal, even a cat.'

He scrunched up his face as though he was going to sneeze, then he gave a short sharp laugh. 'You could say that. Finding cats is a simple matter of knowing where to look. But I can't hang around here with you, Andie. When a woman puts her foot down, you've got to respect that. I'm not allowed.'

I knew about my mother's 'Not allowed'. I knew it was final, the end of the discussion.

'In fact, in a few weeks, I'm moving down to Lindum. More space down there. I'm staying with a friend. I'm just waiting for a few things to fall into place, then I'll come back and get this one,' he jerked his thumb at Tippy, 'and we'll be away.'

I can still hear his tone, flat and businesslike. So many thoughts rushed through my brain. A house at Lindum? What kind of house? My parents were modern people who loathed Queenslanders, which were drafty, filled with dust and white ants and expensive to maintain, painting all that timber. Any time the Deen Brothers tore down another old building in the city made of colonial stone and cast iron, my father told anyone who would listen how lucky we were to have Joh, who was a strong leader and knew how to keep those union grubs and student ratbags in their place, and who alone had the courage and foresight to drag this mangrove-infested shanty town into a gleaming world city of steel and glass.

And he was taking Tippy. Not only would I be losing my father, but the last dog that was the link to my future. Without my father, I would never find Macavity and make up with Larissa and enter high school with friends instead of as an outcast. But the most improbable thing – he was leaving Morningside. I had never considered leaving Morningside; I didn't know anyone who had. I would live here forever, I thought, in a house walking distance from this one.

I opened my mouth, but no words came out.

He ducked to peer into my face. 'You're not going to sook, are you?'

I shook my head.

'Because we don't sook, right, Andie? We hold our head up, we take it on the chin. Never let any bastard see you cry.'

I blinked, and I nodded. 'I know.'

'You're dead on your feet,' my father said. 'Go on, get upstairs to bed and I'll do both of us a favour by not mentioning this to your mother.'

I almost argued, but when he used this tone, I knew he couldn't be moved. It was the tone he used with my grandfather when we picked him up on those Christmas mornings. 'One beer,' my father would say to him when he got in the car, 'and one beer only. If you make it two, you're out. Say a word out of line to Val, you're out. Breathe the wrong way, you're back with your metho-drinking mates in five seconds flat.' And sure enough, before lunch or sometimes just after, something would happen. Once, I remember my grandfather wet himself – a sour, dark patch spreading over his trousers and dripping on the timber boards – and another time he called my mother a stuck-up cunt, and my father bundled him back in the car. It was a shame. I loved my grandfather. I was the smartest girl he'd ever seen, he said, and I'd grow up to be Miss Australia, with any luck.

By now there was a buzzing in my head that jumbled my thoughts and made it hard to open my eyes fully.

I don't remember walking up the stairs to my bedroom or putting my head on the pillow. I slept until past ten and when I woke, everything was obvious. My father thought he was being logical. He expected that I, who was also logical, would agree that doing nothing was for the best. After all, I had always done exactly as I was told.

But what I really thought was this: for some reason beyond my understanding, my father was making a mistake. Some stupid grown-up thing was stopping him from thinking clearly. Perhaps he'd made a promise a long time ago and couldn't break it. Something to do with honour.

But I hadn't promised anything. My mother was wrong and so was my father, and they could not see it. I was mature for my age, everyone said so. I knew it was up to me to fix things.

The young, how arrogant they are. They sit high upon their mountain, they judge and they measure and they find wanting, because of course their life has been simple. They have not yet made the mistakes that will in years to come wake them in the night and gnaw upon their bones.

Chapter 7

At around twelve months of age, a greyhound undergoes what is called 'breaking-in'. This is the beginning of her education, where her trainer or an experienced specialist teaches her to chase, first by hand-slipping, then to jump out of the boxes. They learn to travel and stand for inspection by the stewards and generally behave in a manner to make their owners proud. The breaking-in process depends on handling that is firm yet consistent, and expectations that are achievable and unvarying. Cruelty will never succeed; puppies that are mistreated grow into useless, fearful animals. It is best to be straightforward and blasé, to never present the dog with options. The behaviour required must seem predetermined.

Was I truly as scheming, cold and wilful as my mother would say, all those years ago? Perhaps. In years to come, whenever a colleague talked about their school years, I was astonished by the autonomy they fought for, the battle of wills they engaged in, the sense of childhood as ongoing warfare with a variety of authority figures. My actions, on the other hand, felt as inevitable as a train on a track. In those days, most children regularly copped a wooden spoon or the back of their father's hand, but my parents never struck me. At school, most of the boys got the cuts from Mr Swan, which was a thin cane across their palms or the backs of their calves. Other than Simone, girls never got the cuts. I never received detention or lines or any other kind of discipline. I never did anything to deserve them.

Before this, I recall misbehaving only once. I was small, perhaps five or six. One day we filed into our classroom after little lunch to find a nurse in a white starched uniform and a stiff peaked cap standing with Miss Heather at the blackboard. Sister Something. Visitors were rare at our school. Once a year, we all piled in the library to listen to a policeman tell us not to accept lollies from strangers or get into their car, but that was it. I still recall the novelty of sitting cross-legged on the library floor, paying my usual attention and wondering what out-of-the-ordinary thing was about to happen.

The nurse smiled at us then she began. In her very first sentence, she used the word 'cancer'. I remember that, clear as glass. I'd never heard that word before. Then she said 'death', and I remember being shocked by the bluntness, because while I knew what it meant, most adults around me said 'passed away' or 'no longer with us' or even 'kicked the bucket'. Then she handed around laminated pictures of black and shrivelled lungs, all the while telling stories of men and ladies losing their tongues, or drowning from liquid on the inside of their bodies. If you were lucky enough to avoid death, she said, you were still cursed with bone-jarring coughs and stained teeth. And the cause of all this misery? Smoking.

It was graphic for children our age, yes, and it proved pointless anyway because close to half the boys did smoke by the end of primary school – though perhaps more would have, and some of the girls also, if the nurse hadn't come.

I'd never considered smoking, not for a moment. I didn't like the messy ash or the smell. Still, I was rapt, astonished, appalled, but not for myself. The nurse went on and on, listing grim details in her calm, soft voice. I didn't cry, although I felt like it. Instead, I grew more and more determined.

For the next week, I scooped up my mother's cigarettes and lighter when she turned her back in the lounge room; I slid them down my sock in her car. I crept into their bedroom when my parents slept and pocketed the pack from her bedside table. I had tiny hands and quick, sly movements and no fear. She thought she'd miscalculated how many were left or forgotten them at the pub or in her car. No sooner had she driven to the shops, swearing, to buy more and another lighter than I would palm those also and press them into the narrow space down the side of the lounge cushion or the back of the kitchen cupboard behind the Pyrex. Over days, her aggravation rose. She was itchy all over. She had headaches. She turned out her handbag, stripped the bed, accused my father of smoking them, standing in front of him to smell his breath. I didn't for one moment think I was being bad, and when she asked me,

I lied to her face. I was serving a higher purpose and would have kept it up forever, remorseless, if she hadn't caught me crushing a packet under my shoes in the bottom of my wardrobe. She screamed at me so fiercely, so close to my face, that I wet my pants.

But that was years ago. These days, I was trusted. They never asked if I'd done my homework or where I'd been. I came straight home from school, I ate the food put in front of me. The idea of acting against their wishes, which I thought so self-evidently sensible, never popped into my head until all at once, I was overwhelmed by this determination to restore my family. My parents and I had a pact. I had done everything they'd asked of me, always, without complaint, yet our family was broken. It wasn't fair. I refused to stand for it.

Still, I may have avoided my actions to rid us of Steve if not for parent–teacher night.

Another week or so went by. I woke before my alarm, dressed and made my own Weet-Bix. I was still ignored at school, though now Larissa and the others made up rhymes about me while they played elastic: 'Andie Andie, her legs are bandy, pee on her panty.' I couldn't stop smiling. This acknowledgement of my existence was, I thought, an improvement, a sign they were beginning to weaken. They couldn't ignore me forever. Like generations of children before me, though, I felt safer staying in the library at big lunch, where before long I'd read every book on both shelves – Nancy Drew, the Hardy Boys, the Hal and Roger Hunt adventures, Alfred Hitchcock and the Three Investigators – and started at the beginning again. Soon I could recite large chunks of these books by heart. My father was still arriving home early in the morning and again in the afternoon when I was at school to walk Tippy, but I never saw him. Once he took her away during the day for a race meeting, I guessed, because of her post-race sweatiness and the smell of liniment and the changed position of her bowls and blankets. Just weeks before, when our dogs raced I was told of every decision in the lead-up and I kept an eye on the clock at school so I could hold my breath and close my eyes when the race was underway. Afterwards I asked a million questions about how the day unfolded. Now, I didn't even know when a race was happening.

Meanwhile, parent–teacher night was approaching. For the first time my mother would be the one taking me, so I reminded her the night before and that morning before I left for school. Still, at 5 pm when we needed to leave, I was sitting on the lounge, waiting. At ten past five, a car pulled into the drive and tooted. I looked out the window. It was Steve's blue car, and he was driving.

My mother stuck her head out of the passenger-side window. 'Hurry up, we don't have all night!' she yelled.

I didn't want to get in Steve's car, but my mother yelled again so I locked the front door and scrambled into the back seat. The radio was on, of course: the Olympic Park dogs. My mother's car smelled of smoke and chewing gum, with lipstick-stained butts cascading from the ashtray and half-empty paper bags of Clinkers and pink- and blue-wrapped

Columbines in the footwell. Steve's car was clean in a way that seemed suspicious to me.

'Do up your seatbelt, there's a good girl,' Steve said.

There's a good girl? Who was he, this stranger, to speak to me in that manner? He was no one. He didn't belong here. He wasn't one of us. I stared at my mother – in a moment she would tell him to pull his head in. She swivelled in her seat. I could see a seatbelt across her chest.

'You heard him,' she said.

I felt my face grow red. 'You always said you'd rather drive your car forever than get a new car with seatbelts. They strangle you and squish your boobs, that's what you said.'

My mother shrugged and gave a sly smile. 'And now I'm saying put your seatbelt on, like you've been told.'

Steve laughed. 'Times change. Keep up, Andie.'

'Yeah, Andie,' she said, laughing with him. 'Keep up.'

So I put on my seatbelt, the one on the driver's side behind Steve so I wouldn't have to see him. The belt felt strange and loose around my hips, yet it controlled me so that I couldn't slide across the seat from window to window like I did in my father's car.

My mother kept laughing as Steve backed out of the drive. She was in a good mood, and Steve was also. 'Get a load of teachers, they live in fairyland,' my mother said, flicking a butt out the window, and then she shook her head, wryly. 'I'm missing a shift for this.'

At the Bennetts Road intersection, a woman driving a car in the opposite direction looked in at us. I blinked to freeze her in time like a photograph – grey hair set in tight curls, and cat-eye glasses – and I imagined what she thought she saw. A family. A big dark-haired man driving a newish car, a pretty woman in the passenger seat and a child sitting behind him. The idea of people thinking that Steve was my mother's husband and my father felt insulting to me, and insulting to my actual father. I wanted to jump out and tell her she was wrong, or hold up a sign to the window: WE ARE NOT A FAMILY. Let's see if Steve thought I was a *good girl* then.

At last we pulled into the school. I had hoped my mother would tell Steve to drop us at the bottom of the driveway and that we'd walk home, but instead he drove up to the turning circle and parked.

'We'll be in and out in two shakes,' my mother said to him.

Steve opened his door. 'I might as well stick my head in, seeing as I'm here.'

In the back seat, I froze, my hand on the door handle.

'Oh Steve,' my mother said. 'You don't have to do that. Andie doesn't expect it, do you, Andie?'

'No, I don't.' It would be bad enough without my father. The idea of Steve coming inside, being seen by Mrs Murphy and whichever kids were there, was too awful to contemplate.

'I'd rather be anywhere but here myself, if I could get out of it,' my mother said.

'Still,' Steve said, 'I'd be going to Tracey's if I was there. Begin like you mean to go on, that's my motto.'

My mother looked skywards and clacked her teeth together. 'It's your funeral,' she said.

So Steve twisted his legs out of the car and in one movement, gripped the doorframe and hoisted himself upright with surprising agility, considering his bulk. We walked across the parade ground like the family that we weren't, and up the stairs into the library. Everything looked different at night: the walls decorated with posters made by the Grade 3s of Hector the Road Safety Cat, globes on the ledge, and maps of Australia and counting sheets pinned on noticeboards. The bookshelves were pushed to the side, making space for each teacher to sit at a desk across from parents. Against the wall under the louvres were a row of kids' chairs; we sat. Already at Mrs Murphy's station were Simone and her mother. I couldn't hear what was happening, but from being in class with Simone, I could certainly imagine. Everyone around us – other parents waiting, and other kids, and teachers – seemed to be staring at us. At Steve, I mean.

When it was our turn, Mrs Murphy fetched an extra chair for Steve and we sat there opposite her, with my mother in the middle. Steve's knees had no way of fitting under the tiny desk. Mrs Murphy shook hands with my mother, who introduced Steve with his name, that was all. For a moment it seemed that no one knew how to begin.

Mrs Murphy tapped her pile of papers against the desk. 'Normally Andie's father comes to these. He's the only father, usually.'

'The only man in a room of lonely women, all sick to death of their husbands,' my mother said. 'Surprise, sur-bloody-prise.' She took a new pack of cigarettes from her bag and tore the cellophane wrapper, then flicked open the box with her thumb, worked the foil open, then flicked the box closed again.

Mrs Murphy looked at me, then at Steve.

'He's a friend of the family, all right?' My mother's voice was louder than necessary. The mother at the next table turned to look.

Steve raised his palms, nine fingers in the air. 'I'm just sitting in.'

'Right,' said Mrs Murphy, and she looked away. 'Now, Mrs Tanner, it's always a pleasure to have Andie in class. She's so polite, so smart. She's just a joy. But this time, I want to talk about her work ethic.'

Mrs Murphy wasn't looking at me now. It was as though she'd forgotten I was there.

My mother frowned. 'Righto.'

'Andie doesn't seem . . .' Mrs Murphy trailed off for a moment. 'She ignores the board entirely. She's excellent when you put a book in front of her, but lately in class, she's staring into space.'

If my mother was telling this story, she would see Mrs Murphy's concern as the first evidence of the person I was on my way to becoming. 'See?' my mother might say. 'Andie was always a good girl, always well behaved. Well brought up. But when she was twelve, she turned. Even her teachers noticed.'

But I don't see it that way. I'd expected this night to go like all the others. I remember the shock of all at once feeling as though the ground had vanished under my feet. I gripped the edges of that small chair as if its legs would give out under my weight. There was nothing I could hold onto now. My father, the dogs, my friends were all lost, or at least missing. The last thing I had been sure of was this: I was good at school the way other kids are good at running or catching a ball. And more than that — I was a *good girl*. If I wasn't that, I no longer knew who I was. I wasn't sure how this was happening, how my world had gone from something very predictable to this swirling mess of surprises.

'We've had some . . .' — my mother paused for a moment — 'changes at home, over the last few weeks.'

'I see,' said Mrs Murphy, glancing at me.

'But I don't see how that's any of your business,' my mother said.

'I'm not talking about a few weeks. She was tending like this last year, though now it's worse,' Mrs Murphy said. 'She just doesn't seem to focus.'

'Is she playing up?' My mother folded her arms. 'Because I would find that very hard to believe.'

'No,' said Mrs Murphy. 'It's not that. She's a bright girl. I think she's not being sufficiently challenged.'

My mother ignored her. 'Andie.' She turned to me and narrowed her eyes. 'There will be hell to pay if you're behaving like a ratbag.'

'I'm not,' I said. 'I do everything she says.'

My mother's eyes widened. 'Everything *who* says? She's the cat's mother.'

'Everything Mrs Murphy says, I mean.'

'Andie is weeks away from high school.' Mrs Murphy held her throat in one hand as though her head was too heavy to lift on its own. 'I want her to knuckle down. Starting now. Yes, Andie has earned an A-plus in every subject this year, and her behaviour is excellent. But she doesn't seem to be trying.'

All this time, Steve said nothing. He frowned, his big cockroach eyebrows melding in the middle.

'If she's topping the class, then big whoop,' my mother said.

'I think Mrs Murphy is saying she wants Andie to roll her sleeves up, because her schoolwork's only going to get harder,' said Steve.

'Yes, exactly,' said Mrs Murphy.

I see now that this couldn't have been easy for her. So many kids in our class did poorly; any other teacher would have categorised me as one child they didn't have to worry about. Not Mrs Murphy. She was seeing a problem, even if it was difficult to explain. If she thought I could improve, she wanted me to improve. She wanted the best for me. I wish I had seen that at the time. But I felt only betrayal.

'Tending like this last year, you said. Yet somehow you didn't mention this to Andie's dad before,' said my mother.

Mrs Murphy put her hands on either side of my report card, on the table in front of her. 'It never came up.'

My mother snorted. 'Funny that. Problems are for mothers, I guess.'

Steve cleared his throat. 'I have staff of my own,' he said. 'You can tell when someone isn't giving one hundred per cent.'

'That's exactly it,' said Mrs Murphy. 'Andie's coasting. She's relying on her memory. I'm concerned that if she doesn't learn how to study now, she'll find high school more difficult.'

My mother started laughing then pulled her handbag onto her lap. 'I don't have time for this bullshit.'

'She's got a good memory then?' said Steve. 'And she's bright?'

'Oh yes.' Mrs Murphy's gaze flicked to me then quickly away.

'But she's not paying attention to the blackboard, or working hard?' said Steve.

'Exactly,' said Mrs Murphy.

'She's a bludger, that's what you're saying,' said my mother.

'Do you have any advice?' said Steve. 'Ways to get on top of it?'

'I'd like to see her stimulated,' said Mrs Murphy. 'She's very fond of chess. There might be a club she could join. Or something extracurricular. One of Andie's classmates learns piano?'

'Jesus H Christ, what's the point of that?' my mother said.

Mrs Murphy turned to me. 'What do you want to do when you leave school, Andie?'

In that instant, I experienced something new. It was a deep warning flashing in my mind before I spoke. My first instinct was to answer this question honestly, but I didn't. For the first time I was conscious of measuring what I intended to say against how it would make my mother feel.

'Well?' my mother said. 'Mrs Murphy asked you a question.'

'I'm not sure,' I said.

'Well, I am,' said my mother. 'Clerk typist. That's what I did. You couldn't find a better job. On your arse all day, weight off your feet, always in demand. She can go to secretarial school when she finishes Grade 10.'

This was the first I'd heard of the idea. What did people do all day, sitting at desks? For a moment I imagined a fancy office with carpet and desks, and me in a skirt and high heels. It seemed very grown-up and glamorous, and utterly impossible.

'I think Mrs Murphy is suggesting Andie might go on to Grade 12,' said Steve.

'I'm not talking about a typing pool,' my mother said, resting her hand on Steve's knee. 'I was a *confidential* secretary, working for one boss. It's not for thickees. It's a cut above.'

'I think she could go on to university,' Mrs Murphy said. 'The world's a big place.'

My mother stared at her, then burst into laughter. 'And turn her into one of those dirty shit-stirrers who want to stop the rugby?' she said. 'Thank Christ we're not that kind of people.'

My mother sat in silence as Steve drove us home. Her good mood had vanished. There would be no champagne. No one ruffled my hair. My report card, deep inside my mother's handbag, was still marked with A-plus in every subject with the obvious exception of sport, but I knew there was no cause for celebration. Mrs Murphy thought I was a bludger. So did my mother. That was nothing to be proud of.

'Top of the class,' Steve said finally, his voice cutting the air. 'Pretty special if you ask me.'

'Puts in no effort, that's what the old bag said. Reminds me of someone else I know.' She swivelled in her seat to look at me. 'I wouldn't have invited Steve along if I thought you'd embarrass me. Do you not think I have enough problems?'

'Sorry,' I said, even though I couldn't remember her inviting Steve at all.

She turned around again and leaned her head back on the seat. 'Jesus Christ, Andie, work is all that matters in this life,' she said. 'Knuckle down, get a job, get a mortgage, stand on your own two feet. All the good grades in the world won't help you if you can't roll your sleeves up.'

'Sorry,' I said.

'Do you know how hard I had to work to put myself through secretarial school? I did every job you could imagine – dawn shifts at the bacon factory, cleaning houses, scrubbing toilets at the pub. You won't be following your father and your grandfather in the useless department, I can promise you that,' she said.

'Andie'll be fine,' Steve said. 'I'll help. You'll see.' Then he flicked his indicator on and steered his car into our street.

I did not want Steve's help but I was a passenger, strapped into the seat with a belt. I had my own plans for the future, and neither secretarial school nor university played any part in them.

Chapter 8

You had to finish Junior, which was Grade 10. It was the law. Both of my parents had their Junior, although my grandparents didn't. It seemed unfair to me. I would be fifteen by then, which was so old, considering everything I had to do and to learn.

And what were these important things to do and to learn? I planned to work with my father training greyhounds, and then one day become a trainer with a kennel of my very own.

This was the hard nugget of self-interest in the way I missed my father – I was worried for my own future. This could well have been what my mother would later sense in me, the opportunism at my heart. I longed to see my father, yes, but how could I learn to become a greyhound trainer if he wasn't here to teach me? I already saw myself as his apprentice and I paid attention to every small thing he did. I was more likely a burden to him, that quiet man who treasured his solitude. I was always hanging around, asking question after question, talking endlessly. But I wouldn't grasp that for some years. Back then I considered my father and me to be a team, and that I was irreplaceable. I had yet to realise how easily I could be replaced.

Yet I didn't want my mother to know. She would feel disappointed and possibly angry, because in my choice of work I was favouring my father. Choosing him.

It was the first time I remember feeling torn between my parents. In the months and years to come, if I drank orange juice or ate beans – my father's favourites – I would remind my mother of him. I stopped drinking juice and eating beans. Sometimes when I was doing nothing at all, the expression on my face would set her off. When eventually I began to visit him, when I was in high school, she would drill me with questions: 'What did he smell like?', 'What was in his wallet?', 'Did he pick you up in a car?', 'What was in the glove box?' and 'Did you see *her*?'. Once, when she had asked me to look in his bathroom cabinet and report back, I told innocuous lies – that there was Panadol on the middle shelf when in reality it was aspirin – because any truth at all felt like betrayal. I would feel this constant tension, this monitoring and extrapolating my parents' emotions, for the rest of their lives, and beyond.

But that was in the future. Now, I wondered if my mother would try to stop me becoming a trainer and, if so, what I could do about it. Mrs Murphy had said the world was a big place, but it wasn't. Not to me. The world was our house and my school and the track. I loved watching the races on the rail with the rest of the crowd, but I wanted more than that.

I wanted to be the registered trainer, the one responsible for a dog once they arrived at the track before a race. I wanted to be the one to attend the weigh-in and the vet inspection which cleared the dog of injury, confirmed their identity and checked the bitches weren't in season. I wanted to be in charge of their pre-race routine – to make sure they didn't drink too much water and that they emptied out in good time before the start, to strap them and apply talcum powder or Vaseline to scrapes or chafing, to fit their race rug and muzzle. I wanted to do everything that was done by my father.

The colour of the rug wasn't up to him, of course. It was determined by the box number, which was the same at every track around the country and randomly assigned. I don't know exactly how this box draw happened because I was never there – little numbered balls pulled out of a twirling wire cage like at bingo, maybe – but it's more important than you might think. Dogs have inexplicable preferences just like people and can be natural railers or straight or outside runners. Railers head straight for the inside and so prefer the 1 or 2 box. Straight runners do better in the middle of the pack, so for them the 4 or 5 is ideal; some dogs are so poor at cornering that they're only raced at Capalaba, which is a straight. Outside runners tend to be a little unsociable. They like the 7 or 8 because it suits them to run wide, to feel a sense of freedom away from the others. To this day I have a kind of synaesthesia where in my mind the number one is always red, two is black-and-white stripes, three is white, and so on, right up to eight being pink.

In my plans for the future, I would be the one in charge.

What is twelve-year-old me actually doing when my father the trainer is doing this work? Nothing useful.

I'm standing on the fence near the finish line with a cup of hot chips doused in vinegar, waiting for my mother to walk our dog in line with the seven others in the pre-race parade, showing them to the crowd before the jump. She is usually the only woman. I try to imagine myself in my mother's place, in that white coat, my lovely pup on a lead in front of the crowd. I cannot manage it. My mother could be a model, even wearing the regulation white coat that, many years later, I realise looks uncannily like my future lab coat. I wave at her, but she doesn't see me. I am so proud. Sometimes I say, 'That's my mum' to a stranger beside me, and he says, 'Is she, love?' without lifting his gaze from his form guide. Someone in the crowd might whistle at her. She never turns her head but she likes it, I can tell.

During the pre-race parade, most dogs are calm. They are old hands with quiet temperaments; they've been here before. A few are excited, jumping forward. They need to be kept on a short lead until they reach the boxes, especially if they're showed the lure beforehand, which my mother always did. She believed it helped them understand what was about to happen – which is giving the dog more credit than it's due, in my opinion. Boxing itself requires some finesse and my mother was a natural. The trick is to remove the collar and leash immediately before loading, with the minimum ground still to cover. Straddle the dog confidently, keeping one hand on its chest and the other on its abdomen. And don't drop the lead – it could tangle around the dog's feet – and don't throw the lead behind you because it could hit another dog. And then lift them as far into the box as you can manage, pushing a little further with your hand on its bottom, when and only when ordered by the starter, using the very minimum amount of force. This is because you want the dog to focus on the front of the boxes and not to be distracted by hands or knees or pressure from behind that might encourage their attention behind them, or in the worst case, make them turn around. If the dog escapes during loading or turns in the boxes, its race is effectively over. If a dog's tail is caught in the door, the injury can be severe and it can become box-shy, and then its entire career is over.

Dogs are usually paraded by their trainers, not their trainer's wives, but my father preferred to be the one waiting in the catching pen. I asked him why on one school holiday afternoon when the three of us and two dogs were driving home from Lawnton after a reasonably successful meeting of two placings – a second and a third. The dogs were standing in the back of the wagon with their heads over the back seat, waiting for pats from me.

My mother laughed. 'I'd like to hear you explain that, Eddie,' she said. 'Go on.'

'Your mum's the looker of the family,' he said. 'I like to show her off.'

'Bullshit,' she said. 'Why don't you tell her the truth for a change?'

This was something important about training, something I'd need to know. I shuffled forward and leaned over the front seat, just as the dogs were doing behind me.

My father cleared his throat. 'The truth is this, you can learn a lot by the way a dog pulls up at the end of a race,' he said. 'Muscle soreness. Twinges. And even if the dog's moving fine, you can spot problems early if you pay attention to the way they act. If they snap at other dogs, or look relieved at the end of the race – you know that look they get when they're shitty? When they blow air out of the corners of their mouths so that the inside of their cheek wobbles? And so forth. Sometimes animals are in pain but their brain doesn't know it yet. That's why they're bad-tempered.'

This all made perfect sense to me. *Catching is about paying attention.* I made a mental note.

My mother stubbed out her cigarette in the ashtray in the dash. 'That's a lovely story. Now tell her the real reason.'

'That is the real reason,' my father said.

'The *real*, real reason.' She curved the corners of her mouth upwards and clicked her teeth together. 'Or I will.'

'Well, sport.' My father cleared his throat. 'If I feel good about a dog's chance – and I usually do or else what's the point of starting it – most likely I've set aside a bit of cash to have a little wager.'

I knew this already. Prize money only made up part of a trainer's income. Betting on our own dog also made money for us. This was often done at the last minute when the odds of more favoured dogs had already shortened. The trainer was busy before the race, so this plunge was the job of a trusted friend.

'Go on,' my mother said.

My father changed gears, slowly, and seemed to concentrate on indicating.

My mother swivelled in her seat to face me. 'Your father thinks that if the whole crowd, other trainers and punters, see a female doing the parading and boxing, they'd think that she – me, that is – had a hand in it. The training. And who in their right mind would gamble on a female trainer? No one, that's who.'

I looked at my father, then back at her. I tried to tell if she was joking. Sometimes it was hard to tell.

'I'm trying to get the best odds, Val, using all the weapons at my disposal,' my father said, his gaze in the side mirror. 'No crime against that.'

'So if Mum parades the dog, you get longer odds?' I said.

'I'm not saying it's right, sport,' my father said. 'It's the way of the world.'

'You keep telling yourself that,' my mother said.

'I don't hear you complain about it when we have a win,' he said.

'You're the trainer,' she said. 'I'm just your humble servant.'

This thought had never occurred to me. 'Does this mean girls can't be good trainers?' I said.

They looked at each other.

'What do I always tell you,' my father said, 'about why the dogs is the best sport there is?'

'Because it's the fairest,' I said.

'Is it fairer than the ponies?' he said.

I knew the answer, of course. Horseracing is dodgy. You can bribe jockeys to pull an animal or to interfere. Plus, normal people can't own horses. You've got to be a millionaire. That's why governments always try to shut down the greyhounds but never the horses: because rich bastards all stick together, and they all want to stop working people from having a bit of fun.

'The dogs are for everyone,' I said.

'Rich or poor, teenager or pensioner, new Australian or old,' my father said. 'At the dogs, everyone's equal.'

My mother snorted.

'Do you think I'm wrong, Val?' my father said.

My mother lit another cigarette and blew smoke to the vinyl roof. 'What your father is saying, Andie, is that most punters are idiots. If a bloke thinks you can't do something because you're a girl, just go ahead and let him think that. Being the favourite means high expectations and short odds. It's never a bad thing to be the underdog.'

Over my decades working in universities around the world, I can say that this advice proved to be sometimes right and sometimes wrong.

'When you're a little older, parading them will be your job,' my father said.

'When?'

'Soon. It'll be here before you know it.'

But I didn't want that job, not really. I wanted to be the trainer, to have the biggest kennel in all of Queensland and a wall of winning photos and a cabinet of shining silver cups and ribbons to make him proud, but that would sound like I was up myself. Besides, I knew there was no way I could take my mother's place.

As it turned out, I never paraded and boxed a dog at a track or trained one, because everything about my life changed. All my knowledge about training is theoretical. My only memories of attending greyhound races are as a spectator, standing on the fence.

If I shut my eyes and concentrate, this is what I do remember:

I can't see my mother from the fence once the dogs are loaded, only the green light on top of the boxes. The lure starts up. The tone of the race caller – almost always Mick Cox, who would occasionally pass us in the ring, where he'd nod and say 'G'day, Val' to my mother in that familiar voice – has been all conversational generalities up to now. Once he says, 'The bunny's on the way' though, his tempo and volume and urgency increase.

The anticipation is almost more than I can bear. There are little shivers of electricity sparking through me because our dog is about to show her mettle, what she's made for. I'm jumping on the spot. The buzzing energy overpowers my limbs when at last the lids go up and Mick Cox cries 'Off now!' or 'Racing!' or 'They're away!'

My breath catches.

Those exquisite animals, all that compact muscle and forward propulsion and desperation. The next twenty-five or thirty or forty seconds are the culmination of the dog's whole life with us from the moment we picked them up as a puppy: all that feeding and brushing and walking, all that preparation and solicitous care compressed and concentrated. They are triers, the dogs. They are desperate and straining and giving it everything they have. Nothing on earth can stop them.

And what do I feel?

Standing on the rail waiting for the dogs to fly past – there is nothing like it. I've felt it at dawn when they're only trialling and the trainers are jovial and the air still cool and milky, and I've felt it at serious meetings at night with huge sums at stake, the caller in the background bellowing and strident, the sky a velvet black above and the dogs themselves like darting stars.

As a family, we rarely went to Eagle Farm and Doomben or even Albion Park, and never on Saturdays or during the Carnival, when the whole course fills up with overdressed mugs who wouldn't know how to punt if their life depended on it, and whose stupidity was related to their inbreeding, according to my mother. When you're on the rail waiting for horses to turn into the final straight, you can feel the thud of hooves inside your chest, echoing through every hollow space in your body, making your heart skip. Children especially have to fight some primeval instinct just to stay put. All your senses are warning, *There's a stampede coming! Run!*

At the Gabba or Beenleigh or Lawnton, you don't feel that.

Dogs are weightless compared with horses, and in slow motion it's obvious that to them, gravity means nothing. They hover, stretched horizontal, their mouths open wide within the muzzle for oxygen. The dogs are streaks of light; they are life, flashing before your eyes. The balls of their feet and their toes seem too small to generate the speed of the rotary gallop, which is the fastest of their seven gaits. A dog track is small, so spectators are closer to the action. In winter, you see the mist of their breath, see the sweat sheen on their flanks. Horses are smart when they run, calculating to avoid the whip and a collision, following the instructions and shifts in weight of their jockey. Mostly stick, no carrot. Greyhounds are loveable but they're not the Einstein of dogs. They have no thoughts in their empty heads, not a one. They are fluid instinct; they are molten, desperate desire. They are all carrot and no stick.

What do other children dream of becoming when they grow up? Astronauts and models and firefighters and train drivers? Dogs do not race at the Gabba anymore, not since 1993. Beenleigh closed down in 2003 and even Lawnton – a perfect circle of a track, all grass, with a ring of ten to twelve bookies where over a thousand people would bustle on a Tuesday afternoon – was demolished in 2017. There are now only two tracks in Brisbane and six in all of Queensland, from a peak of fifteen. I'll leave it to you to decide if this is good news or bad.

Chapter 9

From my age now, I can see all the different versions of myself lined up, the traits and beliefs and values that each iteration held and which ones they kept and which they discarded. Sometimes I think Andie at twelve was the original and each subsequent Andie was a photocopy of the one preceding her, and these copies faded and lost colour, blurring and softening over all these decades. Other times, it seems these past Andies are distinct enough to be different people altogether. I pity many of them. I see how hard she tried and how often she failed, and how she was wrong about so many things. And some Andies I will never forgive.

From those years I lived with both my parents, I remember the dogs of course, and the races; watching *Countdown* on Sunday nights with my father, who never showed any interest in music but stared at the screen as though at the zoo; my mother, who once made a special trip to Kmart to buy me elastic so

I could play with the other girls. I remember a watch my mother owned but never took out of its fancy box, which held thin leather straps of different colours and a series of interchangeable enamelled surrounds for the face. I remember my father's football trophies, tarnishing in a heap under the house.

But in those weeks, due to my temporary difficulties at school, I remember time spent by myself either talking to Tippy or in my room, designing my future home where all my greyhounds would live upstairs with me and take turns sleeping in my bed. I read and flicked through my autograph books and played with my Barbies and practised chess against myself. I made jumping beans from tiny ball bearings and bits of aluminium foil flattened with my thumbnail; I decorated sheets of paper with the coloured pencils I'd got for my birthday and folded them into chatterboxes.

I remember the day after parent–teacher night as clearly as anything. I was putting my port in the racks when Larissa and Tammy and Simone and a few others came up behind me. I could smell their breath before I saw them, like warm milk. I turned around.

At first a soft feeling went through me, as though I was releasing a deep breath I didn't realise I'd been holding. Of course they couldn't ignore me forever. Of course not. Then I saw Simone, the ringleader today for some reason, standing in the centre and folding her arms.

'What are you smiling at, Andie? I hear your mum's traded your old man in.' She ripped the nail off her thumb with her teeth and spat it on the ground. She was wearing shorts that I knew to be her brother's and her feet were bare.

I swallowed. 'Rack off, Simone,' I said. 'You stupid bint.'

'"Rack off, Simone",' said Tammy, her voice a high-pitched imitation, her features distorted. Everyone tittered.

'Broken home, hey, Andie,' said Clayton. He was halfway through a cream bun and cream and jam clogged the corners of his mouth. 'Too bad.'

'Yeah,' said Tammy. She pushed out her lips so I could see inside them, wet and pink. 'Too bad, so sad.'

I turned to look at Larissa, who was standing next to Simone with her hands on her hips. 'You know what's too bad?' I said. 'I happen to know where Macavity is. It's too bad that I might just keep that information to myself.'

I can't properly convey my own surprise as I heard those words come out of my mouth. I could say that I was frightened – all these kids in a semicircle around me, menacing. But the truth is, at my school, fights among girls were rare. I'd only ever been in one and that was in Grade 4 with Simone. I remember a wild few moments where we scratched and slapped and pulled each other's hair on the netball court after school, and I remember being angry beyond reason, but I don't remember what about. I can argue I was defending myself when I lied about Macavity. And yet. It was all so long ago. It's equally possible that my anger should have been directed towards my parents, or anywhere except at a little girl missing her cat. That I was waiting with those words, hoping for an excuse to use them. At any rate, I did not waver.

And it worked. I could feel the mood change. The disappearance of Macavity had obsessed the whole school, and now they looked at each other, heads tilted. They were uncertain. Everyone loves a mystery.

The bell rang, yet no one moved.

'She's bullshitting,' said Clayton eventually. 'She's a bullshitter.'

'I put posters on heaps of poles,' I said. 'If you ride over to Camp Hill you'll see them.'

'Posters on poles, big whoop,' said Simone.

'Cats can't read, dickhead,' said Clayton.

'Someone phoned me,' I said. 'A girl. A girl's mum phoned me, I mean. She has Macavity.'

Simone turned to talk to Larissa. 'She's making it up,' she said. Then she turned back to me. 'This girl. What's her name?'

'Tracey.' My gaze was steady and my voice calm and even, without any hesitation. 'She goes to Camp Hill Primary. Grade 5. Macavity showed up at their place. He was starving. They thought he didn't have a home. Tracey loves Macavity, her mum said. But she'll make Tracey give him back if the owner really wants him.'

At first, Larissa said nothing, but I could see her eyes. She was wanting it to be true. She was unsure what she could say next that would make it true. It wasn't that I didn't feel for her. I did. I wasn't trying to make things worse. But I felt myself at war.

'So why don't you have Macavity right now?' said Tammy. 'If this girl's mum called like you say?'

Why didn't I have him? My mind whirled. 'Tracey loves him, see? They have other cats. He fits right in. They want to keep him. I told Tracey's mum I'd think about it and ring her back.'

'He wasn't starving,' said Larissa in a small voice. 'He wasn't. He won't like it there. He likes it with me.'

I leaned back against the port racks, looking as relaxed as I could manage. 'I guess that's up to me to decide, isn't it?'

Mrs Murphy came to the door of the classroom. 'What's this, a union meeting?' she said. 'You heard the bell, move it.'

We broke apart and made our way into the classroom. I kept my gaze down, inspected my nails, stared out the windows. I was usually the one looking at Mrs Murphy as she spoke, being polite, but after the things she'd said to my mother last night, she could suffer.

For the rest of the day, everyone kept their distance – but I was no longer invisible, I knew that. I could see them looking at me, whispering among themselves in the corners of the playground at little lunch, trying to decide if I was telling the truth about Macavity.

Ten minutes before the end of the day, Mrs Murphy stepped outside the room to speak with Mr Swan about something. Alan Greve leaned forward from his desk behind me and threw a folded-up note on my desk. I opened it. It was from Larissa.

I love Macavity more than that other girl, the note said. *Come over to my place, I'll show you. My mum will make a cake.*

This was a victory, of sorts. Now I had an invitation to Larissa's home, with cake, but I couldn't accept yet. Not until I knew where Macavity was. Quickly, before Mrs Murphy came back into the room, I wrote *I'll think about it* on Larissa's note, and almost handed it back to Alan before it occurred to me the danger of Larissa's mother being involved. Mine generally avoided talking to the other mothers because they were stupid, boring cows, but if the news got around, if Larissa's mother told, say, Mr Uhlman the butcher about the imaginary Tracey, and he told my mother – I'd be dead. So I added, to the bottom of the note: *NO telling your mum or you'll never see Macavity again.*

Clayton hung himself with his father's belt when he was barely out of his teens; Simone dropped dead in her mid-forties, a stroke while waiting for a bus with her infant grandchild – she had full custody while her daughter was in prison. I don't know what happened to Larissa. Girls marry, change their names, become impossible to track.

In my mind though, all of them are still twelve or thirteen, with grubby knees and red faces and the smoothest of cheeks. Even those who are still alive and hearty at our age, or at least alive on Facebook, the boys astride Harley-Davidsons and the girls in mother-of-the-bride frocks beside unsmiling men, seem adult facades disguising their familiar child selves. This is perhaps what ghosts are. Perhaps there are no haunted buildings or forests or fields. Perhaps there are no haunted places at all, just memories of younger versions of the dead, or the grown.

I never went into my mother's bedroom anymore. From the doorway, I could see Steve's possessions – a misshapen clay bowl that held coins and cufflinks, a black comb with a thin handle and an oval wooden hairbrush with stiff bristles – on top of her dresser, instead of on the other side of the room between the wardrobes where my father's had been. Just the sight of them was upsetting to me, as was the can of shaving cream, silver-handled razor and extra toothbrush that appeared in the mirror-fronted cabinet above the bathroom sink. The thought of my father's drawers, which I was sure held Steve's underwear and undershirts, and the wardrobe, full of his suits and shoes, was mortifying.

It made me sad for the boys at school who had no choice but to grow up to be men. It would be bad enough having a penis. I remembered seeing my father in the shower and little boys changing out of their togs at the pool, and feeling overwhelmed with pity. I had my smooth, pale front, beautiful and sleek as a seal instead of those dangling, misshapen growths, like an oversized skin tag or a tumour. And I would not be destined to carry my dull belongings to one woman's house after another, where they sat next to pretty doilies and crystal vanity sets and shining gold lipsticks. Every man I had ever known lived without anything pleasing – no favourite dress or shoes, no bangles or flowers. On the shelves above my own bed was a bride doll, the most wonderful thing I owned, and I would take her down from time to time to feel her satin dress and smooth her yellow hair. My bedspread was Holly Hobbie, which wasn't even in the shops yet (my mother knew a bloke who knew a bloke) and my favourite earrings were tiny gold hearts. To live surrounded by everything dreary and worse, to not even notice . . . it was yet another reason to be grateful for being a girl.

Despite my avoiding Steve as much as possible, I began to notice something. He was watching me. It was obvious, because I was used to my parents barely noticing me at all. I began to feel his gaze as I lay in front of the television or read my library book at the kitchen divider. Although I found it unnerving, it didn't make me spend more time in my room. This was my house, not his – that was my thinking. I was the one who belonged here. He can look at me all he likes. If anyone should leave, it was Steve.

Around that time, he went out early one Sunday morning and when he came back, I was reading a library book on the lounge and my mother was in her room, smoking and resting. He stood just inside the front door and winked at me.

'Oi, Val,' he called out to my mother. 'Come out here a moment.'

There was a long pause. I wondered if she'd heard him.

'You come in here,' she yelled back eventually.

'I have a surprise for you,' he yelled again.

'Well, I have a surprise for you in here,' she yelled back.

He cleared his throat and looked at the floor. 'I have a present for you, I mean.'

Soon I heard her door open, then she appeared in the hall. She was wearing her red satin dressing-gown with golden dragons embroidered on it, a present from my dead uncle who'd sent it from Vietnam, and her hair was flattened at the back from where she'd been lying on the bed.

'This better be good,' she said.

He held his two fists out. 'Pick one,' he said to my mother.

She looked down at his fists, then up at his face. 'Don't be a clown,' she said. She frowned, as though she was trying to decide if this game was fun or annoying.

'Fine,' he said. 'If you don't want it, I'll give it to Andie.'

That confirmed it. It was fun, my mother decided. She giggled and touched his left fist. He opened it – empty – raised his eyebrows and put the other fist behind his back. 'Too bad.'

She started laughing properly then. 'No, this one, this one,' she said, reaching behind him to open his other fist. I'd never seen my mother move like that, so fast and playful. She seemed in that moment to be a much younger woman. She was thirty-three then, impossibly old, and I'd never before considered that once she was a girl not much older than me, with her own schoolfriends and her own inner life of strategy and dreams. Now I realise that it wasn't her age that confused me. My mother was often angry or irritable, always exhausted, sometimes resigned and stoic, but I'd never seen her show such carefree joy.

Steve was much stronger than her and stood firm as she wrestled him, laughing and gesturing to me, as though I was part of their game instead of what I really was, which was performatively disinterested, although I couldn't stop watching from the corner of my eye. My mother was being stymied. I'd never imagined her not getting her own way, not being the strongest person in any interaction. She barely came up to his shoulder. I knew I was small because everyone told me, all the time. I didn't realise my mother was also small until I saw her pulling with her whole weight on Steve's arm, unable to move it. He was a tree. All her actions were futile. Then all at once he held his other arm in front and opened his fist so his palm was flat.

'For the colour of your eyes, Val,' he said.

'Oh. Oh.' My mother snatched up whatever was in his palm then rushed to the kitchen where she bent down to look at herself in the oven door, holding something up against her face and turning from side to side. 'Oh, Steve. I've never seen anything so beautiful.'

Steve went to her and plucked the something from her hand. He turned to face me, then held whatever it was up in front of his face.

'Oi,' he called out to me. 'Miss Bookworm. What do you think of these?'

I raised my gaze. From my position on the lounge, I had no idea what it was that he was holding. 'Lovely,' I said, because I'd judged that was the correct response.

'What are lovely, exactly?' he said. 'And what colour are they?'

'Oh Steve.' My mother seized whatever it was out of his hand. 'If you're looking for appreciation from that little miss, save your breath.' She admired them again, then said, 'I suppose I shouldn't take them to a jeweller for a valuation? For insurance purposes?'

He smacked her playfully on the bottom. 'I wouldn't advise it,' he said.

She laughed so hard she could barely stand up straight, as though this was the funniest answer anyone had ever given. 'Oh, you're a devil,' she said, eyes gleaming.

Later, I saw what Steve had given her: a pair of rectangular emerald earrings the deep green of mango leaves, the stones held in place by gold claws. The jewellery of the 1970s was – like everything else about the decade – chunky and oversized and likely costume, but fun and carefree. The earrings I'd seen in *Dolly* were huge hoops and dangling enamel shapes in burnt orange and dark purple, or something made to look Indian. Those emerald earrings couldn't have been more different. They were classic, elegant. I had never seen anything like them.

I have them now, in a matchbox in my bedside drawer. My eyes are green like my mother's but still I never wear them. Even all these years later, I've never taken them to be valued. If ever I feel sentimental about my mother, whenever the feeling of loss and regret rises up in me like bile, I use these earrings as an antidote. I think about the woman who owned them before Steve gave them to my mother.

Sometimes in my imaginings this woman lived in Ascot or Ashgrove, and had come home from the theatre to find the double doors leading to the terrace had been jimmied with a tyre iron and her house was ransacked and everything her husband the barrister had ever bought her – her pearls, the small Blackman that hung over the Louis XV chest – was gone. Other times, the woman lives in Tingalpa or Darra and those earrings were left to her by her own mother, the last precious things she'd owned, that she'd somehow managed to hold onto when they'd lost everything in the drought of 1943, when her husband was in Changi and she'd shot all their cattle and the bank had taken the land. In this version, the grown daughter had been home when the burglars came, and they'd threatened her, or struck her, and she'd been terrified for her life and the lives of her babies.

Steve was not the thief, but that barely mattered. It's a simple economic equation – without customers for stolen goods, nothing would be stolen. And it's a fact as old as humanity that some women own beautiful things and some do not. There are people, I know, who think that this kind of theft works to equalise the fortune that benefits some more than others. Would I think better of my mother if she'd had a militant socialist mindset, if she thought the act of taking earrings from a woman born lucky and passing them to me was justice? Perhaps. Children cling to anything that would posthumously rehabilitate their parents, and I've often found myself, in considering my own life at least, giving too much credit to intentions and too little to actions.

But that was not the case here. I don't recall her ever expressing an opinion about anything to do with political beliefs or values at all. She certainly did not believe in equality. If anything, she believed in the opposite. In doing things the way they had always been done, in *knowing your place*, and in a natural hierarchy of existence.

As well as material wealth, a sense of the fundamental decencies is parcelled out unequally at birth, as Scott Fitzgerald said. One thing I can guarantee about my mother is this: she never gave the smallest thought to the woman who owned those earrings before she did, or the actions that were undertaken to deliver them. I am equally certain that my mother was right in what she said to Steve that night. I have no doubt they were the most beautiful things she had ever seen.

Chapter 10

Meanwhile, the world went on turning. My parents might have bought the newspaper for the form guide, but I read it all, front to back, and as the year drew to its close I knew about the journalists missing in East Timor and that New Guinea no longer belonged to us.

'What's going to happen with Whitlam?' I asked my mother one night when she was making dinner.

'What?'

'The government.' This hadn't clarified things, I saw from her face. Our government was Joh and Sir Gordon and Russ Hinze and the others. 'In Canberra.'

'Oh. Canberra. How should I bloody well know?' She was slicing potatoes for boiling the way she cut all vegetables, with a paring knife against her thumb. I never saw her use a chopping board. I doubt we owned one. 'Why do you waste your time reading about people who wouldn't know you from Adam?

Do you think Whitlam is waiting for his dinner and thinking, "I wonder what's going on with Andie Tanner?" Worry about you and yours, that's my advice.'

Other things in my life were more straightforward. Every mystery, every problem had a solution, at least according to Nancy Drew and the Three Investigators. All I needed was a clue. The earrings Steve had given my mother only solidified my thinking. Like Larissa's treasures hidden inside her white piano stool, I was certain that Steve's bag held a treasure trove of stolen jewels which would prove that he was a fence.

I knew what my mother had really been asking when she wondered if she could take the earrings to a jeweller for a valuation. Anyone who came to our house was amazed by our appliances, and not just the obvious ones like the microwave and the colour television we owned some weeks before the first broadcast. My mother had a battery-powered nail-filer with cuticle attachment, a Lady Sunbeam shaver, a massage gun and a hair dryer with a plastic hood embossed with gold flowers. Like my mother's earrings, they sometimes arrived without a box or any kind of packaging, but not always. In the high part under our house, where there was barely space to crawl between the ground and the underside of the floorboards, was a graveyard of more appliances: a stereo complete with speakers, a toaster oven, a jaffle-maker, a television and two more microwaves. All of these were broken but couldn't be taken for repair in case their serial number was recorded somewhere, so instead they lay mouldering, exposed to run-off and spiders, waiting for the earth to reclaim them. My mother had bought them from an assortment of blokes at the pub.

Our clothes also came from men at the pub; lovely dresses and tops and pants still bearing their Waltons or McDonnell & East tags, which we hoped would fit because they could never be returned. Mostly they did fit. The full-time job of these men was walking into department stores wearing overalls and carrying clipboards, and wheeling out racks of clothes in front of shoppers and staff. They knew a thing or two about fashion, what was likely to be popular and quick to sell, and which sizes would fit which of their customers or their customers' children.

There were no clothes inside Steve's white bag, of this I was sure. Instead I imagined loose diamonds, handfuls of them, like the shattered glass you sometimes found in gutters, and an elaborate emerald necklace that matched my mother's earrings, and possibly a crown like the Queen's with a purple cushion for the head. I had no desire to possess any of these things but if I could just look inside the white bag, all of my problems would be solved. I could tell my father what I found and that would surely be enough to bring my father home, and get rid of Steve for good.

I cannot explain my thinking here. My mother bought the appliances and the clothes with her money, I knew, because she told me often enough how little my father contributed to the running of the household. But my father heated his tea in the microwave when my mother was working, and he wore the clothes. Why did I consider stolen jewellery to be more serious than any of these things? Because it was impractical, perhaps? Or because having a fence living in our home was different from buying things from acquaintances? My best guess is that I saw my father as different from everyone around us. I thought him better. He was my hero, as I've said before. He wouldn't tolerate it, I was sure. He would come home.

That night I sat downstairs beside Tippy in her kennel with a notepad, devising ways of being alone with the bag for a few moments. In stories, the detective would set off the fire alarm or pretend to faint as a distraction, but we had no alarms at home and I doubted I could convincingly fall without hurting myself. I was holding the notepad close to my face, sketching out a way into my mother's bedroom through the ceiling via the panel in the bathroom, when I heard the back door slide open. It was Steve.

Steve rarely came under the house and had almost nothing to do with Tippy. He didn't even acknowledge her. If my mother mentioned her or any of our past greyhounds in his presence, he'd shake his head.

'Understand this, Andie, mug trainers are as bad as mug punters,' he once said to me while my mother was mashing potatoes for tea. 'Your old man had a family to support. What did he think he was playing at?'

Now, on the stairs, Steve was in his normal clothes, a white short-sleeved shirt with a pocket in which he kept three pens, and a pair of shorts and thongs. He stopped at the landing halfway down – he moved awkwardly at the end of the day, as though his weight was too much for his knees – and looked at me like he was waiting for me to say something. When I didn't speak, he sat on the stairs, gingerly. He still didn't say anything, so neither did I. I folded the pad quickly, so he couldn't see my plans.

'Guitar, I reckon,' he finally said.

He wanted me to ask what he meant by that, I could tell, but despite or perhaps because of my mother's rules about making conversation, I didn't.

'Guitars are better than pianos, no question,' he said, after a while. 'More sociable. I don't know a single soul who owns a piano. Where would you even put one? Imagine going camping for the weekend and taking a piano for singalongs. Ridiculous.'

I'd never been camping. We didn't take holidays as a family, though once I went with my parents to the dog track at Bundaberg. We stayed in a motel overnight and the next morning, a tray with toast in paper sleeves and tiny cardboard boxes of cereal was pushed through a trapdoor in the wall. It was the most amazing thing I'd ever seen.

I didn't say this to Steve, though. I didn't want to say anything at all, but the pressure was too much to bear.

'I guess,' I said.

He nodded as though I'd said the perfect thing. 'Guitar, on the other hand. Now that's useful. That's how you make friends.' He looked down at the cement floor. 'If that's something you'd be interested in. Making friends.'

He'd noticed all the time I spent alone, I guess now. He'd also noticed that I listened to music, like every child on the verge of being a teenager. I had a cassette player in my room and two posters on my wall: one of Sherbet and one of Suzi Quatro. I imagined Daryl in his satin jacket and smooth chest singing 'Cassandra' to me, and I imagined being Suzi in black leather singing 'Devil Gate Drive'. At school, we were supposed to have music for one hour a week on Tuesday afternoons. At the beginning of the year we learned the recorder but Mrs Murphy said she wasn't being paid enough to listen to that so now we went to the library instead for quiet reading, which was fine with me. That was the extent of my musical knowledge. I'd seen Larissa's piano but I'd never seen a guitar. The question of which was the superior instrument had never entered my thinking.

Just then, the back door slid open again. I could tell by its speed and force — it hit the stoppers — how my mother was feeling as she came down the stairs. She was working fewer shifts now and was home more often. She had a tea towel over her left shoulder, which I could see as she bent down at the top of the stairs to look through the railing. Tippy jumped to her feet when she heard the noise of the door.

'Andie?' she said. Then she noticed Steve sitting on the stairs. 'What are you two doing down here?'

There were three of us down here, I wanted to tell her: Tippy counted.

'Just having a chat,' said Steve.

Steve's heavy, hairy forearms were resting on his knees. He didn't turn around to look at her, so she came further down the stairs until she was blocked by his bulk. She looked around as though someone else was there, hiding, and she narrowed her eyes at me. 'What about?'

I didn't say anything. What could I say? That guitars were better than pianos? Who would believe we were talking about that? Moments passed.

'Nothing much,' Steve said.

'I was asking Andie,' said my mother.

'Nothing much,' I said.

'Tweedledum and Tweedledee. Down here, just the two of you, talking about nothing much.' Her mouth made a shape as though she'd tasted something sour.

'I'm thinking it might be a good idea for Andie to take guitar lessons at the music school at Coorparoo,' Steve said. 'After school.'

My mother answered him, but she kept staring at me. Her voice was louder than it needed to be. 'That's what you think, is it? What's brought this on?'

'It's good for a girl,' he said. 'School can't teach her everything.'

There was a pause, in which I could hear all of us breathe.

'Oh yes, the whole world revolves around Andie. Funny how no one ever cares what'd be good for me,' my mother said.

Steve made the effort to swivel and looked up to her. 'I'll take her myself,' he said. 'Book her in. Pay for it. Pick her up after school and drive her.'

My mother's face became hard and pale and very still, and time seemed to spread out and pressure built in the air, and I felt that terrible, itchy feeling of something bad about to happen. I didn't know what I'd done – but that wasn't quite true. I knew she'd be furious if she could see the plans in my notebook for looking in Steve's white bag. But that was between me and Tippy. There was no way she could know about that. Still, it's the things you never tell anyone that make you feel the most guilt.

'Look at all this rubbish,' my mother said, waving her hand. 'Empty drums and your weights and all those sugar bags. By the looks of my grass, you might be having trouble finding the mower.'

'It's out of 2-stroke,' Steve said. 'I'll pick some up.'

'I've been in the kitchen mashing potatoes like a mug while you've been down here having a lovely chat about music.' She rolled her tongue around her teeth. 'Guitar classes, hey? Well, isn't that a nice thought. Say "Thank you, Steve".'

'Thank you, Steve,' I said quickly.

She whipped the tea towel off her shoulder and folded it into a tight square. 'Very nice of him, isn't it? When you're not even his kid. When there's nothing in it for him,' she went on. 'It's fair to ask why he's so intent on spoiling you. Especially when he's got a girl of his own that he doesn't even see.'

I didn't see how making me learn the guitar was spoiling me, so I had no idea how to answer this. From the look on his face, neither did Steve.

'Well?' she said.

'It's good for a kid—' began Steve.

'However, Steve is not your mother,' she said to me, as though he hadn't spoken. 'I am your mother. And I am saying no to this guitar nonsense.'

I squeezed the notebook so hard my fingers turned white. I didn't ask for any stupid guitar lessons, and I certainly didn't ask for Steve to stick his nose in or talk to me or look at me. It wasn't fair that I was getting in trouble for this. I twisted to stick my fingers through the door of the kennel and felt the touch of Tippy's grainy nose, and then she licked them. *It doesn't matter what your mother thinks*, Tippy was saying. *You've still got me.*

'I just thought—' Steve said.

'I know what you thought,' my mother said. 'And I've been thinking too. I've already decided to fix this bludging the old-fashioned way. Doreen at the TAB needs a hand on Saturday mornings. Cleaning, putting up the race sheets, marking the scratchings, emptying the ashtrays. I'll drive her myself. No assistance required from you.'

I'd been inside the TAB, of course, and waited while my parents were punting. When I was little we spent hours there, me sitting cross-legged on the floor under the counter with a colouring book while Mum and Dad put their bets on and watched the races on the television high up in the corner. And I knew my mother's friend Doreen. My mother sometimes worked at the TAB herself, on Melbourne Cup and Caulfield Cup and other times when Doreen needed a hand, like when she'd had an entire week off work for her breast enlargement.

Doreen was nice and she liked me. Sometimes at night I had to answer the phone and if it was Alf, Doreen's husband, I had to tell him that my mother was out with Doreen and I didn't know where. But my mother wasn't out. She was in her bedroom, punting and smoking. It was a trick that Doreen was playing on Alf. My mother always used to say, 'What husbands don't know won't hurt them.' Sometimes my mother would come home with a Curly Wurly for me, a present from Doreen for talking to Alf on the phone.

'You've got to be fifteen to have a job,' I said.

My mother clapped me, slowly, sarcastically. 'You're right, Miss Smarty Pants,' she said. 'But Doreen owes me a favour. Several favours. You'll be off the books. Nothing cures bludging faster than a little motivation. You should always, *always* earn your own money. Now do you two want tea, or don't you?'

Steve looked at the ground and stood, wincing. I scratched behind Tippy's ears, and told her goodbye and that I'd be back before bedtime to let her out for a wee, and I followed Steve upstairs and we ate my mother's tea of steak and mashed potatoes and beans in silence, and guitar lessons were never brought up again.

Up until then, Saturday mornings were for cartoons – *Josie and the Pussycats* and *Scooby-Doo* and *H.R. Pufnstuf*, which wasn't a cartoon but was even better. My parents hated cartoons because television was garbage in general and a waste of time during daylight hours, and anything American rotted your brain, but they hadn't strictly forbidden them.

From then on, though, my mother would stagger out of bed early on Saturday mornings and drive me to the TAB at Cannon Hill in her dressing-gown. I was sad to miss the cartoons, but mostly excited. I wouldn't be working with dogs, but it was a chance to earn money of my own which I could add to my savings towards my kennel. My working life was about to begin.

When I was in my twenties and starting my PhD, I took it into my head to take guitar lessons. I had little time and less money, yet bought a second-hand guitar from an exchange student moving back to Italy who'd placed a notice on the board outside the student union. My boyfriend at the time was astonished. I was as unmusical as a person could be. I couldn't hold a tune. He saw this sudden desire as evidence of my quirkiness; another thing he found cute and so different from all our friends, like the way I knew how to gamble at the races, my ability to talk to anyone without shyness and my way with animals.

If my unconscious mind could be excavated, though, I'm sure the answer would be there. Perhaps the day before, I'd passed a dark-haired man on the street who carried weight around his hips, or I'd been at a friend's house for tea and watched her absentmindedly fold a tea towel into ever decreasing squares.

I lasted only two lessons. My fingers – which were sufficiently agile to squeeze upwards of thirty individual samples onto my acrylamide electrophoresis gels with fine tweezers in a perfect line – would neither move to the correct position on the strings nor generate enough pressure to hold them still against the neck. I could not remember the order of the notes; I couldn't tell the sound of one from another. The patient music student who was my teacher told me that anything was possible with time, and stressed the mental benefits of discipline and the value of the journey over the destination, but I knew the window for that specific brain plasticity had well and truly closed. I gave the guitar to an op shop in West End. I hope it found a more worthy owner.

There are people who would give anything to be young again. They bemoan every year that passes, they take their regimen of supplements, they inject their lips and cover every evidence of who they really are as though nothing in the world matters so much as the smoothness of your forehead. These people are mistaken. The number of years ahead of you is not the measure of anything at all. They forget the helplessness of being young, that feeling of being a cork tossed by waves. To be in need of protection again – that is my worst nightmare. Children have no say in anything that concerns them and if they try to exert some control over their own life, they are blamed for everything that goes wrong from that day forward.

—

The morning after it was decided I would begin work at the TAB, I came downstairs to say good morning to Tippy as usual before I left for school. I had heard nothing in the night but from the bottom step I could see her door was swinging open and her leads and collars were missing. I reached my arms inside the kennel, as though there was some way she had evaded my sight. I could still smell her, but more faintly now. Our last remaining greyhound, my darling Tippy, was gone.

Chapter 11

These are some of the things that can go wrong with greyhounds.

Canine distemper and infectious hepatitis, both preventable, but dog-racing was then and is now a sport for battlers who cut corners to their own detriment. It was common back then to wait until a dog was a year old at least to see if they justified the cost of the vaccinations yet unchecked – these diseases can rip through a kennel and in the 1970s were almost always fatal. There was also lockjaw, which sneaks in when pups lose their baby teeth and chew on junk, and Lepto, which isn't usually fatal but sick dogs are poor runners, so it might as well be. Added to these are roundworm and hookworm and fleas, muscle tears and dislocations, track legs and general soreness, strained wrists and toes, viruses and kidney infections, ripped dewclaws and worn pads and bone bruising and spine misalignments and stomach problems and nerves, and many more injuries and illnesses I never knew about.

Compare that with the misadventures of children, which consisted of the occasional tonsillitis or broken bone – I'd had two, due to my general clumsiness – and measles, mumps and chickenpox, which we didn't have the brains back then to fear. Children fell out of trees and ate dirt and had no allergies. We were lined up and vaccinated at school, for what I can't recall, although there was a scar the size of a ten-cent piece on the top of my left arm for decades, and I don't recall my parents being informed or caring, although they were non-negotiable about teeth-brushing and learning to swim.

That children are hardier than professional athletes is, I suppose, not surprising. Small humans grew without being fussed over back then, without consideration for optimising performance. Greyhounds, on the other hand, must be coddled. There are milliseconds between winning and losing, between money and debt and thus between life and death – for the dogs at least.

Yet despite the many problems that plague greyhounds, disappearing into thin air was not usually one of them.

That morning when I came downstairs to find Tippy missing, I sat in front of her kennel for a long moment. It was all I could do not to crawl inside, shut the door behind me and curl up on the carpet offcut where she used to lie and wrap myself in her blanket. I could not bring myself to move. I saw no reason why I ever would. Tippy was the smallest dog we'd ever had and one of the best. In her maiden, she'd drawn the 4 and we'd not had a hope but somehow, while the rest of the field jostled in a pack, she squeezed through a gap not much bigger than herself. She won by six lengths. She was that proud when Dad caught her. She knew she'd done good. Even all these years later, hers is the face I see most often – her coat a soft fawn like butter caramel; her ears, sometimes sticking up like a roo's and other times collapsing down on themselves so they were invisible from the front, which made her look like a bald old man. Her neck and chest were white and soft as though she was wearing a shirt under a suit jacket. She sometimes puffed when she exhaled, making the soft dark corners of her mouth flutter. She hid her head in my armpit when she was frightened. At times I thought she could read my mind.

Eventually my mother came downstairs with a basket of Steve's shirts to put in the washer. She was showered and dressed already in her pink pedal pushers and a button-up shirt. She stopped short when she saw me.

'What the bloody hell are you still doing here?' she said.

'She's gone,' was all I could manage. I was still in my pyjamas, sitting splay-legged on the cold cement. I had no idea what time it was.

'Who's gone?' my mother said.

I couldn't say Tippy's name. I could only reach my arm inside the empty kennel.

'Hallelujah,' my mother said as she hoicked the basket higher on her hip and lifted the lid of the machine. 'Finally he got rid of that useless bitch. That dickhead father of yours would try the patience of a saint.'

That was the first time she'd spoken about my father that way since he left. It was an early sign that my mother's blasé shrug was fading and hatred was building. She was happier with Steve than I'd ever seen her but it is typical of some people, I've learned over the years, to barely feel a wound when it first happens. These people see themselves as tough. For them, the most terrible things are like shallow paper cuts. Over time though, these people do not heal and instead their wounds deepen and bleed more, not less. Because they are not tough. They are merely insensible – so removed from themselves that time must pass before they firstly feel anything, and secondly identify what it is they felt. Their assailant is long gone and has forgotten all about them, yet they turn the circumstances over in their minds and open the wound fresh, and they themselves drip acid into it.

At that moment, though, I only thought about Tippy, and wondered where she was and who was looking after her. I buried my face in my hands so my mother wouldn't see.

'Jesus Christ, keep that up and I'll give you something to cry about,' I heard her say.

That only made things worse. I tried to be a big girl like they always said, to behave like a grown-up. My mother never cried, and neither did my father. I squeezed my eyes, I bit my cheeks.

'They're just animals,' my mother said. 'You eat animals, don't you? What do you think your sausages are made from? Don't be such a baby.'

The dogs weren't just animals, not any more than we were, and especially not Tippy. But there was no way I could explain that.

'All this fuss over nothing,' my mother said. She breathed in and out with the weary air of someone carrying a great burden. 'If you're finished sooking,' she said at last, 'you can get ready for school while I have breakfast and then I'll drive you.'

An observer might think I disgusted her but I knew differently. My mother never drove me to school, and this offer was the equivalent of another woman picking me up and drying my tears and kissing me. I knew to judge her by her actions, not her words. I was grateful. I felt loved.

My mother's breakfast took no time at all. For as long as I could remember, she started the day with a Vincent's washed down by Coca-Cola from small glass bottles she had delivered by the wooden case and that I wasn't allowed to touch. I sometimes brought it to her in bed. It's impossible to explain a Vincent's to someone today and be believed, but they were a pink powder containing aspirin, phenacetin and caffeine, available in single doses inside folded paper sachets, sold everywhere. Women then were trained not to ask questions of men in white coats, and the Vincent's helped my mother get out of bed, gave her a bit of zing. An olde worlde Red Bull. Eventually phenacetin would be banned but by then she had taken at least one a day for all of her working life. Within a few short years she would start complaining of back pain and a strange cloudiness in her urine. It's possible that she was already in the early stages of renal cell necrosis.

I was on my way down the hall when Steve came out of the bedroom. I stopped where I was. He was bare-chested and wore long pyjama pants, because my mother always had the air-conditioning in her room on high. The expanse of dark hair across his chest made me blush and cringe. The hall was narrow and he was wide. To pass I'd have to touch him, so instead I stopped.

'Good morning.' He scratched his stomach and tilted his head from side to side. 'Sleep in, did ya?'

I looked down.

'Are you sick or something?' he said.

'Andie,' my mother called from the kitchen. 'Can you get my smokes? Beside the bed.'

'Righto,' Steve called back, as though she'd been speaking to him. He rubbed his hand over his face where he had tiny whiskers, then he curved his arms and scratched under his armpits, playing at being a gorilla. 'Time to make myself beautiful.'

He whistled and gave a little jump, then he went to the bathroom and closed the door. He would shave before showering, like my father did, I guessed.

'Andie?' called my mother. 'My smokes.'

I had an idea. Inside her bedroom, I didn't have to look hard: Steve's white bag was in plain sight, on top of his side of the wardrobe. My mother's wardrobe door was open and the bed was unmade. One of the pillows was on the floor. There were clothes strewn all over – my mother's, not Steve's. Her beige underpants, her grey skirt from yesterday and a brown bra. There was a strange smell. The sheets looked greasy and dark body shapes marked where they had lain. Steve's side of the bed was the same as my father's – nearest the door, so he could get up without disturbing my mother. I went around to her bedside table where – amid the ashtray and lamp and a packet of barley sugars and the glass for her teeth and a copy of *Australasian Post* and a tube of Vaseline Intensive Care – there was a packet of cigarettes. I opened it. There were six smokes inside.

I took a deep breath. 'It's empty,' I yelled.

'What? It can't be,' she called back.

I took out the cigarettes and scrunched them into the pocket of my skirt, then I wiped my hands on the sheets to get rid of any stray brown curls of tobacco. I felt myself shaking, and I wondered if it was only on the inside or if she would notice. I could hear her steps coming down the hall, heavier as she came closer. The cigarettes were ruined now and there was no going back. In another instant, she was beside me.

'Let me see.' She took the empty packet from my clammy hand. I tried not to look at her, just in case. 'Bloody hell,' she said. She scratched the inside of her wrist where there was a mosquito bite and shook the packet as if she couldn't believe her own eyes.

'Bloody hell,' she said again. She shut her eyes and tilted her head back and for a moment, I felt a twinge of guilt.

I knew it would make sense for her to go to the shop on the way to dropping me at school, or even afterwards. But I had spent my whole life observing my mother and her moods.

Even when she was smoking one cigarette, she was dreaming of the next, and twirling it between her fingers. Being out of smokes for even a few minutes would be too long.

'All right,' she said at last. 'I'm nipping down to the shop but I'll be back to take you to school. Be waiting in the driveway in five minutes.'

Then she left me standing beside the bed while she grabbed her handbag and headed back up the hall.

I stood, frozen, until I heard the screen door smack, until I was alone in the house with Steve, then I ran to the window. As soon as my mother's car reversed out of the driveway, I jumped up on the bed in front of Steve's half of the built-in wardrobe. It was perhaps a metre away, perhaps less. I dug my toes into the edge of the mattress and tilted my body forward, towards the wardrobe, bracing myself with my hands. The door wobbled, but it held. I stretched one arm up to reach the white bag but I was too short and the angle too flat. There were no chairs in here, no books, nothing to pile up and stand on.

I heard the screech of the old sliding shower screen that always fell off its mouldy track, followed by the sound of the shower.

Inside my mother's wardrobe, empty wire coathangers hung among her clothes. I hopped down, grabbed one, then stood back up on the edge of the bed. I stretched as far as I could with the coathanger in my hand, trying to hook the handle, but I still couldn't reach. I tried different arms and different angles; I leaped in the air.

I jumped down again and collected both pillows and piled them one on top of the other right on the edge of the bed and stood on them, but they were too squishy and I gained almost nothing.

Then I heard the shower stop.

I heard the shower screen squeal. Steve was getting out now. He was drying himself with a towel, and soon he'd be opening the bathroom door and walking back in here, and I would be trapped.

I should go back to my room, this second. But I knew I'd never have a better chance.

In the gap between my mother's wardrobe and my father's was a small built-in dresser with a mirror against the wall and drawers underneath. I moved further down the bed and stretched one foot over to the top of the dresser. I managed it, barely. I pressed the sole of my foot down. It was a shiny, slippery surface, like a kind of plastic woodgrain, but seemed sturdy enough. Gradually, half-hopping, I moved all my weight onto the leg on the dresser, then lifted off the bed.

There was a pitiful creak from somewhere beneath me. I gripped the top of the wardrobe with one hand while I reached my other arm up. I groped blindly for a moment, then the tips of my fingers brushed the handle of the bag. I stretched a little further, until the length of my side and under my arm began to burn but, little by little, I managed to wrap the very tips of my fingers around the handle. I pulled the bag towards me. I could get it down now, I knew, and I could find the evidence I wanted.

Then I stopped.

After I looked inside, how would I get the bag back up there? There was no way.

They would know.

Then I heard a noise outside the window – my mother's car, as she pulled into the driveway. She tooted the horn. It was for me. She expected me to be waiting with my port, ready to jump in the car as soon as she stopped. A moment later, I heard the bathroom door open. Steve would stand there for a moment, opening and closing the door to dispel the steam, but he was coming. He would have a towel wrapped around his waist, as usual. He would still be damp, barefoot, gleaming.

He would find me standing on the dresser, with one hand reaching for his white bag.

I let go of the handle and as I did, there was a sharp crack beneath my left foot. I tilted to the side and almost lost my balance. Part of the dresser had caved in where I was standing. I jumped backwards onto the bed as quietly as I could, twisting in midair, landing on my knees. Above me, I could see the bag was a little askew on top of the wardrobe, but only a little. My mother's wardrobe door was still open, so I dived inside. I sat on the floor among her shoes, my knees tucked up tight, and slid the door closed.

The next thing, I could hear Steve. He was in the bedroom. Even from inside the wardrobe I could sense him, smell him, his aftershave and soap, so obviously foreign. I could hear him walking around, singing something I couldn't identify.

There was the smallest gap in the sliding door and through it, he came into view. He was naked. I could see his bottom and the top of his legs, so pale compared with the brown of his arms and feet. I shut my eyes. He moved to stand in front of his side of the wardrobe. I could hear the wire hangers sliding on the rail. He was choosing clothes and getting dressed.

'Andie, for Christ's sake, I don't have all day,' my mother called. She was in the kitchen now, looking for me. Steve continued getting dressed and when no one answered, my mother called again. 'Steve? Are you still here?'

'Yes, love.' His voice was so loud and deep that he didn't have to yell, not the way my mother did. There was only a thin chipboard door between us. He was right beside me. I could feel his voice inside my chest.

'Andie?' my mother called again, louder.

I held my breath. My arms were wrapped around my shins and I was not moving, not a hair.

I heard her stomping down the hall, muttering. Perhaps she would look in my room. I prayed she wouldn't see my port on the other side of my bed. Or perhaps she'd come in here and remember that her wardrobe door had been open when she left. I was thinking of what she would do to me if she found me here. I was shaking so much I pressed my feet into the floor to still them.

'Jesus bloody Christ, what I put up with.' And then my mother was in the bedroom too. 'I told that girl to wait for me and she's gone to school by herself. Not a brain in her head, like her bloody father.'

'She's no trouble, not really,' Steve said. 'You should see what mine get up to. Little monsters.'

'If she keeps this behaviour up, she's in for a rude shock,' she said. 'My mother would have belted me if I pulled a stunt like that, the old bitch.'

'Has old mate been to see her yet?'

My mother laughed. 'What do you reckon?'

I opened one eye the smallest crack. Steve was wearing underpants now, and a shirt. My mother was standing behind him, so I could only see her arms around his waist.

'Hello,' Steve said. 'What's happened here?'

I almost cried out. He had noticed the white bag had moved from where he'd placed it and he would slide the door open and they would find me here and that was worse than anything I could imagine. And I had done this to myself. I had risked everything and gained nothing. I was all at once incredibly sleepy and nauseous. I turned my lips inwards and bit on them. I could taste something curdled in the back of my throat.

'Jesus Christ,' my mother said. 'It's busted.'

They both moved forward, outside of my eye line. They were looking at the dresser.

'How could that have happened?' she said. 'I never put anything heavy there.'

Steve's knee appeared.

'This kind of veneer, it's a joke,' Steve said. 'Cheap build. I'll get a bloke to fix it. I'll ring him now. Be good as new.'

'Have some Weet-Bix first,' my mother said.

'Thanks, love,' he said. 'I'll be out in a sec.'

I heard a scraping above me. Steve was taking the white bag down from the top of the cupboard.

My mother left the room first, then Steve did, and a moment later I could hear noises in the kitchen: rustling, bowls and the clink of a Coke bottle on the divider. Through the crack in the door, I could see the white bag where Steve had left it, on top of the bed in front of me. I lifted the door so it wasn't touching the carriage at the bottom, slid it open then carefully, quietly, stepped out of the wardrobe. I took a ragged breath. I could hear the wireless on in the lounge room, cupboards opening and closing, and their voices. Steadily, I undid the long zip on top of Steve's white bag.

When I finished looking inside the bag, I hid back in my mother's wardrobe. About twenty minutes later, Steve came in to get the bag, then they both left in their respective cars and the house was silent, but I waited a little longer to make sure. I was very late now, but I thought my chances were good that Mrs Murphy wouldn't do anything because it was so unusual for me. I would tell her I left my homework in my mother's room and she was inside with her new boyfriend. Mrs Murphy would likely leave it there, but if she did ring my mother, so what? My mother knew I was late. I didn't think anyone would remark upon exactly how late I was. I would bury the crushed cigarettes deep inside one of the bins at school. No one would suspect a thing.

But going to school at all that day was a waste of time because I couldn't concentrate on anything Mrs Murphy tried to teach me. All I could do was think about Steve's bag, and what was inside it.

The bag was stiff, cavernous, almost empty. There were no loose diamonds, no emerald jewellery, no crown, no evidence at all that Steve was a fence. Nothing that I'd been expecting. There were only three red hardback ledgers like the ones my father used to record the track times of the dogs. I flicked through them; inside were people's names and numbers – some of them in dollars, from twenty and fifty to some thousands, and some of them were odds – pages of them, in columns, in tiny print. And underneath the ledgers, when I lifted them to look, was a gun.

Chapter 12

That night I dreamed of guns. They were lurking in my underwear drawer, my school port, in between the sugar bags in the pile near Tippy's kennel. They were stubby and matt, dark and menacing. I couldn't escape them.

I had never seen a gun, except on television. I knew nothing about them, had never heard the phrase 'the trigger pulls the finger'. But the guns in my dreams drew my hand against my will and by the time I dreamed of one under a chicken when I was checking for eggs, I could no longer resist picking it up. It was warmer than I expected, and much heavier. The grip had the texture of a clutch of tiny pebbles. Somehow I couldn't bring myself to put it down. I woke suffused with dread.

I can still see Steve's gun, clear in the bottom of that white bag – a Smith & Wesson revolver with a timber handle. I could pick it from a line-up, sketch it from my memory, swear to my recollection in a court of law. When you're a child, your memories are fewer and clearer by virtue of your life having been short. Your purpose is clearer also. You are new and the world is fresh and simple, and its heroes and villains behave as they should.

Sometime in the early 2000s, I was travelling for work and flicking channels late at night when I came across *The Great Gatsby*, the 1974 version starring Robert Redford, ridiculously handsome and doltish, and Mia Farrow as a vacant Daisy. I've always loved coming-of-age stories. Does a person cease to become a child in an instant, as the result of one pivotal action or observation? Or is it a gradual process like a diver rising through metres of ocean to reach the inevitable air? *The Great Gatsby* is really a story about two boys, one of whom dies before becoming a man.

Late that night, alone in my room on the 30th floor, I let the movie play in the background while I went over my schedule for the following day. At the end, when George shoots Gatsby, I sat bolt upright, shaking like a child. George's gun was the exact same one from Steve's bag. It was identical in every detail. It took several large room-service whiskeys before I could fall asleep.

The human mind is a fallible thing. I'd seen that film before of course, in the late seventies. If I had been put on the stand and asked to swear to the appearance of Steve's gun, I'd have likely perjured myself because I'm certain now my memory has been overwritten by that film. In reality, I can no longer remember Steve's gun at all.

Part of me knew I should tell someone what I'd seen. But who? Not my mother, who would have asked how I knew the contents of Steve's bag and, besides, was unlikely to be surprised. I wanted to tell my father but still didn't know where he was. Mrs Murphy? My grandmother? It seemed a betrayal to involve anyone else. A friend? Things would soon improve at school, I was confident, but right then I didn't have any.

It wasn't until the next day that I began to wonder *why* Steve had a gun. Perhaps he was dangerous. A killer. I thought back to the day he gave my mother the emerald earrings, how slight and weak she'd been as they wrestled. Perhaps he would murder her. Perhaps I would be woken in the night by a bang that shook the house and would find her bed soaked with blood and my mother lifeless there, mouth gaping and open, eyes cold and staring.

The next day in class, I barely concentrated. Walking out of the school gate heading home alone that afternoon, I was startled by someone calling my name.

'Andie! Goodness, are you away with the fairies?'

I turned. It was Larissa's mother, Mrs Byrne, leaning against her car opposite the top gate. She was in her white dress with the little upside-down watch pinned to her chest and thick white stockings and flat white shoes. Larissa was beside her, with her port. They had been waiting for me. I stopped, blinking, the image of my mother's body fading into the sunlight.

'We never see you anymore, Andie,' Mrs Byrne said. 'We miss you.'

I missed Larissa, more than I could say. But I missed Mrs Byrne too, and the softness of their house with its carpet and piano and bookshelves and spaghetti and family and so many other things.

'I need to pick up Melinda from the plaza,' said Mrs Byrne. 'Why don't you come along? I'll drop you home later.'

My heart began to beat faster. I looked at Larissa. Perhaps this was a trap.

'Please,' Larissa said.

'Or should I call your dad? Or . . . is it your mum at home now?' Mrs Byrne said.

This was something grown-ups did. Asked a question when they already knew the answer. Larissa had told her mother about my family, I could tell by the way she smiled glumly.

'You don't need to call anyone,' I said. 'No one's home.'

We were all jealous of Larissa's sister, Melinda, who was fifteen and already working at Kmart. While we waited for her to finish her shift, Mrs Byrne made some payments on her lay-bys and Larissa and I sat on the benches near the shoe repair and ate hot cinnamon donuts from a paper bag. At first Larissa didn't say much. Neither did I. Then we started to talk about Tammy and how brave she was to shoplift so much compared with Larissa, who only did it very occasionally. (I never shoplifted, though I didn't tell Larissa why: my parents said that only amateurs and idiots risked police attention for something so minor.)

Later, back at Larissa's place, Melinda let us listen to her new Skyhooks album in her room, where we normally weren't allowed, and we ate fat slices of chocolate cake baked by her mother. Then Larissa and I crawled underneath their house, which was close to the ground like ours, and she showed me where Macavity used to lie. It looked just like a squarish hole in the dirt, but I made appreciative sounds. Larissa also showed me everything that belonged to him: his metal food and water bowls, a bed with a rug that Larissa had crocheted, feathers attached to twine that he used to chase and an old teddy bear of Larissa's that Macavity had slept with when he was a kitten.

'I'm keeping all this safe, for when he comes home,' Larissa said. 'I bet he doesn't have his own bear at that other house.'

I didn't say anything.

'We feed him his favourites. He likes the tuna one best. And sometimes Dad gives him a kidney from the butcher's,' she said.

'That's good,' I said.

'You have to keep their water up,' she said. 'It's bad for cats if they don't have fresh water.'

'Dogs too,' I said.

'He belongs to me, not her,' Larissa said.

'Sure,' I said.

Tippy was gone, yes, but at least she was with my father. He would be feeding her his special blend of roo meat and kibble, brushing her from top to toe with his glove with the wire bristles. Her carpet and blanket were still in her kennel at home which was worrying, but he would have found her something soft to lay on. Perhaps Tippy was sleeping in my father's bed with him. And besides, when my father found out about Steve's gun, he would bring Tippy with him when he moved home again. Tippy was missing me as much as I missed her, of that I was positive.

'No one loves Macavity more than me. It's not fair.' Larissa sniffed and pushed her nose up with the back of her hand.

It was a gesture and a sentiment I always found endearing. I have no children of my own. It's nobody's fault; it's just the way my life worked out. I see my nieces and nephews when I visit, and I have my memories of childhood, so long ago. This is one thing I viscerally recall: children believe with their whole being that the world should be fair. When it isn't, they are at first indignant, then enraged. When children cease to believe that fairness is the world's natural state, when they are no longer angry or even surprised that is isn't, their childhood is over.

We were both very much children, Larissa and me. She was right, it wasn't fair. Macavity might be lost and frightened. The longer he stayed away, the greater the chance of something bad happening.

'I haven't said anything to Mum, like you said. I haven't told anyone.' Larissa screwed up her face and made a fist with her little white hand. 'But if you call that girl back and tell her to bring Macavity home, you can be my best friend again.'

Everything would work out, I could see it now.

'I will,' I said to Larissa. 'I'll get Macavity back. I promise.'

Despite my telling her it would be fine, Mrs Byrne insisted on ringing my mother at the pub to ask if I could stay for tea.

'It's the done thing, Andie,' she said, looking the number up in the *Yellow Pages*.

At the Byrnes', everyone sat at the dining table together – which Larissa and I had set with plates and cutlery and serviettes – even Mr Byrne, Larissa's father. Fathers were generally scary back then. If you were playing at someone's house when their father got home, the atmosphere of the house would change. Everyone became edgy, mothers as well as kids, because you couldn't tell what mood he'd be in and you'd be scared to make a noise or even show your face and you'd scramble home, because the last thing fathers wanted after a hard day was someone else's kids hanging around. Fathers yelled and grumbled and generally put the fear of god into you.

But Mr Byrne was different. He told jokes and asked questions and folded his serviette into different shapes: a crown, an elephant, he said, although they looked nothing like that, which was the funny part.

Mrs Byrne made chicken schnitzel coated in crushed cornflakes, and zucchini gratin, which meant cooked in white sauce with cheese on top, and no mashed potato at all. I'd never had zucchini before. It was delicious, though I'd have eaten it even if it hadn't been. Larissa only pushed it around her plate. She wasn't made to sit there until she ate it, even though Mrs Byrne had gone to a lot of trouble and not eating it all was ungrateful and a slap in the face. Larissa and Melinda used their forks like shovels, which was a hanging offence according to my mother, and Mr and Mrs Byrne had a glass of wine instead of beer, which also surprised me because only winos drank wine. Melinda, Larissa and I had orange juice.

'You have beautiful table manners, Andie,' Mrs Byrne said to Larissa and Melinda. 'You both could learn a thing or two.'

Mr Byrne picked up Larissa's crust and wedged it between the bottom of his nose and his top lip, like a bread moustache. 'Yes, you two,' he said.

'Joe,' Mrs Byrne said, trying not to smile. 'You're not helping.'

For dessert, we had Toffee Log, because having me there was a special occasion, Mr Byrne said. Then he pretended he'd had all kinds of famous people in his taxi: Billy J Smith, Johnny Lang from Easts, Jacki MacDonald, and Ray McGregor from 4IP, although of course he hadn't. We all laughed, except for Melinda, who said that he was the most embarrassing father ever, which made everyone laugh even more.

It was one more thing I didn't understand, and couldn't think who to ask. For the life of me, I didn't see what had embarrassed her. It was the nicest night I could remember.

Mrs Byrne dropped me home after tea. Larissa stayed home so she could do her piano practice.

'Larissa is still worried about her cat,' Mrs Byrne said, when she parked out the front of our house.

I froze, but she seemed friendly enough: none of the narrowed eyes or folded arms that adults use when making a point. Casual conversation, that was all, I decided.

'Between you and me, cats get run over. It's sad but true. Earlier this year the Hendersons lost their Minx, and last year it was the Greves. Never saw it again. Such a shame. A beautiful Burmese. I can't convince Larissa, though. She's sure Macavity will come home.'

'Little kids can be quite gullible,' I said.

She coughed then straight away covered her mouth with her hand. 'Sorry, something went down the wrong way,' she said. 'Kids can be gullible, Andie, yes.'

'But my dad says anything's possible. Cats do come back sometimes.'

'Well, your dad would know. You're a well-behaved young lady with an excellent vocabulary, and you're a good influence on Larissa,' Mrs Byrne said. 'And you can tell your mother I said that.'

That was the very last thing I was likely to tell my mother – it would have been the definition of big-noting – but I couldn't ask Mrs Byrne to tell my mother herself.

My mother and Steve were lying on her bed when I got in. She was wearing her new nightie, a rose-pink silk with thin straps that made her skin seem like it was glowing, and reading the form guide for tomorrow. I stood in the doorway of her room to say goodnight.

'What did you have for tea at the Byrnes'?' my mother said. 'Something fancy, I bet.'

'It wasn't fancy,' I said, but of course it was.

She pursed her lips and spoke in her funny high voice. 'We had caviar and drank tea with our pinkies sticking out and listened to Beethoven, didn't we, Steve?'

'Yep.' On his lap was one of red ledgers from his white bag, and his gaze was glued to it.

'And did you eat off of a lace tablecloth like proper ladies? With linen serviettes?'

The Byrnes had a tablecloth, yes, but I couldn't remember what kind it was. We didn't have a tablecloth but my mother had pointed out a lace one at Kmart once and said she'd buy it for my glory box, which was a tea chest she'd begin to fill on my thirteenth birthday, which was when girls stopped getting toys and books for presents and starting getting aprons and tablecloths instead. As for serviettes, the Byrnes' were paper, like ours.

'It's a miracle that Mrs La-Di-Da could bring herself to ring the pub,' my mother continued. '"We'd love it if *Andrea* could stay for *dinner*," she said. "Keep her as long as you like," I said. "Years, if you want." When she hung up, me and the girls laughed and laughed.'

'I like it better here but,' I said. 'They have to sit at the dining table and they're not even allowed to have the television on.'

'That'd be right,' my mother said. 'She's the kind of stuck-up cow that'd have one stupid rule after another.'

'Andie,' Steve said, 'I've left the adding machine at the office. Can you tell me what this comes to?'

'I've got a calculator around somewhere,' my mother said.

Steve shook his head. 'That's what Andie's for.'

He passed me the open ledger, with his hairy finger pointing to a short column of numbers. There was something about the way he asked, as though he was used to giving people instructions and never for a moment considered anyone would say no. I held the ledger close. I was good at maths. One Easter holiday when I was in Grade 4, I'd memorised all my times tables so I could answer questions faster in class but after everyone stared at me, even Mrs Taylor, I began slowing down again.

'Three thousand, two hundred and forty,' I said with a glance at my mother to see if she was noticing. She wasn't. She'd gone back to the form guide.

'Is that right,' said Steve, although I had the feeling he already knew. 'And this one?'

I focused again. 'Eight hundred and seventy-five.'

'Bewdy, Newk,' he said as he took the ledger back.

'You know why she wears those stupid white stockings?' my mother said. 'Mrs La-Di-Da.'

'Because she's a nurse?' I said.

'Because she has varicose veins the size of worms. Giant blue worms. I saw them at the fete last year when she ran the plant stall. What a mug she was, doing all that work for nothing. She was wearing shorts, if you can believe it. Look at these.' My mother pulled up the hem of her nightie so that it was above her knee, then raised her straight right leg. Her toenails were a perfect deep metallic bronze. 'Just look, Stevo. Not a vein to be seen.'

'Looks pretty good,' said Steve, but he wasn't looking. Then to me, he said, 'You're lucky that you take after your mum in the leg department.'

But Steve was wrong. I looked down to where the edge of my skirt sat. My mother's legs were beautiful all right, brown with straight and even knees, not freckled and knobbly with white patches and raised red scars like mine, from all my falls and grazes.

'Never mind, Andie,' my mother said, laughing and picking up the form guide again. 'Being Miss Australia isn't everything.'

I said goodnight and got ready for bed, but I couldn't sleep. I couldn't stop thinking about Steve and his gun, and what he might do to my mother in the night, so I waited until the house was dark and silent and my mother and Steve were quiet, and I crept out of bed.

I opened her door. Inside, her bedroom was lit by the streetlight outside and I could make out their two shapes under the covers. The aircon was loud, pumping full blast. I could see my mother's grinning teeth in the glass on her bedside table. She was snoring.

I settled myself on the floor, just inside the room. I watched, and I waited.

—

That was how I spent many nights over the next few weeks. I'd learned my lesson by being caught by my father in front of Tippy's kennel so as soon as I felt myself nodding, I went back to my bed, shutting my mother's door softly behind me. Some nights I didn't stay long; I could see from the digital alarm clock on my father's bedside table that less than twenty minutes had passed. Other nights I managed to sit there, still as a sphinx, for hours.

On those long nights, I made up strange stories inside my head as though I were playing Barbies without holding the dolls in my hands. Often the stories related to movies I'd seen, either on Sunday night at 8.30 pm, or later on Friday or Saturday nights. *The Poseidon Adventure* or *Paper Moon* or *American Graffiti*, but also older films I've never heard of since, like *Wild Is the Wind* and *A Town Like Alice*, the original with Virginia McKenna. Sometimes I'd imagine what happened after the movie had ended, or I'd change the ending entirely in my mind if I hadn't liked it. Other times, I'd pick out one of the characters that didn't feature much and imagine a whole new movie based around them. Sometimes these imaginings were so vivid I could scarcely remember which was the actual film and what was my own version.

By the time my mother and Steve had been asleep for a few hours, the danger had passed. That was my reasoning, at any rate. Steve would not wake in the middle of the night unprompted, fetch down the white bag and kill my mother with his gun. Provided she was alive right before I went to bed, I was confident she would remain that way until morning.

I was often groggy the next day at school, but that seemed a small price to pay. Looking back, I can't think of anything more ridiculous – a girl sitting on the floor in the middle of the night inventing stories in her head and watching two grown people sleep, believing she could overpower a big man with a gun. Neither my mother nor Steve ever saw me during those quiet hours, and just as well. I can't imagine how much trouble I would have been in. Besides, I might have killed them both with shock had they woken and seen a slight spectral figure in a white nightie watching them, eyes bright in the gloom.

Chapter 13

It was late spring, whatever that meant. We weren't gardeners or bushwalkers or birdwatchers. No one had hayfever. There was the Spring Racing Carnival, yes, but because fashion and glamour meant nothing they were just regular meets to us. It seemed the chill of the Ekka westerlies, the August wind that sliced through our 'winter' clothes, turned overnight into high summer. The end of school was close but now, it was about five in the afternoon on a Thursday. I was lying on my bed doing homework when my mother called out to me.

When I came out to the lounge, I saw that she was wearing a good dress and proper shoes, with her leather handbag over her shoulder. Steve was beside her in a collared shirt and shorts and shoes with long socks, and his keys were in his hand.

'We're going to the Gabba,' she said. 'If you want to come, you've got five minutes.'

Since the dogs began racing there almost three years before, the Gabba had been the most exciting place I could imagine in the world. It was the most competitive track in Queensland, with more prize money and prestige than Beenleigh or Lawnton or even the Tweed. Trainers came from New South Wales for races like the Gabba All-Star Invitation. The dogs raced at night, under lights. It was rare that one of our dogs got a start there, so my parents and I were usually spectators. Granted, there wasn't much else to do on a Thursday night, but more than five thousand people would come to watch the greyhounds race and there'd be around forty bookies, some from interstate. It was a different crowd from other tracks. There were fewer typical punters of the type I remember – sinewy, roughly shaven men with heavy earlobes and heavier stainless-steel watches, white-ish singlets visible under their thin shirts. At the Gabba, women dressed up, couples were on dates. Upstairs was a seafood restaurant with a wall of glass windows looking over the track, and if my father or mother won we'd go there for supper after the last race. I would order a seafood crepe, which was prawns and oysters and scallops in white sauce wrapped in a thin pancake, which I doubt still exists on any menu anywhere in the world but I thought impossibly sophisticated.

'It's a school night, but,' I said. The last race was after 10 pm.

'What a wuss.' My mother winked at Steve. 'Sometimes I think there was a mix-up at the hospital.'

'Come on, kid,' Steve said, jangling his car keys. 'Live a little.'

I wanted to go, of course. I loved it, but there was another reason I rushed back to my room and threw on my best dress and filled my purse with some, but not all, of my savings. I thought my father might be there.

'Whacko,' said Steve, when I came back outside. 'Now let's have a little fun.'

I sat in the back of Steve's car as he drove. He held hands with my mother all the way except when he changed gears, then he parked in the school grounds next door. Steve queued at the window, asked for two adults and one child and paid for our admissions, and again I was conscious of being there with my mother and him and wondered what people would say if they saw us. If anyone would ask why my father wasn't with us. And then we walked through the turnstiles.

I had never been inside a church. We celebrated Christmas with a tree and presents and Easter with chocolate; my vertical learning curve about religion would come later. My parents didn't discourage talk of Christianity, it just never came up. In class, I stayed at my desk while we chanted the Lord's Prayer in unison every morning, unlike the Brethren kids, quiet boys in collared shirts and girls in long skirts and scarves, who waited outside the door. I never gave that prayer a moment's thought. In my mind it was just another of the poems we memorised, and the most boring one at that. But that didn't mean our family had no religion.

Gambling was more than a pastime to us. Gambling was my family legacy, an ideology of living, the way brave people expressed their optimism about the world. It was a sign of engagement and of hope, of a belief that life would get better if only you had sufficient courage to take risks. I was proud of understanding the intricacies of betting on the horses and the dogs – the difference between a double and a quinella; how to understand odds and calculate returns – but gambling was more than animals or statistics, and more than money. Gambling lived in our hearts. I was brought up to believe that people who didn't gamble were sad cowards who hoarded their money, pessimistic and mean. For years into my adulthood I thought gambling – and with it, the stoic acceptance of good times and bad times without complaint – was the only honourable way to live. It was obvious that any boyfriend of my mother's would need to share this philosophy. Steve did.

He paused as soon as we were through the turnstiles, and took a deep breath. The air was heavy with the smell of cut grass and the sweat of the ring and money and cigarette smoke.

'It's a magic sight, this, isn't it, love?' he said.

My mother shrugged. 'If you're winning.'

I also thought it was magic. Even having Steve with us instead of my father wasn't enough to dampen the thrill – that first sight of the green track, glowing under the brightest lights I'd ever seen.

My mother fumbled in her purse and brought out five dollars in notes. 'If you win big, you can take us out for lobster,' she said. 'But if you run out, don't come looking for any more because you won't get it.'

She didn't mean it, not always. On my unlucky nights if I found her in the bar, she'd sometimes slip me another two dollars, or even another five if she was winning. And I'd brought some of my own money anyway, which she didn't realise I had, saving being inconceivable to her. Bookies would take a bet of two dollars, but begrudgingly and with eye rolls; it was an embarrassing amount, a bet for babies or mugs. To be taken seriously by a bookie I'd have to bet all five dollars a place on the one race – and if it lost, I'd be cleaned out. I could bet two dollars a place on the tote of course, which was a kind of on-course TAB staffed by women behind barred windows, but that was infinitely less exciting. It was where old ladies punted.

Steve seemed to read my mind. 'That's not enough to have a proper punt,' he said. He pulled out his wallet and flicked through a wad of notes before handing me another five dollars.

'She'll need a form guide of her own as well,' my mother said to him. 'Or else she'll be borrowing ours all night.'

Form guides were forty cents but Steve just nodded and headed to the form-guide seller standing over to one side in his white coat, calling out, his pile of guides beside him. Steve also bought pencils for my mother and himself. I already had one in my bag.

When he was gone, my mother pulled me close. 'Listen,' she said to me, 'check in with us every couple of races. I don't want you vanishing.'

I nodded, but I had one eye already on the betting ring. It was magnetic – and besides, my father might be in there.

Steve came back and handed me a form guide. 'If you get any good tips, let me know,' he said, and he winked.

With that, I headed off.

First I walked as far as I could in both directions, peering through the windows into the members' bar, skirting the betting ring, zigzagging up and down the stands. I couldn't see my father anywhere, but it was still early, before the first race. He might show up later.

For now, I had work to do.

The Gabba had a childcare centre, but I never went there. There were always other kids roaming in packs and playing games of their own, but I never joined them. I found a quiet spot in the stand where I could concentrate and, holding the form guide an inch or two from my face, peered at it.

First I looked for dogs I knew and liked. Even now, decades later, the names of my favourites from those days pop into my mind: Alpha Brava and Jalna's Star and the great Coorparoo Flyer, the beautiful fawn dog with the strange gait that was Greyhound of the Year in 1975 and that I once saw come from behind to win, although exactly when I cannot recall. I'd memorised the arcane language of abbreviations that described how each dog had performed in previous races. MDN, for example, meant the race was a maiden, for dogs with no previous wins; W meant it had run wide. I also considered trainers I knew my parents admired; dogs with winning streaks or unlucky past runs; and odd patterns in a dog's history, like lots of wins at regional tracks or fast times when placed second or third. After all that calculation, I decided to put my money on number 6 in the first, and so headed to the betting ring.

When I was very small, the ring was a frightening place: dozens of people jostling and rushing from bookie to bookie as the odds changed, or waiting until the final moments before a race to surge forward. I was frightened of being crushed. As I grew bigger, though, I learned to love it. The energy of the ring, the dance of punters and their hopes and dreams and triumphs and failures.

There were close to thirty bookies here tonight. The bookies themselves were in charge, standing high on their benches, calling out the odds and adjusting the dials next to the dogs' names on the board, but my attention was always on the pencillers, those funny and droll mathematical geniuses. They stood on the ground at the front of the stand with their bags slung across their bodies, joking with the punters yet never distracted, shouting behind them so the bookie could write the bet in their ledger. The nature of the job meant that pencillers were quick, because any money left untaken before the jump was a potential loss of profit. When a rush was on, they barely looked up – they could often recognise a punter by the sound of their voice – and they were chatty and funny, because if two bookies had the same odds, punters chose the one they liked best.

I found a spot on the outside of the ring and squinted, looking at the odds for the dog I wanted and trying to see if anyone I knew was here.

The pencillers couldn't take my bet directly from my hand, I understood that. It was the law. But they never talked down to me. They made me feel respected, important. I never had difficulty finding someone to place my bet; I never had a bookie refuse a bet that was clearly mine. The penciller would write the ticket solemnly and hand it to the adult, who would then hand it to me. I never lost my ticket, which is more than I could say for some of the men. I sometimes won, but never more than ten dollars, which an adult had to collect on my behalf. This was exciting without being noteworthy, which was lucky for me. If I lost all of my money and my mother wouldn't give me more, I would pick up discarded tickets off the ground in the hope some drunk or clueless man had thrown away a winner. This never happened.

I was standing on the edge of the ring when a couple stopped in front of me. I'd noticed them in the crowd earlier: he was thin and stooped, probably in his fifties, with threads of dank black hair and loose skin around his throat and pleated, sagging trousers held up with a belt. He had a similar look to my grandfather, and I knew what that meant. A drinker. The woman was about the same age, plumper, with blue-rinsed hair and a huge bosom, in a floral house dress with buttons down the front and a pair of glasses on a chain around her neck. A white plastic belt squeezed her waist in a way that looked uncomfortable. I noticed them because I thought them old-fashioned and out of place here, as though they belonged at the daytime tracks or at bingo or the RSL, and also because of the man's face. One eye was closed and purple and there was a deep bruise along the line of his jaw. A sprinkling of small dark red scabs were sprayed over his forehead. If my face looked like that I'd stay home, or at the very least wear sunglasses. But back then, for people in our circles, your appearance wasn't something that entered into your thinking.

The woman reached out and touched my arm, lightly, as though she were petting a dog. 'Well,' she said to me. 'You're here at last. That's a very good thing.'

'A very good thing,' the man said, although moving his mouth seemed to pain him, and he didn't look me in the eye. His skinny body tensed as he spoke, the sinews in his forearms like wires. 'Very good. But overdue.'

'Overdue, dear,' the woman said. 'But small mercies, yes? Better late than never.'

I had a good memory for acquaintances of my parents but I couldn't place them. Were they from the pub? Or did they have dogs? Owners, maybe, not trainers. My mother knew a lot of people and I couldn't be certain they wouldn't report back to her – but speaking politely to adults was by now so ingrained that it wouldn't have mattered.

'Thank you. It's good to see you.' I hoped that inspiration would strike as to who these people were, or that they would give away some clues.

'And where are the boys? Being minded, I guess?' the man said.

I didn't know what boys he meant. They had confused me with someone else, I was beginning to realise. I wished I could find a way to extricate myself or the race would start before I found someone to put my bet on.

'I don't know what your mother was thinking,' the woman said, without giving me a chance to speak. 'Far be it from me to criticise, but.'

'We would never,' the man said. 'Hardest job in the world, being a mother.'

'People forget that a father has rights. Some blokes couldn't care less, that's true, but your father isn't one of them. Especially when he's paying the bills and there are boys to consider.' The woman touched her husband's arm in the same way she'd petted mine, and she adjusted her weight to her other leg.

'He's moved back in, I gather. Or at least she's come to her senses. Sons need a father.' The man was looking at the ground as he spoke, mumbling through his stiff face.

The woman nodded. 'Oh, they do. Men and their sons, it's the way of the world. Daughters are a different story, no offence. Daughters are for mothers, sons are for fathers. Your mother needs to let bygones be bygones, that's what I said since the beginning.'

'Your father's been back to his old self over the last few weeks. Much happier. More . . . reasonable . . . in terms of allowances to his good customers, and so forth,' he said.

In a sharp movement, the woman's elbow jerked towards him, and though she didn't connect, he winced. Then she smiled at me, wider, and I could see a gap where one of her incisors was missing.

'Not that he isn't always reasonable. I wouldn't want to give that impression,' she said, her eyebrows knitting together. 'That we're not grateful. He's a patient man, your father, and very understanding about the unexpected turns in a person's life that aren't anyone's fault. A generous man.'

The sound of the race caller describing the field and the odds had probably always been there, background noise until now, when something changed – the volume or the clarity. The energy in the ring began to increase; the tempo of talking and walking and betting. The race was close to starting.

'We saw him buy you a form guide when you came in. Plenty of blokes wouldn't be arsed. He's a gentleman all right.' The woman smiled at me again, but seemed more doubtful. 'On your way to see him now, are you? He's in the bar. We didn't want to interrupt him.'

They each took a step backwards.

'Make sure and give him our best,' the man said. 'And tell him I'm right as rain for Saturday.'

I nodded and thanked them. In a blink, they had melted into the crowd. I understood then. They weren't friends of my parents. They thought that Steve was my father and that I was Tracey.

'Hello there, chickadee,' another voice said, right beside me. 'Thinking of how you'll spend your winnings?'

I looked up. It was my mother's friend Lorraine, who used to work with her at the pub until she got married and her husband didn't let her work there anymore. I explained to her I needed an adult to put my bet on.

She held out her hand. 'Not a drama,' she said. 'Who'dya fancy?'

I gave her my five dollars, told her my dog, and followed her into the ring to the bookie I'd chosen. Lorraine put the bet on for me. I distinctly remember it lost.

Chapter 14

Looking after children wasn't considered a job for men back then, not even when the children were their own. My grandmother and her siblings, aged two to eight, were dropped at an orphanage when their mother died by their alive-and-well father. My own mother told stories about sleeping in a basket underneath my grandmother's ironing station at Fish Steam Laundry in the Valley when she was only a few weeks old rather than being left with her father, my grandfather. And I, in turn, spent the occasional Saturday at Doreen's TAB when my mother worked casual shifts there. No one minded. Even as a toddler I was no trouble, or so everyone said. I always did what I was told. What my father was doing at the time, I couldn't say.

Back then, punters queued in front of the TAB operators – only two or three in a small agency like this, and always women – and recited their bets from memory or notes on the back of an envelope or their markings on the form guide from the newspaper, and the operators would write the tickets in their own hand. I remember being fussed over while waiting for my mother in the back, behind the grill and the heavy security door in the small private section not visible to the customers. Against one wall was a safe, twice my height, ideal for dropping on Wile E Coyote's head, with a massive dial in the centre that I longed to twirl. I remember the huge wooden frame where Doreen would sort copies of each ticket by the number of each horse or dog, waiting for the phone call from head office when correct weight had been declared, after which she would scoop up the losers and secure them with rubber bands and calculate the dividends on an adding machine with its long tongue of paper.

By the time I started work, the first computers had been installed, though some things remained the same. Even now I can shut my eyes and conjure the TAB: punters murmuring to themselves in their secret language against the low volume of the races on the TV in the corner of the ceiling; the smoke and ash, and the tickets stacked in thick piles in crevices on the benches in front of the felt-board walls; and everywhere the pervasive smell of bundles of old-fashioned notes counted by hand by Doreen and piled up in the safe. Money reeked of ink and leather wallets and saliva and the dirt and sweat of a thousand hands. At the end of the day the girls all scrubbed their fingernails with toothpaste to remove it.

The next Saturday morning, I was excited beyond words that my working life had begun. I wore jeans and a striped shirt and carried my shoulder bag, which made me feel grown-up. My mother woke early to drive me, still in her dressing-gown and thongs.

'I never got driven to my first shift,' she said, as she pulled onto Richmond Road. 'Your grandmother would've sooner given me a clip over the ear. And no one handed me a job on a silver platter. I had to go door to door, asking for work. You're spoilt, Andie, I hope you know that.'

I nodded. My mother's first job had been as an usherette at the Metro Cinema in Albert Street, which had since been gutted and split into three to make the modern Albert. She was soon fired for smoking but I'd always imagined her in a tight-fitting suit and pillbox hat, and thought it the ideal job for someone as glamorous as my mother.

'There's something I want to talk to you about,' she continued.

I gripped the edges of my seat. Could she know that I'd seen inside Steve's bag? Or lied about knowing where Macavity was? No, she couldn't. She wouldn't be calmly driving me if that was that case.

'There are dickheads around, and plenty of them,' she said. 'If ever a man comes in with a weapon and asks for money, you empty out your drawer. Quick and with no arguments. Just give him the money.'

At first I thought she was joking. I had years of memories of my mother in the car yelling, 'Get stuffed' at other motorists in carparks, or telling off women in the supermarket who frowned at her language. If there was one thing I was certain of, it was her bravado and her courage. And now she was telling me to give up. It was another part of my life that felt upside down.

'Women will always be weaker, Andie. Being smarter doesn't count for anything. Just hand over the money, no cheek. Do you hear me? I mean it,' she said.

I told her I did, but I knew this was another thing that wasn't fair. Going along with everything, doing what everyone else said, just because I was weaker. *One day,* I thought, *I'm going to be the one in charge.*

'And be ready out the front at one o'clock for me to pick you up. On the dot. I'm not parking.'

I swallowed. 'I forgot to tell you, Larissa's mum is picking me up. We're going to the movies. Is that okay?'

'I couldn't give a shit what you do,' she mumbled, holding the car lighter to the cigarette in her mouth as she steered with one hand.

Had she asked me what movie we were seeing, I would have said *Escape to Witch Mountain*, the matinee at the Hawthorne. I'd seen the advert that morning in the *Courier-Mail*. I'd also seen the film itself earlier in the year and remembered every little detail, if she asked any questions about it later. She wouldn't have known if I was telling the truth or not; despite or perhaps because of her job as an usherette, my mother didn't like movies, which was a shame because the Hawthorne had a glassed-in smokers' room so she didn't have to miss a thing. If she asked the following day, I was prepared to tell her that Larissa and I had sat in the scooped canvas chairs at the front, and about the Fantales that Mrs Byrne bought us. I even had a spare Fantale wrapper in the bottom of my bag as casual evidence.

You can see that by now I was quite the accomplished liar.

But she didn't ask, not then and not later. If she'd looked in my bag, she'd have seen I brought some of the money I'd saved, an apple and a sheet of paper upon which I'd traced a page from the Refidex that lived under the front seat of her car. But she didn't look. My mother wouldn't expect me home until dark. I'd made my decision. As soon as I finished work, I was going to find my father.

Those first TAB computers were monstrous, beige and unreliable, frequently jamming no matter how carefully the tickets were fed through. I was nowhere near old enough to legally process the bets but my tiny fingers were ideal for flipping open the cover and reaching inside to release a ticket, squished and bent deep in the guts of it. Imagine the most temperamental printer you've ever used, with the smallest copy paper and the most complicated series of internal sprockets and dials. A jammed machine was offline and the bet lost inside it was probably, but not always, unprocessed and had the potential to throw off the balance of your drawer by the end of the day. Jams also needed to be fixed quickly. Serious punters wait until the last minutes before the race to place their bets. If stymied, things could turn ugly. Doreen said she'd like to take a sawn-off .44 to the computers, that they were evidence, along with today's terrible music and corrupt politicians, that the world was going to shit. But I liked fixing them. I never became frustrated or flustered; I liked understanding things, figuring out the way the world worked. Punters also had trouble marking their crosses in those tiny squares on the betting tickets, especially the old-timers. They needed someone patient and not intimidating to stand beside them, showing them which box they wanted and reading their bets back to them.

'You're a wonder, Andie,' Doreen said on that first morning. 'But if anyone asks, you're fifteen.'

I barely looked twelve, but no one asked. Instead, the customers said things like, 'Val's kid? She's a chip off the old block' and 'She's a good little worker, isn't she? Wouldn't mind one of them around my place' and 'Good to see a kid these days who's not a smart arse. One who knows their place.'

Doreen was a funny, cynical mathematical genius who'd left school when she was not much older than me. She'd worked her way up from typist at the TAB head office to managing her own agency, usually worked seventy-hour weeks and, I would learn, had a series of boyfriends younger than her that everyone knew about except her husband. This husband, who I never met – although I had, of course, spoken to him on the phone when covering for her – did a few shifts a week at the pet food factory and was otherwise drunk while Doreen ran the house and paid the bills. Once, later, I asked her why she didn't divorce him.

She laughed. 'Jesus, Andie, if you want to run your own business, you need a husband,' she said. 'Everyone knows that.'

She went on to explain that without a husband's written letter of approval, you couldn't get a bank account or a credit card. You couldn't get a business loan or a mortgage.

'You need one that doesn't interfere, but. Signs on the dotted line where you tell him. They're not the brightest knives in the drawer, blokes, as a rule. Never show them how smart you are, that's the first thing,' she said.

I can still hear the depth and timbre of her voice. Doreen is long gone now but much of what she told me over the years has stayed in my head: 'Green is the unluckiest colour, so never wear it while punting'; 'Never have more than one laundry basket or else you'll be swamped by unfolded clothes'; 'You only need two sets of sheets, one on the bed and one in the wash'. And 'A bloke raises his hand to you just once, he's out on his arse. Because it's never just once.'

Doreen was the perfect first boss, and her advice through my teenage years, if not exactly correct in a literal sense, always taught me something important about the world. She was brusque sometimes when under pressure, but never cruel or patronising. She knew almost every customer by name.

'You're a serious kind of kid, aren't you?' she said that first day.

I'd never seen myself that way. Inside my head was always rich with imaginings and plans. But I wanted to do a good job for her, and for her to tell my mother.

My other responsibilities were sweeping the floor, emptying the bins and ashtrays, marking up scratchings on the race sheets – always a cause of groans and complaints, as though

I was responsible for withdrawing the animal myself – and refilling the ticket holders. I checked and replaced the ballpoint pens, tied to the counters with black string and sometimes stolen or snapped in frustration. I ran to the newsagents to pick up copies of the *Sporting Globe* all the way from Melbourne and to the Chinese takeaway next door for dim sims or the fish shop for steak sandwiches, Chiko Rolls and Cokes. I sometimes made change when one of the girls had to pee. I learned to check the vicinity of the door that lead to the carpark before leaving the back office, where the girls were and the money was kept, by crouching down and looking for legs of men hiding behind the parked cars. It'd been years since Doreen had been held up, and she wanted to keep it that way.

'Does no one ever win?' I asked her at some stage, because every single punter in the place was so glum.

'If they did, you wouldn't know it,' she said. 'Only wankers make a fuss, good times or bad.'

In those days the TAB was always busy on Saturday mornings, with a queue waiting before Doreen opened the door. Some punters were there all day, every day – sad and tired men on the pension, mostly; thin, stooped and fumbling with hollow cheeks and white hair. Doreen knew them all. They'd been her customers for years; it gave them somewhere to go during the day. For others it was merely a transaction, like going to the shop. These were often tradies on their break or men in suits, rushing, hoping no one noticed they're away from their desks. Taxi drivers, but never Mr Byrne. Some younger men were professional gamblers, either on their own or part of a syndicate, and they were very charming and flirtatious at the start but were gone in a few weeks. They were slick, all ego, and liked to be thought of as winners, so after too many bad days – and there were always too many bad days, eventually – they would move to another TAB.

The customers were mostly kind, with a gallows humour that revealed they knew they were trapped in a prison of their own making. In years to come, they would bring me flowers from their gardens and remember my birthday. When I was in my twenties, one old lady named Florence left me a moth-eaten fur coat in her will.

These days, I feel sick at the thought of punting even five dollars a place on the Melbourne Cup.

That suburban TAB, and many others like it, is long gone. The premises itself is a real estate agency, or it was last time I visited, but somehow the Chinese takeaway next door survives unchanged. They still have combination chop suey on the menu, which would become Doreen's and my favourite after long Spring Carnival days in my teenage years.

TABs in general are not as lucrative as they once were, except for those in pubs – alcohol loosens every good intention. Punters are mostly young men these days, I'm told, preyed on by gambling companies who present it as a way of being with their friends without the awkwardness of conversation or connection. Expensive, lonely mateship. Even the sense of community is gone; they do it at home alone, on the app.

The customers of the TAB may have been sad, but this seems even sadder. Pathetic, desperate masturbation as opposed to tawdry group sex.

But back then, I didn't consider any of that. When I finished my shift that Saturday, Doreen handed me the first pay packet of my life – a long brown envelope with my name written in her hand on the front.

'You're a good girl, Andie,' she said. 'Same time next week.'

Inside the envelope was twelve dollars and some change, the same amount I would have been owed had I been fifteen, which speaks to Doreen's character because she could have got away with paying me less. It speaks to my naivety that, despite what my mother had said about it being my own money, I hadn't imagined I'd be paid at all. I was helping a friend of my mother's and was being treated like a grown-up, both of which I liked. I wish I still had that envelope. I wish I'd framed it.

I remember it being a long walk to Morningside station. My father was moving to Lindum, he'd said, to stay with a friend who had a house. I'd caught the train before, though never by myself, but knew it was only a few stations away. As to what I was planning to do when I got there – I felt certain I would know where to go. My father was like home to me. I would find him, as surely as if I were a baby bird returning to the nest.

Chapter 15

As well as my first pay envelope, I wish I had kept the birthday cards my mother gave me. Not that they contained any of her thoughts or feelings. They were not letters. She never to my knowledge wrote a letter to anyone. The cards she gave me from my next birthday onwards were designed for adults. I suppose that in her eyes, I had voided the right to be treated like a child. Inside they were indistinguishable from anyone else's cards, printed with *Happy Birthday*, and her handwritten message, *To Andie, love Mum*.

But the design on the front was always memorable. They were cards designed for friends or siblings in their sixties or even older, with photos or cartoons of elderly women holding martini glasses or wearing adult nappies, with rolls of sagging flesh and blue, sparse hair in rollers. The text was something like: *Age is just a number. In your case, a really high number* or *It's all downhill from here!* or *I wanted to get you a dryer for your birthday, so you could come out wrinkle-free and two sizes smaller.* As a teen, I was confused rather than offended but they were snide, meant to hurt, there's no escaping it.

The gifts that accompanied my mother's cards, though, were perfect treasures, some secret wish I barely knew I had. When I was small, she ordered the toy of the moment weeks in advance. The exhilaration of opening a gorgeously wrapped box at the foot of my bed to find a Barbie Country Camper Van or a huge box of novels has never left me. Even after everything happened and she was living under a court-ordered budget, choosing cigarettes over food, she somehow managed gold hoop earrings for my sixteenth, a CD player for my eighteenth and then a French dutch oven for my twenty-first. None of my boyfriends nor my eventual husband could compete.

My mother loved me. I have never doubted that. I have also never doubted that she never forgave me for what I did, not even on her deathbed. This is what I think now: all those years I thought she was strong, but really she was weak. She could not bear to let her feelings rise up and swamp her, destabilise her, make her vulnerable. She could not give in to either her anger at me for the way I ruined everything or her love for her only child, and she spent years balancing the thin line between these, sometimes slipping from one side to the other. The gifts were from the part of her that loved me, and the cards and the way she spoke to me were from the other.

I've lost those cards, all of them, in moves from house to house, following break-ups and new jobs, across borders and oceans. But now – and this is something I never would have anticipated – I long for the sight of her handwriting, which was rounded and even, like cursive in a child's workbook. She never wrote anything that was not prosaic, yet all those years of shopping lists and betting lists and school notes when I was absent for tonsillitis were thrown away without a thought. It was not the hand you'd expect from someone who lived the life she did. When I think of my mother as a child in the 1950s, tiny and barefoot and beaten at home, hunched over a slate and concentrating on this one skill, my heart feels like it will break.

But that year, I was cursed with laser focus. She was the one who stayed. She fed me and clothed me, yet other than my fearful nights sitting on the floor watching her sleep and my escalating lies to avoid her disapproval, I barely noticed her at all. I could only think of my father.

The air was still that Saturday afternoon when I got off the train, and I held the image of him in my mind like a beacon. Everything was quiet because the shops closed around lunchtime, the banks didn't open at all and there were no ATMs, of course. Credit cards weren't common or often accepted, so if you didn't have cash on Friday afternoon or couldn't find someone to take a cheque, you couldn't do anything until Monday morning. There were no food delivery bikes and the few coffee shops were closed. Even the TAB would be slow from lunchtime. Weekend pursuits included sitting in the pub or fishing or sleeping or playing 500 or, for families like mine, punting at the track or over the phone. League was played on Sundays. You could watch the Aussie Rules from Melbourne on television, but for that you had to be *really* bored.

I'd seen no people from the windows of the train, only rows of identical backyards: brown grass divided by a cement path leading to a Hills hoist and, a little further, a dunny. At Lindum train station there was not another soul, not even a lady selling tickets inside. It was much flatter and dustier than Morningside, almost rural. I could smell the sea and the rotten egg of mangroves and what I know now to be diesel. The sky above was the brightest blue dotted with puffy clouds. I watched the train pull away and I felt brave, excited. I was a working girl on an adventure to find my father and rescue my family. I'd come this far. There was nothing I couldn't manage. But where to begin?

The station itself was at an intersection of four roads. With my traced Refidex page in hand, I began methodically, walking along the first street to the left. The houses were mostly double storey but without obvious stumps: the front door on ground level. They were newer than Morningside houses but less sturdy, and without gardens or trees. More front fences, mostly chain link. A few white tyres cut into swans, the odd fernery. Some blocks were empty, overgrown with grass, but most were mowed to an inch of their life. I remember scrub right to the edge of the road, and drains underneath, and ovals, and mangroves. No concrete footpaths of course, but we didn't have them in Morningside either. I ate my apple as I walked and wrapped the core in a tissue and stashed it in my bag rather than litter. After a while, a posse of bored kids in Wynnum-Manly jerseys on bikes followed me, chucking wheelies and calling, 'Show us ya tits', but they didn't come close and gave up before long. I looked up every driveway for my father's car; there were hardly any garages, thank goodness. I listened for the sound of Tippy barking.

One hour passed, then another. I must have walked by 200 houses. I was thirsty and beginning to regret the whole scheme. If my father was out for the afternoon somewhere in his car – swimming Tippy at Colmslie Reach, for example, or at the pub, or on a treasure hunt at the dump – then I wouldn't find him at all. This was a terrible plan. I wasn't nearly as smart as I thought I was.

I was almost ready to give up when I saw it: my father's white station wagon, parked in a driveway a few houses down. I would have run if I didn't already have blisters from the straps of my sandals. The house was khaki-coloured fibro, single level with a flat roof that extended over the carport. It had a yard of brown grass and a couple of cactuses in pots near the front door and lots of cement. The roof was rusted and there were tall tufts of something growing in the gutter. There was no fence and no sign of any dogs.

I walked up the driveway and, making binoculars with my hands, held my face to the station wagon's side window. It was the same inside as always: clean and neat, nothing like my mother's. There was the wire grate along the top of the back seat to keep the dogs from climbing over. I knew the glove box would have his notepad for jotting down mileages and his dustpan and hand broom for cleaning the grill along with assorted rags and a glass jar of change and a plastic bottle of water in case one of the dogs was sick in the back. My father was here, and somewhere out the back was Tippy.

A thrill went through me. I was shaking. I rushed up to the screen door and knocked, and then I knocked again.

'Hold your horses,' called a voice from deep inside the house.

It wasn't my father. It was a woman's voice.

Inside was dark. Through the screen door, I could see a fuzzy shape approaching down the hall, very slowly, as though she were swimming. She was a big woman, I could tell that much. Every so often she stopped and put her hand on the wall before continuing. This was undoubtedly the wife of my father's friend, the one he was staying with.

The big woman opened the screen door. Now that I could see her in the light, it was clear that she was even younger than my mother and not that many years older than me. Her hair was blonde and short and it curled damply around her red, puffy face. She wore a huge lime floral house dress with a white rounded collar. Her legs were skinny and her feet were bare. I'd thought she was fat through the screen, but she wasn't, not exactly. She was the most pregnant person I'd ever seen. She seemed to defy the laws of physics just by standing.

'Yeah, what do you want?' she said.

I could hear her breathing and she was standing strangely, tilting back and pushing her hips forward. In one hand she carried a washer that I guessed was cold, and she was patting it around her neck where the skin was crimson and blotchy.

All at once, a possibility entered my head. There were no noises behind her, no movement, no evidence that anyone else was home. Possibly my father was out with his friend, this woman's husband. If her husband was friends with my father, she might know my mother. This woman might wonder why I was here on my own. She might decide to ring my mother and tell her I was here, and – what with the taking off on the train by myself and the lying about the movies – I would be in very big trouble. I might be forbidden from working for Doreen ever again, or from going to Larissa's.

'What?' she said again, as though she was too tired to complete another sentence.

I had found where my father was staying. That was the most important part. Now that I knew how to get here, I could come back whenever I wanted and next time, he'd be here.

'I'm looking for my cat. He's lost,' I said.

She made a face as though she'd burped. 'No cats around here.'

'Are you sure?' I said. 'He's black with white feet.'

'No cats, I said. Probably flattened, the way the local yobbos hoon around.' She gestured to the street even though no cars were passing, then she rested the washer on one shoulder and lifted up the edge of her dress, swinging it up and down to generate a breeze. She wore huge footy shorts underneath and as the edge of the skirt billowed up, she flashed the white expanse of her stomach. Her skin was taut and the colour of raw chicken. The woman looked at me; I looked at the ground.

'Do I know you?' she said. 'You live around here?'

I shook my head. 'Can I have some water?'

The woman jerked her head in the direction of the front yard. 'There's a hose. Help yourself.'

She watched me as I walked across the yard, yellow grass crackling under my feet. The hose was lying loose like a dead green snake. I put my hand on the tap then jerked it away. It felt as though the imprint of the tap was seared into my palm. I knew what water from that hose would taste like: warm and metallic, a bit like dirt. But before I could try the tap again, this time through the fabric of my top, she called out.

'Hey,' she said. 'Wait.'

I turned.

'Do you want to make a quick dollar?' she said. 'I'll throw in water with ice, in a glass.'

Inside, I followed the woman as she swayed down the dark hall. There were no pictures or photos, just a dull green telephone like the one we had at home with the same twisty spiral cord, on an old-fashioned low stand, the kind with the built-in seat. Doors led off on either side but they were all closed – her and her husband's bedroom, I imagined, and a nursery for the baby with a cot and a mobile, and at the end of the hall, a spare room where my father probably slept.

At the back of the house, the hall opened up to a kitchen on one side with a dingy curtain on the window over the sink filled with dishes, and a lounge room on the other. Every window was screened yet there was a squadron of flies beating themselves on the walls and ceiling. There was one small wicker lounge with cushions covered in a pattern of green palm trees, still indented from where she sat, and two black peeling bean bags on the floor in front of a big square television with long bunny ears. There was a cardboard box making do for a coffee table. Next to the television was a table fan balanced on a pile of phone books, whirring as it turned from side to side. At the back was another screen door leading to the yard.

'I got them up okay this morning,' she said. 'But now I couldn't be fucked and they've got to come in before the storm.'

Then she handed me a plastic laundry basket and opened the back door.

In the backyard, the Hills hoist was heavy with laundry. I fought my way through the sheets to wind it down; it stuck and squeaked alarmingly. The woman was right. A storm was coming. I could smell it now, and see the greenish tinge to the clouds.

I scanned the yard for a kennel but there was only a tin shed in one corner next to a rusty wheelbarrow on its side, a pile of bricks spread near the fence and a few pots with shrivelled dead plants. Maybe Tippy was living inside with my father, and perhaps this afternoon he'd taken her for a swim using someone else's car. The woman had followed me outside and was sitting on the back steps in the western sun with her legs spread wide and her dress lifted above her knees. She was supervising, to make sure I didn't steal her clothes or drop them in the dirt.

'Many dogs around here?' I said as casually as I could. 'I'm thinking about my missing cat.'

'A few.' She straightened one leg and then the other, and peered at her feet as though she'd never seen them before. Even I could see that they were swollen, almost spherical.

'You don't have one? A dog?'

'My bloke wanted a dog. No bloody way, I said. Not around the baby. When he's older, sure. Dogs are good for boys. Not that I know it's a boy, but I've always been lucky. My fella's pretty keen on a boy. Carrying on the name and the rest of it. You know what men are like. They want sons, don't they? Even the ones that pretend they don't, really do.' She rubbed her stomach lovingly, as if it were already a baby. 'If it's a girl, we'll be stuffed because we've only picked out boys' names. But that's beside the point. Get rid of the dog, I said.'

There were always stories in the *Courier-Mail* of kids being mauled by Rottweilers or pit bulls, but greyhounds were wonderful with children. I'd hoped she might say, 'We've got a friend of my husband's staying with us, and he wanted to bring a greyhound, and I told him no.' But she didn't say that. And if I asked her about greyhounds specifically now, she might get suspicious. I could see how it had unfolded: my father's friend, let's call him Wayne, saying, 'Of course, mate, you and your dog are both welcome.' Then this woman overruled him and turned Tippy away. She was likely in a boarding kennel until my father found a place of his own, or she was staying with a professional trainer. Tippy would hate it. We'd visited places like that when my father made friends with other trainers so he could see their operations. Too many dogs, barking and darting up and down their runs like ratbags, my father had said. All the more reason for me to bring him and Tippy home fast.

'Plus, I don't need the extra work,' she continued. 'My mother, the old bitch, says I couldn't work in an iron lung. Shows how dumb she is. Babies sleep most of the time, I told her. But I'm not picking up dog shit as well.'

While she was speaking I started with the sheets, folding each one using my chin, being careful not to let it touch the ground, and replacing the pegs in the little plastic basket hanging from one corner.

'My mother still does sheets in a trough with a mangle,' the woman said. 'Machines make you lazy, she says. I told her to stick it up her bum.'

I started on the clothes: a few big house dresses for the woman, some huge old-lady underpants, some tops and shorts. Bras, the stretchy kind, without underwires. The clothes were all stiff from being in the sun too long. The pregnant woman would have to sprinkle some water before she ironed them.

'In my next life, I'm having a pool,' the woman said. 'In-ground, above-ground, kids' blow-up, I couldn't give a shit. Any kind of pool. I'd go to the Wynnum baths if it wasn't full of screaming kids pissing in the water. I'd get in the bath right now, I'd live there, but if I got in, I couldn't get out again.'

'A pool would be good,' I said.

'Let me give you some advice. Never be up the duff in summer.'

She spoke as though she were old enough to be my mother, but she was a teenager, I guessed. Nothing about her made pregnancy look enticing to me, not in any season.

The next shirt that I reached made me freeze. My mother and I had gone to Kmart and bought it together for his Father's Day present last year. I wasn't sure he liked the shirt when he unwrapped it. It was cotton, long-sleeved with pale blue and brown checks. He called it his cowboy shirt. My father liked practical thing for gifts. Socks and undies and a hat for when he did the mowing. On the line next to it was his favourite t-shirt, with the XXXX logo on it. Then some shorts that were his, and his socks and undies. I'd seen them on our line a million times.

At home, I didn't do any housework. My mother had given up asking me. She would take one look at what I was supposed to have done – the kitchen benches or stovetop or the ring around the bath – and say, 'Do you call that clean? What are you, blind? Your poor husband, that's all I can say.' And I took too long. At the rate I did things, it'd be quicker and easier to do everything herself, she said.

So I took extra care with each piece of my father's clothes. I felt the fabric with my fingers, every fibre. The clothes no longer smelled of him. They smelled of OMO and sunlight and grass. I folded each piece, smoothing it before I put it in the basket. Despite the approaching clouds, the glare from the sun made my eyes sting. When I draped the shirt over my forearm and pressed it with my other hand, it was almost as though I was touching him. I was out in the backyard for a long time. I must have seemed trustworthy enough, because after a while of watching me fold, the woman hoisted herself to her feet and lumbered back inside. I thought she might have said something about how slow I was at folding, but she didn't.

When I finished and all the sheets and clothes were in the basket, inside the house seemed hotter than the backyard. The woman was sitting on the wicker couch with her round feet up on the cardboard box. I put the basket on the kitchen counter next to a glass of water and a stack of five 20-cent pieces.

'Cheer up, love. It might never happen,' she said when she saw my face.

I nodded.

'Cats show up when you least expect it. Sulking about it won't help.' Then she nodded towards the glass on the counter and put the washer on her head. Tiny rivulets of water ran down her forehead. 'Out of ice cubes, sorry. I chew them faster than that shit fridge can make them.'

'It's fine,' I managed. The glass was a washed-out Vegemite jar with scraps of the label still stuck on it. I drank the water straight down and scooped the coins into my pocket.

'You'll feed them to the Space Invaders, I guess.'

I was less than three months away from being a teenager myself, and I'd expected it to be a weighty and important transition, a graduation into a bigger life. I hadn't envisaged that this also was a way of being a teenager: alone in a hot house and pregnant and dreaming of swimming pools and ice cubes. The woman shook her head as she spoke, as though she were an old lady complaining about young people instead of what she actually was – someone who should have been playing video games herself, or at least listening to music or doing something fun.

'Maybe,' I said.

It was a short interaction, that first meeting between her and me. She never asked my name and never told me hers. It would be years until I learned it, and sometime after that I would meet her for the second time in very different circumstances – on a warm Saturday afternoon on her family's farm some distance out of the city. She had been lucky. Her baby would be almost three and the sweetest boy anyone could imagine, and by then she'd have a tiny plump girl with a swoop of blonde hair as well. She had long forgotten that hot stormy afternoon late in her first pregnancy when a girl looking for a missing cat folded the clothes on her line for five 20-cent pieces. Which was understandable. The day we were properly introduced was her wedding day after all, and she had many other things to think of. Still, she took the time to make her children give me a cuddle, and held my hand and said how happy she was to finally meet me. That she'd heard about my grades at my posh private school, about my prizes in maths and debating. She would have no memory of meeting me before that at all.

'Thanks for the dollar,' I said.

'You can let yourself out. I'm not getting up again. And good luck finding your cat,' she said. Then she leaned her head back on the edge of the lounge and closed her eyes.

Chapter 16

Greyhounds have two names. One is their home name, given by their trainer or their family, like Tippy, Shep, Crumbs and Sally, the darlings that I loved, my gentle little children.

They also have a racing name. When I was a child, registering a greyhound meant providing a long list of possibilities for the control board to choose from, because you couldn't know if a name has already been taken. My father's first choice for Tippy, for example, was Andie's Treasure, but she raced under the name Tenderfoot, which my father only included to make up the numbers, because as a puppy she'd whine when walking on gravel. Shep's racing name was Mister Malarkey, not Prince Val.

A dog's racing name is a secret to her. Otherwise she's tempted to run towards the crowd, thinking the punters are calling her when yelling her name in desperation or relief or fury, the way punters do.

At this point of my story, the pieces of the puzzle are racing towards me – the man watching me, asking me to add up the numbers in his ledger, and the man I cannot find who is not watching me at all; the woman careless with lunch money and betting money, and the woman who doles out 20-cent pieces; the missing cats and the missing dogs – but I'm only twelve and I haven't put them together, not yet. I don't know who can be trusted. The truth is, of course, that everyone can be trusted and no one can be, depending on the circumstances. The truth is that greyhounds are two animals at the same time – Tippy and Tenderfoot, the gentlest of animals unless you are a small furry creature. It's simplistic to think that people are either good or bad. People behave the same way dogs do – their nature depends on whether you are a small furry creature or not. That is what you need to figure out.

The moment of clarity, when it comes, will make me feel very stupid, and very weary.

It was late, probably five or six, when I got off the train and began the long and hilly walk home. The air was tightening and the clouds were still building but the wind had picked up, squally and fierce. Those summer afternoon storms were a staple of my childhood and I knew it would soon rain or even, by the greenish tinge to the clouds, hail. My bag was plastic so at least my pay envelope and savings would be dry.

My mother was working at the pub this afternoon and tonight, a double shift. When she'd finally make it home, smelling of beer and second-hand smoke, her arms would ache from tilting glasses at the perfect angle under the tap to control the size of the head. Behind the bar she was jolly and flirty, taking everyone's minds off their troubles, but at home, worn down by the sad stories of the sad men she served, she would run herself the hottest Radox bath she could stand and lie in it for hours. At least that's what she did when my father lived with us, before Steve came along.

'Poor stupid bastards,' she would say, sinking down so that the back of her neck turned mud-crab red. 'They never had a chance.'

She was talking about the young men at the pub who'd been friends of my uncle, my mother's brother who I don't remember, and had been with him in Vietnam, but they'd come home. She liked hearing them talk about my uncle, even though they told the same stories over and over.

'Did the government give a shit about those boys?' she'd say. 'Not on your life. Politicians will fuck you over as soon as look at you, Andie. Remember that.'

There were old men in the pub as well, and many of them had fought in New Guinea and others in North Africa. Others hadn't been in any army but still seemed to live at the pub.

'Never marry a drinker, Andie,' was another thing she'd say to me at the end of a long shift.

Everybody, I realise now, needs to see themselves as the hero of their own story, to imagine a line they wouldn't cross. The more trouble they're in, the more they need this. My mother, unbeknownst to me, would soon be in a fair amount of trouble and the faster she sank, the more she needed to draw that line. And on the other side were people who were not her, who were worse off, either by the bad luck of their circumstances or the unfortunate choices they'd made in their unfortunate lives. She thought the men who drank across the counter from her were the world's most miserable souls, yet those same men who spent every session of every day on their bar stools might well have seen my hardworking, pretty mother and gone home and said to their sons, 'Never marry a gambler.'

On that walk home from the station, I thought it unlikely my mother would realise I hadn't been at the movies or the Byrnes' either. I was often lost in thought in those days, carried away with either imaginings or in trying to understand something and turning it over in my mind, and I was often surprised to find myself at my destination without any memory of the walk itself. This afternoon though, I was a little jumpy. On edge from that strange encounter with the pregnant woman and the heaviness of the approaching storm. The energy, building under the low clouds. I decided to take the backstreets home so I could stop under trees if the rain came.

I had just turned off the main road at the corner shop when I saw a car on the crest of the next hill. I froze and I squinted.

There was no mistaking the colour, that distinctive blue. It was Steve's.

The storm was nearly upon me. Warm rain isn't the same as cold rain, I know now after having lived in cities that were properly cold, but I'd walked a long way on only an apple and the pregnant woman's glass of water, and the blisters on my heel were bleeding. Steve was my mother's boyfriend. He lived with us. The logical thing to do was wave him down and slide inside his dry car.

I can't explain why I didn't. The gun, I guess, and the beaten face of that man who'd stopped me at the races. So instead I darted behind a hedge in someone's front yard and ducked. It was a childish gesture, like when we kids formed into teams to hunt each other with slingshots at big lunch, yet I couldn't shake the feeling of menace stalking me, of not being safe in the world. It was ridiculous. I felt disappointed in myself, like my day of adult work and unsupervised train trip had been an aberration and I was still a baby at heart. It began to rain then, big fat drops that came at an angle with a swirling wind, and a huge clap of thunder made me jump.

I peered around the side of a bush as Steve's car passed. It was cruising, leisurely, and Steve had one arm out of the driver's side window, incongruous with the urgency of the building wind. As though he wasn't headed anywhere particular, or like he was looking for something.

Somehow I knew what he was looking for. Me.

Every inch of Morningside was familiar, every house and every street. There was a back way home that avoided the roads, up through the corner of the Greysons' yard. I had to beat Steve home and not be alone with him in his car. It was crucial, although I couldn't have said why.

I steeled myself, then ran up the hill as fast as I could manage. The thunder was loud and the water made the blisters on my heel sting. The gutters were filling and the grass was slippery and soggy. I ducked up the Greysons' driveway and under their front verandah, then darted across their yard. I held my plastic handbag over my head when I could. I fell once, mud splattering my leg and my good work clothes. I cut through gardens and waited under trees, because it was the kind of rain that made motorists pull over if they could, or find an undercover park. I saw no one.

When I could finally see our house, I was sodden all the way through, gasping and shaking. I stopped at the bottom corner of the backyard and looked up through the fog of rain. Steve's car wasn't in the driveway. I ducked along the back fence and, once under the house, dried myself roughly with one of Tippy's clean towels my father had left behind. Then I used the key on the chain around my neck to let myself in the back door. I threw my bag in the bottom of my wardrobe and shut the door, then I bolted inside the bathroom and turned on the shower.

About ten minutes later I was back in my bedroom, in a tracksuit, lying on my bed with a book, when I heard Steve's car pull in. He came up the back stairs and straight to my room. He looked surprised when he saw me on my bed, looking for all the world like a girl relaxing. He couldn't hear my heart.

'Oh, hi.' He was dry, wearing long pants and a short-sleeved shirt. He didn't step inside my room but the size of him blocked the whole of the doorway. 'When did you get home?'

'Ages ago,' I said, as airily as I could manage.

He nodded slowly. 'Ages, eh? Where've you been?'

I placed my book down deliberately, so he could see he was disturbing me and asking questions that were none of his business. 'At the movies. I told Mum.'

'Your mum thought the movie finished a while ago,' he said.

I tried to keep my breath steady and even. 'Yep, sorry. Lost track of time.'

'She phoned here and no one answered. She was worried. I thought you might have been walking home from your friend's place. It's absolutely shithouse outside. I thought I'd give you a lift.'

I picked up the book again. 'I was fine, thanks.'

It's amazing, the confidence that I was completely safe here in my room. My mother only came in to leave clean clothes on the end of my bed and to vacuum and change the sheets. I couldn't recall my father in my room, other than tucking me in and turning off the light at bedtime. No boys had ever been in my room and Steve had no business here, seeing my bald kewpie doll on a stick with its purple tulle skirt and flaking glitter that I'd kept from the Ekka last year, or my stack of *Dolly* and *MAD* magazines, or my Barbies spread all over the floor.

Steve looked around my room, taking it all in. 'Like living here, do you?' he said.

I didn't know what he meant. Here, in our house? Or here in Morningside? There was no answer to either question. Here was where we lived, that was all. Morningside was where our house was. I understand how incomprehensible it sounds now, but I had never heard of anyone buying a house, or selling one.

I shrugged. 'I guess.'

'I used to live out Greenslopes way,' he said. 'It's nice out there, near the hospital. There are more places in the world than Morningside. Better schools, for example.'

I shrugged again. He was trying to raise the topic of moving, perhaps into a new house, with him. That's what happened when parents divorced – the house was sold and divided in two. I can't fathom how it hadn't occurred to me that we wouldn't go on living here forever, waiting for my father to come home.

'How was your first day of work?' He folded his arms and leaned against the doorjamb. 'Sell any winners?'

'I'm not allowed on the counter yet,' I said.

'Right, of course,' he said. 'Only a matter of time but. You'll be running the place before long. Just remember that having a flutter is just a bit of fun, Andie. A hobby. It's like the difference between having the occasional beer and being a derro. The only way to properly clean up is to be on Doreen's side of the counter. Take the bets, don't make the bets.'

'I know,' I said, even though I didn't. Then, knowing that wouldn't be enough if he reported back to my mother, I added, 'Doreen's a great teacher. I learned a lot.'

'Well, you're a bright girl. And you like learning, I can tell. I liked books and shit too, when I was your age. Maths especially. I even had a teacher who wrote a letter home, asking my parents if I could stay on.' He screwed up his nose as though he was about to sneeze. 'I would've, but Dad wanted me to be a butcher. You can see for yourself how that worked out.' He held up his hand with the missing finger and wiggled the other four at me.

It was more common those days to see men with missing fingers. Standards weren't the same. Industrial accidents, but also young men being stupid. Fireworks had been banned for three years, but I still remember my father setting off Roman candles and Catherine wheels in the front yard on cracker night, with a beer in one hand, while making me stay on the front steps. My own mother had a raised, lumpy scar across one wrist which, my parents told me, was from when she had tried to mow the yard while my father was out, but the blades clogged and she reached underneath the mower to clear them. One of the boys the year above me at school had lost a finger while trying to stop his younger brother riding his bike – he'd tripped while chasing him and grabbed the bike by the spokes. Missing a finger wasn't a big deal. I wasn't impressed.

'Although I did end up working in maths, funnily enough.' He chuckled. 'I'm a kind of accountant, you could say.'

'Right,' I said.

'They treated apprentices like shit, back in those days,' Steve went on. 'I could tell stories that would curl your hair.'

I knew about that. My mother said the same thing, and my father also. But I was planning to apprentice as a trainer with my father, so it wouldn't happen to me. I didn't reply.

'You like the flicks, hey,' he said after a while. 'I loved them too when I was a kid.'

'It must have been a thrill when talkies came in,' I said.

As soon as it was out of my mouth, I regretted it. I was absolutely not allowed to be a smart arse. Besides, I needed to be polite, to not antagonise him, but I was still only considering him from my own perspective. Steve as a young, bullied apprentice, panicked and fearful as he lost his finger; Steve as a father, missing Tracey and his boys – those versions of him never occurred to me.

'You're funny,' Steve said, but he didn't smile. 'I remember when I felt like that, that all grown-ups were a hundred years old.'

He *was* old. Other than my grandmother and Mrs Murphy, he was the oldest person I knew. Older than Larissa's father, definitely older than both of my parents. He would have been in his early forties, I guess. He would be dead by the time he was fifty, but I couldn't have known that.

He wiped one big hand over his face. 'But seriously, Andie, it wasn't only the rain. I was looking for you because there's somewhere I wanted to take you. It's too late now, they'll be closed. Never mind, we'll try another time.'

I gripped the edges of the book so hard my fingers turned white. The face of the man at the Gabba rushed back at me – the purple eye and welts on his forehead and his wife's strange, cringing deference – but perhaps I was being ridiculous. The movies, that was what he had in mind. He'd just said he liked films and my mother probably wouldn't go with him. The Hawthorne cinema, that was probably it.

'Where?' I said. 'Where did you want to take me?'

Steve held one finger to his lips. 'It's a surprise,' he said. 'No need to say anything to your mum.'

Chapter 17

A few months earlier when everything had been normal, or what seemed normal to me, my parents had dressed up to go out for the evening together. Not to the pub, where my father sometimes sat at one end of the bar while my mother worked, or the races. Out, like on a date. My grandmother was even coming over to babysit.

I couldn't recall this ever happening before. It was as though the separate spheres of my parents' only occasionally intersecting lives were, for some reason, stuck in synchronicity and were moving in the same direction for once. My father was by then already seeing his life differently and had at least dreams, if not concrete plans, of a new beginning away from my mother and me. When you're married to someone, you're also married to their previous selves, the earlier steps in their evolution, and you remember their history of flaws and mistakes, the mortifications and shame we all carry. I don't believe there's a human alive immune to the attraction of starting afresh with someone who sees only our best, newest version. It's a seductive thought, especially for someone like my father, so self-contained and focused and, I was to realise, unfulfilled, heavy with hopes for his life yet married to someone like my mother, wilful and extravagant and sensuous, incapable of plans that went beyond the next hour.

That night though, I was ignorant to all of this. I lay on top of their brocade bedspread, entranced, propped up on my elbows, and to me it seemed like they were like Faye Dunaway and Steve McQueen. My father was unbearably handsome in his ironed short-sleeved shirt and polished lace-up shoes. My mother stepped into the long emerald dress that hung at one end of her wardrobe. She asked my father nicely to do up the zip, which started low, in the small of her back. Then she clipped gold earrings to her lobes and sprayed the air with Charlie before walking through the mist.

It never occurred to me that my mother, who dressed up so rarely, might be anxious that her dress was wrong or her lipstick or the shape of her body. I never considered she might be self-conscious about her broad way of speaking, with her dropped g's and slang and swearing. She never showed the slightest hint of weakness or doubt. I thought her the expert in everything and paid close attention to her every action. I knew I would never be as beautiful as my mother, but this was how a woman prepared to go out with a man and I'd need to do that. At least I hoped I would, some day.

To add to the strangeness of that evening: the trannie wasn't on. The odd quiet made the house seem creaky, as though every window rattled and every door squealed on its hinges. I asked where they were going. Dancing perhaps, because even though I'd never seen them dance or imagined they could, on that night anything seemed possible. Or maybe they were going to Lennons, which was where General MacArthur had stayed and was the poshest place I could imagine. I'd never been there, and neither had my parents to my knowledge, but my grandmother had a saying whenever anyone rested on their elbows at the table or was generally slovenly: 'Couldn't take you to Lennons.'

My father was adjusting his paisley tie in the mirror between the wardrobes. 'To see a man about a dog,' he said, which was his standard answer to any questions about his movements.

My mother was facing the other way, sitting in front of her dressing table. She'd been playful up to now, blowing kisses to me and my father, fluffing her hair in an exaggerated way. She twisted her gold lipstick and leaned towards the mirror. 'To a casino in the Valley,' she said, as though he hadn't spoken.

He blew air into his cheeks and puffed it out, then turned around and looked up at the ceiling. 'Jesus Christ, Val, don't tell her that.'

I froze, but my mother went on applying her lipstick, slicking red, pursing, touching up the corners of her mouth with her fingertips. Seconds passed. Perhaps she hadn't heard him.

But she had. Slowly, she set her lipstick down with a sharp clack on the dresser, then narrowed her eyes at him in the mirror. 'Don't. You. Tell. Me. What I can say in my own house. Who the bloody hell do you think you are?'

The realisation that things were all at once different showed on his face, his skin stretching tight over his temples, his throat tensing for an instant, making his Adam's apple bob. Now he was a lion tamer in a cage without a whip or chair, keeping his voice soft.

'Val, it's my house too. Let's just keep this between us, hey?'

She turned back towards the mirror and snorted. '"See a man about a dog". What the bloody hell does that mean? That you're a big man with big secrets?'

It was a perfect microcosm of the pair of them, a snapshot of why they had always been unsuited: him, giving away nothing, understated with the barest glimpse of a deeper disapproval; and her, revealing every thought and every feeling, zero to a hundred in two seconds flat.

'Not every bloody thing needs to be broadcast,' he said.

His voice was calm which, looking back, was less a sign of his nature and more one of resignation, as though the ties of their relationship had already slipped and her speaking to him that way had no more impact than if a stranger had, or if someone else's dog had barked at him and pulled on its leash.

'"Broadcast"? Telling your own child the truth is not *broadcasting* anything. Jesus Christ, you have a yellow streak a mile wide. I'll shout it to the street if you keep this up. See if I won't.' She stood and took two steps towards the window.

'She's a kid, Val, and she doesn't need to know every little detail of everything.'

'I didn't raise an idiot, unlike your mother apparently,' she said. Then to me, in a sweet voice to contrast with the way she spoke to him, 'You won't tell anyone where we're going, will you, Andie? It's a secret.'

Whether I was an idiot or not would prove to be debatable, but one thing was true: I knew how to keep a secret. I also knew there were no casinos in Queensland. Not legal ones, at least. There weren't even any pokies. Occasionally on a Sunday my father packed the station wagon and I slept in the back seat while he drove us all the way across the border to Tweed Heads. My father hated the pokies and never played. There was no skill in it, that was his main complaint, and no animals, no blokes and no sunshine, none of the things that made punting on the dogs or the horses so enticing. He dropped my mother and me off, then went to the beach.

She, on the other hand, could spend the whole day on a stool in the dark at the Bowls or the Services Club, sipping a Coke and pushing buttons, with me playing the machine beside her. No one checked the age of gamblers in those days, or perhaps parental permission was considered more important than laws. I learned to drink in the same manner at sixteen, out with my mother and her boyfriend of the moment who would order me something extravagant to show off his largesse – a Japanese Slipper or a Grasshopper. Drinking took some practice but I loved the pokies at once, and for good reason. It seemed for all the world like a child's game: all those spinning dials and pretty lights. The Japanese Slipper of gambling. As I grew though, it was the first type of gambling to bore me, and by the time I was twenty, I would have rather done anything than sit in those dismal, smoky rooms among those sad people. My mother continued to love the pokies until the day she died.

Was my mother talking about a proper casino though? With roulette wheels and baccarat and martinis, like a James Bond movie? I'd never imagined one in real life. I'd heard rumours of illegal casinos in the Valley, but the National Party and police denied their existence, and the *Courier-Mail* was dismissive of this wild conjecture spun by a loose consortium my parents called ratbags and shit-stirrers, the 'hairy armpit brigade', those who weren't loyal Queenslanders. They were Cockroaches, which were southerners, and communists and feminists and Labor voters and university students and dole bludgers, all of whom were too stupid to know how good they had it and were out to cause trouble. If they didn't like it here, they could piss off. They would soon regret taking on Joh.

But if my mother was telling me casinos were real, then they must be.

'She'll be coming with us before too long,' my mother said, nodding at me. 'You'll love it, Andie. Lots of games. And dancers in sequins. Very pretty.'

Lying there on my parents' bed, a horrible idea dawned on me. What would happen to them if the casino was unlucky enough to be raided by police that night?

My parents and all their friends hated the police. They were not to be trusted. I was taught to keep my head down if I ever saw one and never, ever to speak to one. I thought of my mother in her emerald dress, arrested and behind bars, thrown against a wall; my father, bruised and bloody and locked up for years. What would happen to me? To the dogs? I astonished myself by burying my face in my mother's pillow and bursting into tears.

My parents were as shocked as I was. I had never seen either of them cry, and the fact that I wasn't a sook, not even at the dentist or when being vaccinated, was a source of parental pride. Now I understand that they had trained me into never crying by making a fuss of my bravery since I was a toddler, until it was part of the way I saw myself. Right at that moment, though, there was nothing I could do.

They stared at me blankly.

'What the bloody hell is that about?' my father said to my mother.

'How the bloody hell would I know?' my mother said, louder. 'I thought she'd like games and sequins.'

'Queenslanders don't cry, Andie. If you don't stop that racket . . .' my father trailed off, unable to think of a punishment.

'Andie, I'm not in the mood for your nonsense,' my mother said. 'Stop being a bloody baby.'

'Do we have any ice cream?' my father said to her. 'Get her some ice cream.'

'Am I your slave? Get her some yourself,' said my mother.

'A toffee.' He opened the drawer of my mother's bedside table, fished one out and handed it to me. 'Here.'

I took the toffee. Even wrapped it steadied me, and I blurted it out – all my fears that they would go to jail, and my terror of what would become of them. How would I get enough money to feed myself and the dogs while going to school at the same time? And how could I walk all of them by myself? I didn't know how to pay the mortgage or go to the bank. I wasn't allowed to turn on the stove. I ended with, 'Please don't go.'

There was a moment of silence. My parents looked at each other, and then they began to laugh. To their credit, they turned their lips inside out and bit down at first, but it soon overtook them. I was so astonished that I stopped crying. Eventually my mother wiped her eyes and sat on the bed beside me.

'Oh Andie, you poor little dummy,' she said kindly. She took a tissue from her purse and handed it to me. 'That's not the way the world works at all.'

'Listen to your mother,' my father said.

I wanted to listen to her. At that age I wanted to know everything: which stars were distant suns and which were planets, how to read a betting ring the way they did, the name of every country on the globe in the school library. I wanted to see every movie, speak every language, visit every dog track in the country because every new thing I understood was as though a small piece of an enormous jigsaw was clicking into place. Yet my parents rarely taught me anything, at least not deliberately. They did not go in for speeches or lectures; they generally answered my questions with, 'How the bloody hell should I know?' and 'Look it up in the *World Book*,' which was the encyclopaedia to which they'd subscribed when I'd been too annoying, and which I often read before bed. And now, at last, my mother was about to tell me how the world worked. I turned towards her and listened hard.

She took my hand, which was special in itself, and gave it a small squeeze. 'Some people are suckers, and some people know what's what. Me and your father are not suckers and we will never end up in prison, I can promise you that.'

Despite everything that happened, she was right. Whether this was precognition or just dumb luck, I don't know.

'It's safe, Andie. I promise,' my father said. 'Cops are hired thugs. They only raid what they're told to raid. Very clever people take care of that.'

'And we're friends with very clever people,' my mother said. 'Just don't tell anyone, or we'll all be in trouble.'

I never did tell anyone about the casino. I consider myself to have been an imaginative child yet I could not envisage any fate worse than being In Trouble. If anyone had asked me what that specifically entailed though, I couldn't have answered. My parents never hit me, as I've already said. Confined to my room was no punishment – that was where my books and dolls were. As a child herself, my mother had suffered her mouth being washed out with soap and having the strap and being sent to bed with no tea. She considered these to be barbaric, and she harboured lingering resentments towards her own mother, my grandmother, revealed in snide comments and asides about cruel mothers transforming into doting grandmothers at they aged. In general, my mother believed that naughtiness in a child was a reflection of many years of incompetent parenting and that if a child required any kind of punishment or even course correction, the parents were always at fault and it was likely too late to do anything about it.

'Training children is no different to training dogs,' I once heard her say when an acquaintance complimented her on my excellent behaviour at the shops when her own children were careening a trolley down the aisle. 'Be kind, be firm, leave absolutely no room for interpretation. If you do it right and start early enough, you never have to raise a hand.'

My mother had a cutting tongue and a voice so sharp it made me wince, but the way she screamed when she lost her temper was mostly unrelated to any action of mine, I knew, and more to do with the hours she worked, her exhaustion, the way life had ground against any part of her that had ever been soft. When she was a girl, she didn't have any of the advantages that I had – she told me that often enough. It was her disapproval I feared above anything else. The idea that I had let her down. After our conversation about the casino, I was left wondering what being In Trouble could mean to grown-ups, and who they could be in trouble with. In my mind, the whole point of being an adult was that no one could boss you around ever again – never scream at you or tell you off or tell you that you're useless. When I was a grown-up, no one would ever speak to me that way, not ever.

But I was still a child, and the night after coming home in the storm I felt as though the world had narrowed around me. I was out of options. My mother was changing. She and Steve had stayed in last night, a rare occurrence, and my mother had made Oysters Kilpatrick and scallop vol-au-vents and roast beef with roast potatoes, and had set the table for the two of them, which showed how much things had changed since he had arrived. The fridge was packed with pâté and pork pies and moselle – of which I was allowed half a glass and thought disgusting – and green olives stuffed with almonds and French onion dip and tiny dry toast imported from Europe and after-dinner mints, so fancy, each in their own envelope. My father would have hated all of it.

That night I stayed in my room until the lights went out, then I waited on the floor beside my mother's bed as usual, watching her and Steve breathing by the light of the streetlamp filtering through the venetians. I thought about him cruising around in his car looking for me and what would have happened if he'd found me. Where he wanted to take me that was a 'surprise'.

It seemed as though I would have to risk being in very big trouble.

The next morning, I was sleep-deprived and worried about every single thing in my life. Anxiety wasn't something anyone talked about. My mother sometimes talked about old women she knew who were 'nervy'; it was a term of derision reserved for those without the character to get on with things. At all costs, I didn't want to be that. Yet that morning I felt that if I didn't do something to fix things, the tension in the air would peel away my skin and leave me raw and naked, facing the world with no protection, and further – that I was the only person in the world who'd ever felt this way, and if I told anyone, I'd fall so low in their estimation that they'd never want to see me again.

It's difficult to explain this next part but I've put this off for as long as I can. Now I have to tell of the decision I made and the action I took to protect the everyday life that I knew. No more explanations or justifications. Just the facts.

I headed out early, on my bike. My mother and Steve were still asleep. I left a note on the kitchen counter, *Out riding with Larissa*, although of course I wasn't. I could have gone to the pregnant woman's house where my father was staying, but I didn't. I thought that things had escalated past that point, and that setting those particular gears in motion to bring my father home would take too long. I saw no other option. I was riding my bike to Tammy's house, but I wasn't visiting her.

As my mother said, I was young, but I wasn't an idiot – not about some things at least. I knew that the numbers in the columns in Steve's ledger were dates, odds and amounts, and that the names were punters. They were bets. Steve was an SP bookie. And Tammy's father was a policeman. Despite all my father's warnings about the untrustworthiness of coppers, he was the one I was going to see.

Chapter 18

I had my chances to stop. A magpie swooped me, half-heartedly, which I might have taken as a sign. But I was young. There was something magnetic about the line that I'd crossed, and I found myself propelled almost against my will. I was brought up to believe that fear was something to be overcome, not surrendered to. One thing I've learned is this: the image of yourself you hold in your head is solid and difficult to shift, even when all evidence points to it being wrong. I'd always thought of myself as a loyal and smart person, and the fact that I was acting in the most stupid and disloyal way possible towards my own mother did nothing to change that view. I was accustomed to keeping secrets back in those days. I told no one about my parents' stolen goods, or that Doreen was out with a boyfriend when her husband called. I was happy to lie about my age while working at the TAB. I considered these secrets an honour, and the trust of adults a compliment. Back then, a dobber was just about the worst thing a kid could be, and I would have fought any kid who called me one. Still, here I was, pedalling the few dozen blocks to Tammy's house.

It was the longest ride I could remember. I was frightened, of course, but only because I was submitting myself to the very thing that had so petrified me the night my parents went to the casino – making myself known to the police and so disobeying all of their instructions. Perhaps Tammy's father would arrest me. I wondered how long I could hold out under questioning before telling him everything he wanted to know – in my mind, forever. I was an earnest girl looking for a trial to prove myself worthy. I would save my mother and myself, because I knew my gentle father could not protect us from Steve. No one could. With every turn of my pedals I thought of my parents as they used to be, living together in our house. Their soft voices at night through the wall we shared; their excitement when a race call ended with a surprise victory. We may not have eaten together, and my parents certainly knew almost nothing about the details of my life, not the names of my teacher or friends or the books I was reading or anything I was learning at school. But I was their moon, secure in my orbit around the planet of their marriage and without them together I would be flung, alone and helpless, into the emptiness of space. I had to do everything in my power to restore things to rights.

The root of my mistake was this: my father had told me to always remember that cops and crooks were 'two sides of the same coin'. I took that to mean that, although their methods were awful and they weren't to be trusted, cops were still on the opposing side of criminals. And Steve was clearly a criminal.

In reality, the police and the criminals were on the same side. The illegal casino my parents had visited was one of several in the Valley back then and part of a web of gambling, prostitution and corruption that spread to the centre of political power. Queensland was and had been for some time a police state, where brothel owners, bookies and drug dealers paid police for protection and that money filtered upwards through layers of their superiors onto heavy teak desks, in brown-paper bags. It would take years, brave reporting and a Royal Commission for it all to come out, and by then, a police commissioner would be convicted of corruption and stripped of his knighthood, ministers of the Crown would be imprisoned for misappropriating funds and the premier himself would narrowly escape conviction in a verdict that was later alleged to have been the result of jury selection manipulation.

The fact was this: in choosing someone to tell about my mother's boyfriend the SP bookie, I couldn't have made a worse choice than a serving Queensland police officer.

Tammy lived on the other side of the school from us, in a cul-de-sac of newer brick houses encircling a small park. She only went to our school, according to her, because she'd arrived in the middle of the year and her mother had decided it wasn't worth settling into a private school for only a few months. Next year she'd be attending the convent school on the hill overlooking the river instead of the local state high with the rest of us.

We felt sorry for her. We were all a little scared of the convent school: the gothic buildings that were rumoured to be haunted, the gargoyles and statues, the high brick walls topped with pikes and the chained iron gates – whether to keep non-Catholics out or to keep the convent girls in, we didn't know. There were no boys at that school. Some of the girls, I'd heard, were boarders from cattle stations out west or plantations in Papua New Guinea. We'd see them at the Plaza sometimes in their calf-length skirts and stockings and ties and hats accompanied by tiny nuns in pairs, unsmiling and grim, like bats in their black habits and veils. There were day girls as well, but we didn't know any of them. They'd gone to Catholic primary schools and they walked to and from the station in groups, never lounging around or smoking like other kids. No minis or dyed hair, no dangling earrings, no sandshoes. No freedom at all. I'd told my mother about Tammy and the convent school, and she said it takes a special kind of idiot parent to pay for something that the government gives you for nothing, and that those girls were brainwashed god-botherers and stuck-up little bitches and Tammy would fit right in.

I pulled up on my bike in the park across from Tammy's house. As was the fashion, there were no trees or shade of any kind – nothing that would make the park harder to mow – and the early sun reflected off the grass, blinding white, the heat turning my arms pink even at this hour. The whole street was quiet. Everyone was probably asleep. I waited on the swings until I saw the curtains twitch in what I guessed was the kitchen, then I left my bike in Tammy's front yard and knocked on the door.

After a while I heard footsteps, then some unlocking sounds. The door opened two inches and Tammy's mother appeared in the gap, clasping her dressing-gown closed at her throat with one hand. She was closer to my grandmother's age than my mother's, with a flat round face like Tammy's and thin drawn eyebrows and narrowed eyes. Wiry auburn hair with grey roots curled around her face. She asked me what I wanted.

I pulled myself up to my full height and stood evenly on my feet with my hands behind my back. 'Good morning, Mrs Monaghan,' I said, and I told her my name. 'I'm in Tammy's class.'

'And what time of the morning do you call this? Tammy's busy. Come back later.' She began to close the door.

Later would likely be too late. 'Wait, please,' I said. 'It's Mr Monaghan I need to see.'

'Go home, why don't you? I'm not in the mood for stupid games,' she said.

'It's not a game,' I said. 'I want to report a crime. A very important crime.'

She stopped, then opened the door a little wider. '*Mr* Monaghan?' she said. 'Do you mean, Senior Sergeant?'

I nodded.

'It's a Sunday morning, madam, in case you didn't realise.' She waited for me to say something and when I didn't, she rolled her eyes. 'Wait here.' She shut the door.

A moment later, the door opened again. This time it was Tammy, in a dress with a bow around her waist and her hair in two long plaits. There were boys behind her; her brothers, I guessed. She screwed up her face.

'What do you want, Andie?' she said. 'D'ya wanna move in? Gonna ask my mum to adopt you?'

'As if,' I said. 'If you were my sister, I'd slit my own throat.'

'Tammy?' her mother called from behind her. 'Leave that girl alone.'

Tammy laughed, and called back, 'Yes, Mum.' Then she leaned closer to me and whispered, 'My mum's lovely. Ever wonder why no one comes to play at your house, Andie? Because your mum's a scary witch, that's why.'

'Rack off, Tammy,' I said.

She laughed again and closed the door.

I sat on the front steps for twenty minutes, watching ants scurry backwards and forwards along the side of the coir doormat. I thought I'd been forgotten. Then the garage door swung up and a car backed out, driven by Mrs Monaghan wearing a hat. A boy, one of Tammy's brothers, was in the front seat, and Tammy and her other two brothers were in the back. The driveway was close to where I was sitting, so I could see the three in the back seat sticking out their tongues at me before Mrs Monaghan drove off.

A minute later, the door opened again. Standing there was a heavy-set older man with wildly bushy eyebrows wearing a pair of blue striped pyjamas and red tartan slippers. He opened the screen and asked my name.

'Well, Andrea Tanner, come in if you're coming, I don't have all day,' he said. 'You got me out of mass so I suppose I should be grateful.'

I dusted myself off and wiped my shoes and followed him to the dining room, where the table was set with pikelets and strawberry jam and a pot of tea and fine china cups, none of which we had at our house. No one smoked in this house, that was clear right away.

It was not how I'd pictured any of this. The police force, I imagined, was like the army. I expected to be somehow transported to an interview room, like on *Division 4*, where a stern, official-looking man in a blue uniform with shiny gold buttons and a hat and a gun, or else a dark suit and thin tie and pork-pie hat, would sit in front of a typewriter recording my statement. Instead the pyjamas made him look gentle, like a grandfather in a picture book. He pulled out a chair for me then sat himself and yawned extravagantly.

'Tea?' he said, then he poured it without waiting for an answer. He added two teaspoons of sugar and milk, stirred it, and slid it across the tablecloth to me.

'Thank you,' I said.

We were both silent. He picked up his teacup with both hands and sipped from it.

'It can be hard as a young person to know exactly what to say,' he said. 'Whatever's on your mind, just spit it out.'

I sat there glumly. Now that the moment had come, I couldn't find the words.

'I can't help with pencils and rulers and such,' he said. 'You should know that. Schoolkids are forever nicking each other's belongings. Little buggers. And if someone's bashing you at school, your teacher's the best person to chat with. It means they like you, generally. Boys will be boys, that's the fact of the matter.'

I didn't know what else boys could be expected to be.

'Shoplifting is a phase all kids go through. Just don't do it again. Or are you having problems with Tammy? You'd best speak to her mother,' he said. 'Or perhaps you've come about something else. Something more . . . delicate.'

I nodded.

'I see.' He leaned back in his chair and lifted both slippered feet onto the chair at the head of the table, then he clasped his hands behind his neck. 'You know, when I first joined the police force,' he said, 'my job was to visit schools to tell students about Stranger Danger. Do they still have that, Stranger Danger? I had to stand in front of these kids, who were always playing up, little ratbags, and tell them not to take lollies from people they didn't know or get inside cars to look at puppies and so forth. Very important work no doubt, but I couldn't help but think that kids who didn't know that by the time they started school were a little on the dim side, if you take my meaning.'

'I do.' Most kids were thickees, my mother said, but I had no idea why he was telling me this.

'Kids who get themselves into bother have to take some responsibility,' he said.

The tea looked like dirty water, but I didn't think I could ask for a Coke so I held it in my two hands to give them something to do. We never had hot drinks at home.

'I'm not the best person when it comes to things of a private nature,' he said. 'We have lady police officers these days. Lovely girls. If you made an appointment to come down to the station during business hours, I could get one in to chat with you.'

Now I really had no idea what he was talking about. I was at school during business hours.

'Although I think you'll find, and I'm thinking about your best interests here, that letting bygones be bygones is the right idea. Turn the other cheek, as the good book says.'

I didn't know what book he was talking about. I'd certainly never read that in any of my Enid Blytons and I couldn't think of any books better than that. I took a sip of my tea. It was strangely tinny and, despite being liquid, somehow made my mouth drier than before.

'Is it about . . . that kind of thing? Or something else entirely?' he said.

'Something else entirely.'

'Then it's best to get it off your chest,' Mr Monaghan said. 'You haven't touched your pikelets, young lady.'

The jam was dotted with little seeds visible through the glass jar, which had a handwritten label on the front showing it wasn't a proper bought one. My mother always said homemade things were for women with too much time on their hands, or else for poor people who couldn't afford to buy proper things from the supermarket. 'Those stupid bitches spending hours making *Women's Weekly* birthday cakes with swimming pools filled with green jelly when they're eaten in ten minutes by ungrateful kids need their heads read,' she said. The tea was a milky brown and smelled of grass. The lounge, which I could see through a curved doorway, had lace doilies on its arms and here in the dining room, the wallpaper had a repeating pattern in fuzzy gold that I now know to be flocking. I was still frightened, but there was something peaceful about this room. Steve couldn't get me here. I felt I could stay forever.

'Perhaps you should come back when you've sorted yourself out,' he said. 'No harm done.'

My parents always told me how brave I was. I thought of Tippy, the way she jumped out of the boxes without knowing what was in front of her, her sharp focus on what she wanted. She'd raced many times and never caught the bunny once, but she was undaunted. She was pure of heart and never afraid to do the right thing.

'My mother's boyfriend has a gun in his penciller's bag,' I said.

His bushy eyebrows raised. 'A gun? Is that right? How would you know something like that?'

Over the next half-hour, I told him everything: not just the gun, but about Steve's ledgers filled with bets in the bottom of his white bag, and about the extra telephone line in my mother's bedroom. I described the two heavy-set men who'd delivered Steve's belongings, who must have been his muscle, and I described Steve's car and told him the rego, which I'd memorised, and the names I remembered from his ledger. I even confessed to hiding in the wardrobe to look inside the bag, because I guessed there was some kind of rule that allowed for doing the wrong thing to uncover a crime, but I left out the part about breaking the dresser because I thought I might be arrested for that. Once I began it was easier than I expected, sitting in that quiet room in front of the cooling tea. I had never been to confession at that stage of my life but now I understand the peaceful release of handing over all your troubles to someone bigger.

I finished with, 'And he wants to take me somewhere, and I don't know where.'

Mr Monaghan took a long sip of his tea and swished it around in his mouth. 'I see,' he said. 'You're an unusual girl, I'll give you that.'

It was only then I realised that Mr Monaghan hadn't taken any notes. Not only did he not have the typewriter I'd imagined, but there was no cassette recorder, not even paper and pen. He'd only nodded from time to time, and sipped his tea.

'Aren't you going to write this down?' I said.

Mr Monaghan smiled. He wasn't handsome like my father, but he was solid and kind, and I thought Tammy was lucky having someone like him to look after her.

'Don't you worry about that, Andie,' Mr Monaghan said. 'I'll take everything in hand. I promise.'

Chapter 19

Once, back when Sunday drives were a thing, my parents took me to visit people they knew who were once trainers but had now retired. I must have been eight or nine, I guess, an age when being alone with my parents with no races on the radio, no punting, no competition at all for their attention, was heaven.

Unusually, on this particular day my father needed no encouragement to talk. As he drove, he told my mother and me about the complex these people – their name escapes me now – had once owned, which was close to ten acres near Beenleigh with a house for themselves and kennelling for twenty dogs. They had an oval for galloping and a rotary walking machine, the first my father had ever seen, like a huge Hills hoist with dogs tied at the end of each arm by the lead so they could walk themselves in endless circles without any need of human involvement. There was a kitchen bigger than a restaurant's, with a wall of refrigerators and storage for all kinds of supplements and powders, and whelping kennels and a private uphill straight track.

'The kind of place that dreams are made of,' my father said, as he drove. 'Uphill! Think how fit those dogs must of been, training with that kind of resistance. Flat tracks would of been a breeze by comparison. Must of broke their heart to sell.'

After a while I fell asleep along the back seat and woke up only when the car slowed, light dancing on my closed eyelids.

'Andie,' my father said when we stopped. 'Front and centre – we're here.'

I raised my head. I'm not sure what I was expecting to see out of the window. These people had retired, yes, and sold their complex, but their lives and hearts and minds had revolved around greyhounds. They would never be able to give that up, I thought, because training dogs was not just a job that could be retired from. There would be dogs to meet, I was sure, and exciting things to see.

Yet we'd arrived in a flat, dry outer suburb, at a small fibro house with a cement front yard and screen door that slammed in the wind and no dogs at all, not even a Pekingese or a pug, and no equipment or kennels. During our visit, my parents and I sat in a long thin lounge room shaped like a sleep-out. There was a portable television on a card table in one corner of the room but none of the heavy tufted lounge chairs faced that way. They didn't face each other either. Instead, all the chairs faced one long wall, and on this wall were dozens of framed photographs of dogs.

These were mostly the official ones the track gives the owner when your dog wins or places, with a picture snapped at the precise moment she crossed the line in the lower half of the frame and above that, a post-race photo of you and the dog together. The owner's name, and the trainer's, and the dam and sire, the distance and the time, were all printed there, usually on the bottom. Interspersed among these photos were shelves holding shiny silver cups of all sizes that reflected our faces when we examined them, and trophies of dogs, and trophies of men with dogs, and yards of shiny blue and red ribbons hung from nails along the wall like bunting. On the coffee table in front of us were photo albums fat with newspaper clippings big and small: every mention of every one of their dogs, kept under plastic film.

We admired it all, while my parents nursed glasses of beer and I sipped lemonade in an anodised cup and swung my legs until my mother told me to stop. She said little, but my father asked about cod-liver oil and B12 shots and which muscle man was best and whether they used Radox in the dogs' baths or not. (Not. It over-relaxed the muscles and took the dogs days to recover.)

When it seemed my father had run out of questions, I asked one of my own.

'How come you don't have any dogs?' I asked. My parents would approve of this, I knew. They liked it when I joined in on adult conversations.

'She's full of questions,' my father said, laughing.

The woman laughed too. 'We're retired, thank god!'

'But don't you miss them? Don't you want just one, as a pet?'

'Oh love,' the woman said. 'The first thing you've got to learn is this – they're not pets.'

'Best to think of it this way,' the man went on. 'When our lads were teenagers, motorbike races were all the rage. Not for us. It's a sport for young blokes. But greyhounds are like the motorbikes. Or pushbikes, or those little boats that the kids across the road race, what are they called, Gwen? Mirrors.'

That's right, I remember now. Her name was Gwen.

'People like to race all kinds of things,' Gwen said. 'The thing itself isn't important.'

'Kids,' my father said. 'They love dogs.'

'She'll grow out of that soon enough,' the man said.

In the car on the way home, my father shook his head and said, 'That wall. All those wins. A man could die in peace with a career like that.'

As to growing out of my love for animals? Well, it's true that I haven't had a dog of my own for many years. This is because of the life I lead, the hours I keep, the travel. It wouldn't be fair on a dog. It's because I still love dogs too much.

All these years later, at last I understand what my father meant by 'die in peace'. At the moments of my greatest professional successes I've never felt exhilarated, or even happy. Instead my overwhelming feeling has been relief. I haven't squandered my chances and let down any of my mentors, although most of them are long dead now. There's a peculiar calm that descends when the battle is won and we've earned our rest.

From this distance, it's tempting to look back on myself that Sunday morning as being as doomed as Judas in the garden, with the active part of my betrayal over and only the kiss to come. Yet at the same time, it's difficult to describe my relief. The sun was bright and the morning was fresh and clear after yesterday's storms, all the gutters clean, the grass that iridescent shade of post-rain green, fences heavy with bougainvillea and star jasmine, and the jacarandas and poinsettias were both out, which I'm not sure is even botanically possible and might instead be a false memory of nature joining in the celebration of the weight lifted from me. The streets were empty and I pedalled in lazy curves, zooming down the steepest slopes, past the school, feet lifted, hair streaming behind. Handing my troubles over to a grown-up was the right thing to do. I was proud of being independent, but I was still twelve. I felt so relaxed, I was almost sleepy.

At home, my mother's car was missing – she sometimes went to the hot bread kitchen on a Sunday morning for a fresh white loaf, if she'd bought prawns or a cooked mud crab home from the fisho the day before. Steve's car was there, though.

I was too relaxed, that was the problem. The world took too long to come into focus. As I rode down the driveway, I all at once realised Steve was sitting behind the wheel of his car. I pedalled backwards to brake but it was too late. I pulled up in line with the passenger window. Steve looked up from the newspaper he was reading. I knew he'd been waiting for me.

Time stopped for a moment. Then he stretched across the front seat and put his head out of the open window, folding the paper as he spoke. 'Andie, park your bike and get in,' he said. 'You and me are going for a drive.'

I straddled the bike, heart thumping, mind racing. 'Where's Mum?'

He opened the passenger front door. 'Not home. It's better to ask forgiveness than permission, love. Get in.'

I thought fast. 'I can't. I don't have my purse.'

'You won't need it. Come on, stash the bike.' He smacked the side of the door with his palm: *rat a tat tat*. 'I don't have all day.'

'I have to go to the loo.'

'Two minutes then. Quick, or I'll come up and get you.'

His voice was flat and definitive. I considered for a moment turning the bike around and pedalling hard down the hill. He'd be taken by surprise. I could make it across the bridge, maybe, and he couldn't follow in a car.

But he was big and I was small. I dreaded the thought of being picked up by him, being suspended off the ground in the grip of his meaty hands. Besides, I only had a bike, and no money. I could only ride so fast and so far. I'd have to come home some time. And if he told my mother I'd disobeyed him, I'd be in all kinds of trouble.

These are all logical arguments, and not false, but the truth was probably this: I was the kind of child who'd been trained to do what she was told by adults, at least to their faces. I rebelled in the same way I played chess, by strategising and sneaking around and trying to make things happen without any kind of confrontation. That was a habit that took me many decades to break.

So I put the bike away and went upstairs to the loo. I waited, looking at myself in the vanity mirror, praying that my mother would come home. I heard Steve's horn toot once, then twice, so I steeled myself and decided to be brave. I locked the front door behind me, crossed the yard and got into his passenger seat. He was dressed up in nice tan slacks and a blue shirt, and he waited for me to put on my seatbelt then started the engine, resting his hand on the back of my headrest as he swivelled in his seat to reverse out of the drive.

'You were up and at 'em early this morning,' he said.

I nodded. I sat as far away from him as I could, against the passenger door. For some reason, the thought that I held close was this – that one day I would have a boyfriend. I'd always hoped I would, but for some reason now I was certain. And not just someone I kissed occasionally like Darryl Gould – whose hand was damp when I held it, and who once gave me a necklace I later learned he'd stolen from his sister – but a real boyfriend. And once I had a boyfriend, nothing like this would ever happen again. It was exactly as Doreen had told me about husbands and bank accounts – boys enabled difficult things to be possible. They kept all the inconveniences, and worse, of life at bay so we girls could get on with things.

'Not a churchgoer, are you?' Steve said, laughing. 'Because that would be a shock to your mother.'

People sometimes ask why I live in an apartment in the centre of a city instead of a house in the suburbs. 'I'm lazy,' I tell them. 'I see a backyard and I think mowing. I think weeding and watering and raking up leaves.' It's true, as far as it goes. It's also true that I love the energy and the vibrancy of a city, and the hidden nooks and the age and beauty of the buildings, and the style and youth of the people. But the truer answer might be this: I love the anonymity of life there. I love that no one knows me, I love living where I feel small, where the weight of people means that nothing is my particular responsibility.

I also remember the thrill of my twice-a-year childhood visits to town — once to the dentist followed by lunch in the Coles cafeteria with my mother, and then again in December for the compulsory *Peter and the Wolf* concert for children in the City Hall, which was presented as a privilege that would benefit us culturally when, without any prior exposure to classical music or knowledge of instruments, the orchestra seemed boring and screeching to us, and so much less exciting than the real highlight of the day, which was travelling on an actual bus. When I learned, decades later, that *Peter and the Wolf* was only thirty minutes long, I was astonished. If someone had told me it took six hours, I wouldn't have been surprised.

That morning, Steve drove us towards the city. That should have made me happy but I felt sick with panic. Half a dozen times I considered jumping out at the lights and making a run for it. Somehow he'd discovered where I'd been and what I'd said and to whom. I turned every moment of the morning over in my mind. I'd been careful that I hadn't been followed by riding across the pedestrian bridge to Tammy's house, and I'd left no notes, no journal or diary. I'd told no one my intentions. I felt exposed, revealed, as though he could see into my mind. He was taking me somewhere to shoot me, I was sure of it.

'You're quiet this morning.' He hadn't shaved, so his face seemed dark.

I turned to look in the back seat. The white bag wasn't there, but it could be in the boot or he could have taken the gun out. He might have it in his pocket right now. I wished now I'd left a note for my mother to tell her that I loved her, and that I loved my father and Tippy, and I was sorry for telling Larissa I knew where Macavity was and that she could have my purple dress with the spaghetti straps and my poster of Sherbet.

'We didn't tell Mum where we were going,' I said. 'I don't want her to worry.'

'We'll tell her later,' he said. 'Mind if I listen to the radio?'

I shook my head. He switched it on: a replay of a league game at Lang Park, I realised, between the Dolphins and the Tigers. Steve was listening to each play, talking back to the radio with 'Go you good thing!' or 'Put him down, put him down!' just like he'd done to the race caller the first day I'd met him, but this time in a normal speaking voice, not yelling, and seemingly not caring that the game had already been decided.

'Nearly there,' he said, as we drove across the bridge.

Learning my way around the city was one of my projects. Earlier that year I'd bought a map from the newsagents, stuck it to the wall above my dresser and tried to memorise the street names and their positions: the girl streets of Adelaide and Queen and Elizabeth and Charlotte running in one direction; the boys of William, George, Albert and Edward the other. It seemed a sophisticated thing to me, to know the city as well as I knew the streets of Morningside. But on that day, street signs were blurs from the windows of the car and I was so dull with fear that I had no idea where we stopped. All I know is that Steve found a park on the street – such things were possible in those days, before the mall – in front of a tall building. He levered himself out of the car, newspaper under his arm, and came around to open my door, then put his heavy hand on my shoulder and steered me inside a building. We stood in the foyer and waited for a lift.

'In you go,' Steve said, holding the lift doors for me.

When the lift doors opened at the twelfth floor, we turned to the right and walked down a long corridor, passing offices that all looked the same but were different: lawyers, accountants, orthodontists. There were no people anywhere. When Steve stopped at a door at the end of the hall, he stood in front so I couldn't read the sign.

'After you, Miss Tanner,' he said, holding the door open.

Inside was a small reception room that could have been in any office, anywhere. There was a desk with a small silver bell and a desk calendar in a plastic frame, the kind with pages that flipped over every day. There was a limp plant with brown-tipped leaves in one corner and a series of steel-tubed chairs around a coffee table. In the other corner was a magazine stand and a box of shabby-looking toys. On the far side of the desk was another door.

'Terry?' Steve called out.

The inner door opened and a man, Terry, came out. He was drying his hands on a towel.

'This her?' Terry said.

Steve nodded.

Terry was a thin man, taller than Steve, and older. He wore running shorts and sneakers and an old-looking t-shirt with sweat stains under the arms, and he looked nervous to me, darting his eyes around the room, his face pinched and frowning. He opened the door we'd entered and looked out along the corridor in both directions. Then he closed the door and locked it. He didn't acknowledge me at all. Instead he looked at Steve and raised one eyebrow. 'And after this, we're square?'

'As square as can be,' said Steve.

'And that's the end of it?' Terry squeezed the back of his neck with one hand. 'No blokes at my place, no showing up here? Nothing said to the missus? I have kids of my own, you know.'

Steve grinned at Terry, then at me, as though this were all a big joke. 'You're making us feel a little unwelcome, mate. Provided you keep your nose clean, this marks the end of our arrangement.'

Terry nodded. 'Good, fine. Bring her in, I don't have all day. Carol thinks I'm training for a marathon.'

'Go on, Andie.' Steve ushered me forward with his hand in the small of my back.

The inner room looked almost like a dentist's. In the middle was a large chair with a complicated mechanical device beside it. On the other side of room was a smaller desk and chair. There were charts with letters and symbols all around the room and, on top of a cabinet, a huge model of an eyeball. Steve had followed me in; he sat near the desk.

'Don't mind me.' Steve took a folded form guide out of his back pocket.

Terry frowned. 'Okay then. Hop in, young lady,' he said, waving to the chair.

I hesitated.

'Go on, Andie, give it a whirl,' said Steve.

Steve was unlikely to kill me here, I thought, in this office, in front of this nervous man. Also I was curious. What were these machines? What did they do? It was all so *interesting*. I did as they asked. Terry lowered himself onto a small stool on wheels and rolled in front of me. His hands were trembling, and his breath smelled like beer. He still wasn't looking at me. He kept blinking, then looking at the ceiling.

'Let's begin,' he said. 'This won't hurt a bit.'

Chapter 20

I won't go through every test that Terry performed in that deserted office on that quiet Sunday morning so long ago. I can't remember them in any detail anyway. But I've been to many optometrists and eye specialists and surgeons in the years since, as I imagine many of you have, so I suppose it happened like this: Terry first adjusted the chair for my size and then asked me to sit back. At some stage he tilted my head and squeezed drops into my eyes, unless that's a modern thing that I've transposed, then he held up a thin torch while telling me to look up and down, this way and that. He likely swung a heavy metal arm in front of my face and slid lenses into it – my right eye first while covering the other, occasionally swapping the lenses for different ones – while asking me to identify and judge the diminishing symbols and dots and letters of differing colours and sizes and clarity on the wall in front of me.

'Better now, or now?' he said. 'One or two?'

'One,' I answered. Or two, as the case may be.

I expected him to say if I was right or wrong each time. That was the point of answering questions after all – to show a teacher or a parent how hard you'd worked to understand and remember, to have someone say, 'Good girl'. But Terry said nothing. He couldn't. Unlike every other test, this one had no right answer. Or rather it did, but I was the only one who knew it. What if I was wrong? I had to stop myself from asking Terry to go back to the earlier images so I could double-check. And what if Steve, quiet in the corner of the room, saw me make a mistake? The whole thing was unmooring.

Eventually Terry sat back. 'Two shakes,' he said, as he wheeled his stool across the room and made up a heavy and cumbersome pair of glasses with lenses that he chose from a shallow drawer. After some fumbling, he wheeled back and rested them on my face, slipping the temple tips over my ears.

'Now, young lady. What do you think of that?' he said.

Over the course of my life, there have been moments I will never forget, bright as glass in my memory: the unnatural, eerie beauty of giant ice sculptures filled with neon in Harbin; the slow drift of the current past a houseboat lined with coir in Kerala. Others have a more obvious significance and can be seen in retrospect as turning points in the story of my life: a job interview where an overworked doctoral student took an illogical chance on me; meeting a man at a party and falling in love, thus changing the trajectory of everything. Yet before or since, there has never been a moment like this one.

Terry slipping those glasses in front of my eyes was like the moment in *The Wizard of Oz* when the black and white of Kansas becomes glorious technicolour. I could see every letter and symbol on every poster on the wall. I could see buildings through the window, their ledges dotted with pigeons and the white streaks of their poo, and I could see clouds, which were not uniform blobs but three-dimensional, with their own depths and shallows. When I looked down, the fuzzy grey carpet was a chevron pattern of darker grey speckled with cream and above my head, the fluorescent tube hanging from the ceiling by two chains was layered in dust that would have given my mother a fit. Terry's forehead was sweaty and pitted with acne scars. Wiry hair sprouted from his ears.

The world that I had known – that was the normal world. Before that moment sitting in Terry's chair, I had no reason to suspect that my reality was different from anyone else's. Our own narrow life is the only one we know. I laughed out loud from the shock of it.

'What's the verdict, doctor?' said Steve.

Terry was grinning, almost despite himself. 'Well, mate, in technical terms, and I don't want to bamboozle you with science here, the girl's as blind as a bat.'

'I knew it,' said Steve. 'Didn't I tell you, mate? I told you. Andie? What do you reckon?'

Now, of course, none of this seems magical. At home I sat as close to the television as I could, on the hard timber floor instead of the couch; I held every book to my nose. I didn't pay attention in class or notice what was written on the board. Add my general clumsiness, my bruises and scabbed knees and inability to catch a ball before it hit me in the head – sometimes I think I should have realised myself.

But I couldn't have, and even had my parents been less preoccupied with their own troubles, they couldn't have either. It takes fresh eyes and a new perspective to notice something that was obvious all along. Above all, it takes someone willing to look.

'They'll be thick, no getting around that,' Terry said. 'But she doesn't have to wear them all the time. Only when she needs to see something. In class, at the cricket. Driving, definitely.'

'Andie?' Steve said again. 'What do you think?'

I turned my head and looked at him.

He remained a big man, but his cheekbones were more defined than I'd realised and his chin was divided by a long, thin dimple. His face was firm rather than fleshy and loose as I'd thought. His eyes, too, were different. They were hazel, and small, but somehow not lost in the width of his cheeks. They beamed, as though a ray of light was exiting his eyes and entering mine. The cartilage of his left ear was missing a sharp triangle and there was a blurred blue swirl on his left bicep as it peeked out from his sleeve. His name was Steven John Lynch, and he was my mother's boyfriend for a time, and somebody's husband and someone else's father. These things my mother told me later: he was an SP bookie and a former amateur league player for Valleys and an ex-con, and for some years he was one step ahead of his competitors and the law until, one day, he wasn't. In that office, at that moment, my fear of him fell away like mist.

The logical side of me argues this was a straightforward result of my improved eyesight – that Steve, like the carpet in Terry's office, was one more thing in my vicinity that I could now see clearly. Or perhaps the events as I recall them never happened at all. This might be another example of my memory editing things retrospectively, considering how much about my life was about to change because of him.

But this is what I think now: Steve became a different person because he had noticed me in a way that no one else, before or since, ever had. In the act of seeing me, I could also see him.

'She's speechless,' Steve said.

Terry chuckled. 'Not much choice in frames, considering the strength she needs. She can pick them up in a week or so.'

Steve tilted his head to one side. He waited, as though expecting Terry to say something else, then said, 'You can do better than that, I'm sure.' His voice was relaxed, almost lazy yet smooth, with a kind of inevitability.

'That's how long it takes,' Terry said.

Steve folded his form guide, deliberately, precisely, and wedged it in his armpit. Then he stood and walked over to Terry, still on his little rolling stool, and stood close beside him and folded his giant arms.

'Andie's done without for long enough.' He leaned down, as though whispering in Terry's ear, and his voice was a heavy purr. 'I'm sure you can do better than that.'

Terry closed his eyes for a moment. I could see his eyeballs darting beneath his closed lids, calculating.

'I do have a kid's pair here, and they're close but not perfect,' he said. 'Not exact, for her astigmatism and her prescription.'

'Still, better than nothing, right?'

Terry nodded. 'Yes, but mate, they belong to another kid. He's picking them up next week.'

'And I'm sure you'll do an excellent job explaining the delay. She'll take good care of them until hers are ready. Won't you, Andie?'

I told them yes, I would. And I did.

Perfect or not, the world was sharper straight away. Terry had frowned as he adjusted my loaner pair, tightening the arms inward. He warned me not to run in them, or ride my bike, but they seemed secure enough. I remember staring out the car window as Steve drove us home, and the sound of him laughing at my wonder. I remember blushing at pedestrians: compared with the privacy of blurry, indistinguishable faces, seeing the fine details of a person's expression – the signs of their emotions and character – seemed an extraordinary act of intimacy. Stopped in traffic, I saw the reflection of our car in the window of a shop. I could see a girl in the car. It was me, caught unawares.

This is how I look when people meet me, I thought. *I am meeting myself.*

'What's that say?' Steve said, nodding ahead. His big hairy hands, with part of a finger missing, were splayed on top of the steering wheel. He wore a gold ring with a black oval stone on his pinky.

It took a moment to realise he was nodding at the writing on a building through the windscreen. 'Foggit, Jones and Co, Limited,' I read.

A few blocks later: 'And that one?'

'Moreton Rubber Works.'

'Spot on,' he said.

As we left the city, I was struck by how shabby everything became, the peeling paint on houses and unkempt yards. I could differentiate cars by their make and model instead of their colour. Trees had hundreds, thousands, of individual leaves, all of them fractionally different in tone and shape. A Solo can lay in a gutter, glinting gold and yellow. As we waited at a stop sign, a lizard was sunning itself on top of a brick fence, neck arched, and around the next corner, a woman was kneeling on a red cushion on a footpath picking out bindis with a weeder and dropping them into a bucket with a crack down one side. Birds, it turned out, were of different types: pigeons and sparrows and others I didn't know. I saw a lorikeet in a grevillea when we slowed down to turn at the level crossing.

The other astonishing thing was that I could barely remember my actions from the morning. They seemed to have been something I'd imagined, or had read about in a story. I certainly would never have done such a thing.

This strikes me now as evidence of my childishness. Maturity does not rise smoothly like water filling a tank. Instead our coming of age is a jerky, unpredictable process, a wild tide coming in on a ragged beach. First an adult characteristic (say, a certain resilience towards things we cannot change) shows itself, then another one (perhaps a new-found tendency to fulfil our obligations). One or two great forward lunges – then all those gains lost in an instant as we recede back into childhood, into impulsivity and recklessness, into dependence and egocentricity. Some parts of this story mark me as astonishingly mature while other parts reveal me as little better than a baby.

This is the frustrating nature of adolescence. There are few photos of me from my childhood, for which I am grateful. I feel for young people these days, heavy with the evidence of themselves at every age, so easily tricked into believing that growing up is a calm and inevitable process; that we have always been the same person, only smaller. In truth we are many different people over the course of our lives, often unrecognisable to ourselves or others. We are entirely inconsistent. I try not to be too hard on myself.

When we pulled into the driveway at home, I was still laughing and so was Steve. From this angle our house looked happy: the garage door with the spotlights in the far corners were its broad, smiling mouth; my window and my mother's were its eyes, and my holland blind, halfway down, made it appear to be winking. My mother's car was in the driveway. I couldn't wait to tell her everything I could see.

'Prawn sandwiches, hey?' said Steve. 'I could eat the horse and chase the jockey.'

Then I clocked her, my mother, standing in the middle of the front yard with her legs braced and her arms crossed. It's possible she'd heard Steve's car coming from some distance and rushed outside, but she might have been waiting for a long time, a public declaration to make clear the severity of her feelings. I was used to reading my mother's body language. Her arms could bend backwards a little at the elbow like mine, which meant something was building inside her. Her slender fingers likewise stiffened and arched backwards, a sign she was making a decision. Now though, I could clearly see her face. It was tight and swirling, her mouth twisted and her eyes narrowed. My chest began shivering as though it were full of bees.

Steve switched off the engine and waved at her. My mother didn't move. Her face didn't change.

'Oh boy,' he said softly, looking at her. 'I'll handle this.'

We got out of the car. I walked behind Steve up the stone stairs towards her, I could see her hair was damp and her skin was pink from being in the sun. Even from here she smelled of soap. She unfolded her arms and passed her cigarette from hand to hand.

Steve coughed and cleared his throat. 'Hiya, love.'

She threw her half-smoked cigarette on the grass and ground it under her foot. 'Don't you "love" me,' she said. 'Where the bloody hell have you two been?'

'It's quite a story,' Steve said. 'Wait till you hear.'

I stepped out from behind him, but she didn't even glance at me. I'd never noticed before how tight my mother's throat was at times like these, with sinews that jutted like wires. How she squeezed her mouth so hard that little lines threaded outward from her lips so her lipstick looked like blood seeping into her flesh. I wished I couldn't see any of this. It was my first hint that clarity wasn't always a good thing.

'You must think I'm a bloody joke,' she said.

'Of course not,' Steve said.

'You two must have a good life. Mugsy me thought it'd be nice if I made you lunch.'

'Lunch'd be ripper,' Steve said.

'Did I feel like queueing at the hot bread kitchen for you pair? I did not. Serves me right. Won't make that mistake again. You can both eat sand for all I care.'

He opened his mouth, but she continued.

'And, Mister Big Shot, you think I'm going to spend my life sitting around waiting for you?' she said. 'Is that what you think?'

He opened his hands wide towards her. 'Of course not, darl.'

Steve was going about this all wrong, I knew. He was as good as agreeing with her. He was practically apologising. It was fine for me to do that but whatever happened, he shouldn't. My father shouldn't have, either. Both of them would have been better off having a proper fight, telling her that they could go wherever they bloody well liked, and take me if they wanted, and they didn't need her permission. If Steve had stood up to her there'd be more yelling, but it'd be over quicker.

'I get plenty of offers, you know,' she said. 'Down the pub, at the track. Plenty. Every night. If you take off, I could replace you in two minutes.'

Her voice was a deep growl, but loud. There was a movement in the corner of my eye: a curtain twitched in a side window of the Shepherds' house across the road and a pale face appeared. It was Mrs Shepherd, who had two boys a few years older than me. She wore voluminous floral house dresses that were lumpy in the front on account of the assorted hankies she kept in her bra.

My mother saw too. She stalked over to the edge of the yard. 'What are you looking at, you interfering old biddy?' she yelled, even louder now, so that the whole street could hear. 'Turn on the television if you want something to gawk at.'

The curtain twitched again and Mrs Shepherd's face disappeared.

'I didn't think we'd be gone so long, that's all. I shoulda left a note,' Steve said. 'Won't happen again.'

'You'll keep,' she said, as though he were a worm. Then for the first time she looked properly at me. 'What the bloody hell is that on your face?'

'Val, listen, you remember that bloke, Terry? From out Kenmore way? Fancy eye doctor, couldn't stay away from the horses, got himself in a bit of trouble?' He told my mother where we'd been, and the state of my vision. 'Terrible, it was. That's what Terry said.'

'You're a mug and a cretin,' she said. 'Terry woulda said anything to get off the hook.'

'She could see better right away,' Steve said. 'Couldn't you, Andie? And everything's paid for. You don't have to do a thing.'

My mother let out a bark of a laugh. 'You think you're a big hero but you're a bloody idiot,' she said to him. 'Or else there's something wrong with your eyes as well.'

She took a step forward, reached out and grabbed me by the chin, then she tilted my face upward.

I froze. She was not a toucher, she never had been. 'Only lezzos touch other women' is something she used to say if I'd try to hold her hand at the shops or cuddle her on the lounge when I was little.

'Glasses,' my mother said. She jerked my face from side to side, and my chin hurt where she squeezed it. 'I've never heard anything so ridiculous in all my life. Take a good long look at her. Go on.'

From that angle, I could see a dot of an aeroplane high against the blue. I'd never seen a plane mid-flight before. I'd never known anyone who'd flown in one. What could a person see from its windows? Us three standing in the yard, my mother's thumb and forefinger pincering my chin? All of Morningside, or all of Brisbane even, and my father and Tippy, wherever they were? The whole of the earth, curving away into black space?

Steve shrugged. 'What?' he said.

'She's no oil painting as it is,' she said to Steve.

He winced, as though it were him she was talking about. But she wasn't. She was talking about me.

'And glasses,' she continued, 'are only gunna make it worse.' Then she jerked my chin up and stared into my eyes. 'You think you're old enough to go somewhere without my say so? Well, let me tell you, you're not. I brought you into this world.'

That was true. It was fair she had some say in my life, because I was once a part of her. She made me from her own flesh, and I was her creature.

'It was my doing,' said Steve.

She ignored him. 'Go to your room,' she said to me. 'Now.'

I sat beside my bed playing Barbies for the rest of the afternoon. From my bedroom windows, I heard them yelling outside for a while, then I heard the screen door bang. I heard them stomping down the hall to the bedroom. The door slammed. There was more yelling, muffled by the wall. I heard my mother say, 'And who's going to look after her if she doesn't get married? You?' I could hear Steve's voice, but couldn't make out his words. After a while, their voices became softer. Eventually, my mother's bedsprings squeaked. 'Don't even think about it,' I heard her say. Then I heard her laugh.

Of all the things that are impossible to explain all these years later, one of the most startling is this: at twelve, I had no awareness of my physicality or my appearance at all. I had a mirror in my bedroom but can't recall looking in it except to check that nothing was wildly wrong. I lived entirely in my head and was utterly unselfconscious, genuinely, blissful unaware of my place on any hierarchy of attractiveness at school. I didn't consider my looks any more than I did the length of my first toe, other than the knowledge I would never be as pretty as my mother. I'm not sure a twelve-year-old alive could say that now.

So this was the first time I realised I wasn't pretty, that I would never be pretty, that I would never grow to be a woman who was courted or desired or valued for anything other than my character and the things I said or did or made.

My mother could not envisage a way of being – of travelling or owning a house or a business or having children of your own – without a husband. This wasn't because of any deference she had for men, or any belief in their superiority. To the contrary – she often said that men were generally stupid, which made it easier to make them do what you wanted yet have them think it was their idea.

No, my mother simply saw marriage as the best way to work the system, which was stacked against us and always would be. She would never have asked herself if such a system was fair. It would never have occurred to her to try to change it. It was the way things were and that was that. Every woman for herself. She loved me. She was worried that glasses would further narrow my husband pool.

She was right, by and large. The unwanted male attention that plagued my friends through their teens and twenties never happened to me. But at twelve, I had no desire to be thought pretty by anyone. Since I was little, my games with dolls revolved around warrior queens and witches and Amazons. My Ken dolls were always Steve Trevors waiting to be saved by Diana, and in my plans for the future I was alone, surrounded by my dogs, in an empire of my own making. Do young girls today still long for righteous power? The most surprising and electrifying part of growing old was the realisation that my fertile years were a passing aberration. Now that I've stopped bleeding, I feel like myself again.

I came out for a glass of water at about five. The air was cooler now; a change had come through. Through the windows on the western side of the house, which were narrow to protect us from the afternoon heat, I could see a dark cloud of flying foxes heading for the river. My mother's bedroom door was still closed. There was no sign of either her or Steve until the morning.

Chapter 21

Years later, when I was sixteen and in my last year of high school, I disappointed my teachers by deciding not to enrol in medicine. I had no special inclination for it, I told them, and life and my good education had taught me many things, one of which was just because you *could* do something, didn't mean you *should*.

But that wasn't the whole truth. By my mid-teens I had lost much of my decisiveness and confidence, and I allowed myself to be swayed by my mother. She was right, I decided, all those times she said I lacked compassion and was interested only in myself, that even my 'good' deeds were expressions of my own ego. Untrustworthy, a backstabber. And more, that I'm sure you can imagine. 'The likes of you, Andie,' she said often, 'has no business looking after anyone.'

This was, of course, a circular argument. If I truly deserved such a character assessment, then I was the last person likely to heed it.

By then it was clear that I was going to university, but what should I study instead? Anything business- or finance-related held no interest. I had grown up, changed. I was no longer the girl who saw punting as central to her world. I still worked for Doreen at the TAB part-time after school during busy times and on Saturdays, but this is what took me years to realise – the more people gamble, the less pleasure they take from it. The punters who were at the TAB all day had exchanged every cent, their families and their pride for that brief moment of infinite possibility that was like heroin in their veins, until finally their fellow customers and we staff became their only human contact. At that point, if they quit punting they would lose us also. Poor people gamble not as a demonstration of their optimism, but precisely the opposite – because they see no other way to improve their life. Experience has taught them that working harder or longer, if that's even possible with unemployment so high, makes a hard life worse. Economising on food or drink or fags, too, makes a hard life worse. Clever, rich people know this. They use it. Gambling is a sleight of hand that distracts you while a rich person picks your pocket. Now I see gambling for what it is: an insidious and savage business designed to transfer money from the poor to the rich; a feast for the few laid out on other people's bones.

The love of money was the root of all evil — that's what they taught me at high school. Also, I had no incentive to choose a career based on income. I had no interest in clothes or fancy food or cars, and needed so little to live.

Teaching? I was bossy enough already; choosing a career that put me in a position of authority over others seemed like tempting fate. Law? I couldn't see myself arguing with anyone, at least not to their face. A Bachelor of Arts was out of the question. I had no aptitude for art at school, for painting or drawing or sculpture, and had no aesthetic sense of any kind. (No one explained to me that arts didn't mean 'art' in that context — my middle-class teachers also had difficulties imagining a different kind of life.) In the end I enrolled in science, more by elimination than design.

Perhaps psychology would have been a better choice. I might understand my inexplicable state of mind that next day, following the eye test.

I woke at the normal time, dressed and made breakfast. I headed to school like always but, wearing my loaner glasses, was delayed by the sights of this walk I'd done every day for the past seven years: the patterns of curtains in windows and the strange swirls in the bark of trees; the designs made by cracks in cement in driveways and the miniature gardens growing out of gutters on roofs. I made it just as the bell was ringing.

I stashed my port and hurried to my seat, pushing my glasses higher on my nose with my middle finger. Mrs Murphy stared at me. The whole class stared at me.

'Well well, Andie Tanner,' Mrs Murphy said. 'That explains everything.'

I couldn't wait for little lunch. They'd have to notice me, have to speak to me now, because of my new glasses. There was no way they could avoid it. I beamed at Mrs Murphy and at the board. The lesson went on for about half an hour when all at once she stopped in the middle of summarising the first law of logarithms on the board and turned around to face us.

'Anything you'd like to share with us then, Andie?' she said. 'Good news, perhaps? Did you win the Casket? Hava Hearts for everyone, on you, is that it?'

I shook my head.

'Well, you're interrupting my train of thought. Please stop grinning like a chimpanzee every time I say something.'

The class thought this was the funniest thing ever, but I didn't care. I never minded being the centre of attention and besides, I was fine. Better than fine. Nothing that happened in the past had any relevance. Everything had been explained. I was a different person now and I could see everything. It's ironic that this kind of wilful amnesia, this complete denial of the events I had set in motion, had an inverse relationship to my actual vision. If I'd studied psychology, I'd know the name of it.

It wasn't until little lunch that it all came back to me. No one spoke to me when the bell rang, no one looked at me, like usual. I went downstairs and bent over the trough for a drink and when I straightened, a group of kids was standing behind me in a circle. Too close. Normal suburban kids who were my friends at one time, in shorts and skirts, shoed and not, hair wild. Exactly the same as me. I looked at their faces, one by one. Tammy was in the middle. No one was smiling, not even Larissa. They would notice my glasses any second. They would ask me about them, what happened, where I'd gone to get them. I would get to tell them the whole story.

'You'll never guess who came to over our place yesterday,' Tammy announced to her audience.

My first thought was, *Who?* Then it came to me in a rush. It was me.

I was the one who'd gone to Tammy's house yesterday. I'd waited until she left for church, and sat in her dining room and sipped tea and told her father about Steve. Betrayed him, and my mother, and broken the rule about talking to cops. I felt my face become hot. How could I have done that? I looked down, not so much in shame, but to check that I was still in the same body.

None of the other kids seemed in any doubt who Tammy was talking about.

'Hanging around like a bad smell,' said Ross. He was ripping his brown-paper lunch bag into little circles and chewing them.

'Maybe she has a crush on your dad,' Sharon said.

'Gross,' said Sandy.

'I have glasses now,' I said.

'Big whoop,' said Sandy.

'You're not special, Andie,' said Sean.

'She said she knew where Macavity was,' said Larissa. 'That was ages ago, and nothing. She's a bullshit artist.'

She was right, of course. I didn't know where Macavity was. That would come later.

As quick as a snake, Tammy grabbed my forearm. She was strong for her size, and her fingers were sticky and hot. 'What were you saying to my dad? Were you dobbing me in?' she said. 'D'ya want a Chinese burn?'

Dobbing to her father about her shoplifting, Tammy meant. The lip gloss and earrings and bits of rubbish that girls slipped into their pockets at Kmart. I tensed my forearm, but Tammy only gripped tighter.

'Maybe I did tell him everything you've been up to. Maybe he's going to arrest you,' I said. 'Sucked in, dickhead.'

'If you breathed one word,' Tammy said.

'Yeah,' said Darryl.

'Come on. I'll bash your fat head in,' I said. 'All of youse.'

'Oh yeah?' said Tammy.

'Fight, fight, fight!' yelled some of the others.

I wasn't frightened. The realisation of what I was capable of, of the kind of person I was – I felt dangerous, unpredictable. I was not only happy to fight Tammy, I wanted to. I'd fight my mother, my father, anyone. I could feel my hands tightening into fists. I'd always loved tests, the satisfaction of measuring myself against the others. I'd already done much worse than hit another kid and at last I was ready for the fangs and claws of the world. My only concern was my glasses, because I'd promised Terry I'd look after them.

'Come on then.' I pushed my glasses closer at the bridge of my nose. 'Newsflash, Tammy – you're no oil painting as it is. And you'll be a whole lot worse when I finish with you.'

Perhaps she could feel this change in me also. My lack of fear, the way I leaned towards her instead of away. She dropped my arm, leaving white marks on my pink skin where her fingers had pressed hard.

'Who cares about you.' Tammy stepped back into the ring of kids. 'My dad says kids lie all the time. He won't believe you anyway.'

She could be right, I realised. There was no way either of us could know what her father thought, or what he'd do with what I'd told him.

Just then, the bell rang. No one moved, no one spoke. It was as though we were still waiting for something else to happen – for me to hit someone, or someone to hit me.

'Hey, you lot!' yelled a voice above us.

We looked up. Mrs Murphy was leaning over the upstairs railing, looking down.

'What's this, bush week?' she said. 'Get up here, or I'll keep every one of you late, you little buggers.'

When we were finally sitting at our desks, I could still see the dark marks of Tammy's fingertips on my forearm. Inside, I was trembling. I had set something in motion that would change everything; I had betrayed someone who was on my side.

Or perhaps, as Tammy suspected, I had done nothing at all. Perhaps her father hadn't believed me, and what I'd said to him would have no lasting impact at all. All I wanted was for the day to be over – yet at the same time, for it never to be over.

Just after big lunch, I couldn't stand it anymore. I was sick, I told Mrs Murphy. I was going to spew any second. I was the last person to lie about something like that, she knew, so after asking me if someone would be home, she let me go.

As I walked, I had an image in my mind of our street blocked with sirens and flashing lights and all kinds of cops with all kinds of weapons laying siege to our house and of Steve being carried, bleeding, across the yard. My mother, arms cuffed behind her, or weeping and bruised in the yard, beating the cops with her fists. It crossed my mind to go to Tammy's place instead of mine. I could wait for her father and tell him that the kids at school were right, that I was a bullshitter and everything I'd said about Steve was a lie, but that might make things worse. I wanted to be home, but also to walk and walk and keep walking and never arrive because until then, everything was suspended and everything was possible. Until then, the police were there and they weren't, and Steve also. My father might be there too, and Tippy. Oh, Tippy. As long as I kept walking, she could be waiting for me.

But time doesn't work that way. When I reached the top of the hill, I saw there were no cop cars at home, no sirens. There was, however, a familiar ute in the driveway.

I ran flat out, port at my chest, as fast as I could down the hill.

When I got there, it was plain what was happening. The world was running in reverse: the same two burly men who'd brought everything those weeks ago were now loading everything back. Already packed and tied down with ropes was Steve's huge recliner and his weight bench and bars and dumbbells.

My mother was standing in the front yard in her dressing-gown, watching them, smoking furiously. Then she clocked me on the edge of the drive, with my port.

'Fuck this life,' she yelled out, looking straight into my eyes. 'Fuck this entire world and everyone in it. I cannot get a break. I'm the unluckiest bitch in Morningside.'

The men, who I would learn later were Steve's debt collectors, lowered their heads and diverted their gaze. I couldn't find any words to reply. I stood, frozen to the earth by the weight of what I'd done.

My mother tilted her head back to look at the sky. 'I wish I was dead,' she screamed at it.

Then with no warning she jumped down onto the drive and ran around the ute towards me. I stepped back, but her nails dug into my arms. Her dressing-gown fell open and I could see she was naked. My port fell to the ground. She was going to kill me, I thought, right here in the driveway. She knows what I did and she will make me pay for it, and I have only myself to blame. I closed my eyes.

'See this? See what's happening?' She had wild eyes and wild hair, and she spoke in a low, determined growl, as though she was telling me the secret of the universe and lives depended on my hearing her. Perhaps she thought it was later in the day, because she didn't blink that I was home. 'People fuck you over no matter how hard you try. You do the right thing, and what do you get for it? A kick in the bloody teeth.'

The screen door slammed. I opened my eyes as she let me go and turned around. It was Steve. He was on the landing with one of his suitcases in each hand and the white bag across his body.

'Enough of that, Val,' he said. 'Leave the girl alone.'

'Don't you tell me what to do, you arsehole,' my mother said. 'Fuck off and find yourself some ugly slag and spend the rest of your life wishing you were back with me.'

Slowly, breath began to enter and leave my body. *She didn't know*, I realised. She was angry at Steve, not at me. The thought of owning up, of telling her it wasn't his fault, never once entered my head.

'It is what it is, Val,' Steve said. 'No need to make a big song and dance.'

'You stuck-up prick,' she said. 'You think you're so much better than me, but you're not.'

Steve walked to the back of the ute where the two men were finished, hands cupped in front of their bodies as though they were gravediggers waiting for the ceremony to finish. He handed his suitcase to one of them.

'That's it, fellas,' he said. 'Off you go.'

I shook myself free from my mother's grip and followed him.

'Don't.' My back was to my mother, and I dropped my voice to just above a whisper. 'I'm sorry. I'm so sorry.'

'Nothing to be sorry for, love,' he said, and for a moment I thought he was telling the truth, that his leaving the day after I'd dobbed was a coincidence. But he watched the men get in the ute and didn't look at my face and his mouth was tight, and I knew.

'Please.' I took the edge of his shirt between my fingers.

Steve sighed then squatted down to face me.

I'm sorry, I mouthed.

'Listen to me, Andie. I have to go.' He pried my fingers off his shirt. 'It's a hard lesson to learn, sweetheart, but everyone backs the wrong horse sometimes.'

There was nothing I could say, no way of justifying anything. The motivations that seemed so pressing just days ago were ridiculous to me now.

'Please,' I whispered again.

'You dickhead,' my mother roared into the air. 'You think you can treat me this way? Nobody treats me this way. Don't even think about crawling back. Don't you ever show your face around me again, do you hear me?'

He ignored her, as if she hadn't yelled anything. She was inconsequential to him now.

'Andie,' he went on, 'you're one of those people who makes up your own mind and doesn't wait for the world to make decisions for them. That's not your fault. It's just the way you're made.'

I squeezed my eyes tight. 'No,' I said.

'We're not so different, you and I,' he said.

'That's right,' my mother yelled out to him. 'You've got all the time in the world for her.'

The look that passed over his face then only lasted an instant, but in it I could see his depths, which held everything I'd feared. I could see the person he could be when he felt wronged. He was dangerous, and he was also afraid: of himself and what he was capable of doing. For a moment I thought he was going to walk over to my mother and I wouldn't have wanted to be in her shoes.

But that expression passed like a breeze. After that, he seemed very tired, as though the weight of his body was pulling him down to the earth.

'You've got a rough road ahead of you, Andie. Anyone can see that. And, all things considered' – here he nodded in the direction of my mother – 'who knows, you might have done me a favour.' Then he smiled and reached out his hand and touched my shoulder, lightly, for no other reason, I thought, than to make my mother even wilder. 'Tell you what. I'll send you a little helping hand, how about that?'

I could only nod.

'Look after her, Andie,' he said, nodding towards my mother. 'You're all she's got.'

Then the ute backed out of the drive, and Steve got in his car and drove off also. I never saw him again.

After that, my mother went straight to bed for an hour or so. I stayed in my room. Then I heard her door fling open and her footsteps in the hall. She opened the back door. I followed, quietly. Steve had told me to look after her, and I would.

I found her under the house yanking clothes from the laundry chute. She'd turned on all the lights. My clothes and hers were landing on the floor; she was hunting for anything of Steve's. She found a pair of undies and some socks and a white singlet. The singlet she tried to rip. When it wouldn't give way under her hands she tore it with her teeth like an animal, until a great strip peeled away from the middle.

'I want every skerrick belonging to that cunt out of my sight.' She bunched all the clothes together and handed them to me. 'Stick these in the incinerator.'

I did. When I came back inside, she was sitting on the stairs in her underwear, smoking.

'I was too good for him, that's a fact,' she said. 'Wasn't I?'

I nodded.

'I can do better. Way better that that prick.'

She stood, then froze.

'More of his rubbish,' she said.

I followed her gaze to the corner of the garage. One of Steve's smallest dumbbells was there, on the floor. The blokes with the ute had overlooked it, I guessed. In those days, dumbbells weren't covered in a coloured plastic coating. They were iron cast in one piece, dark grey. It was only two kilograms, maybe three. Much too small for a man his size. I don't know why he had it.

'Put that in the bin,' she said to me, pointing at it. Then, 'No. Put it in one of those bags.' She pointed to the pile of sugar bags still on the garage floor, left over from when my father and the dogs lived here. 'I'll see if one of the girls from the pub wants it for her kids.' Then she went back upstairs.

I picked up the bag from the top of the pile. It was no different from any of the others, hessian with stains the colour of iron, thick and coarsely woven. I carried the bag over to where the dumbbell sat. I opened it. I lifted then dropped the dumbbell inside.

It thudded on the cement, but I also heard a tiny 'ping' sound. It was not the sound of a dumbbell against hessian, or against the garage floor. It was the sound of metal on metal.

I already had my hand around the neck of the bag when the sound registered in my brain. I stopped. I knelt and opened the bag and looked inside. At first I couldn't see anything. Then, caught on threads in the bottom seam, I saw something red and shiny, flashing in the fluoro glare. I put my hand inside the bag and unhooked it. It came away easily, and I knew what it was before I brought it out and held it up to the light. I recognised the colour, the shape. It was a disc, and I knew exactly what was engraved on it but still I turned it over in the flat of my palm.

Something acrid and sour rose up in the back of my throat. *Macavity*, it said. And under that was Larissa's phone number.

Chapter 22

There are things that no one tells children, at least not in so many words. If, however, you're even slightly observant – and all children are; their entire reality has been constructed piecemeal from things they've seen and heard – unsaid things float in the air, in inferences and winks, and are absorbed like oxygen.

In the back of my mind I knew that a feed of milk and sugar an hour and a half before a race will slow a greyhound, which is useful if it's the favourite and your money is on a dog with longer odds. Black dogs and brindles, whose patterns can be indistinguishable, were more often ring-ins than anyone suspected – successful city dogs with duplicate papers running against weak competition in country maidens. In smaller meets, a steward might be encouraged to wipe honey inside the box to distract a particular dog before the jump. And I knew that some dodgy blokes made their living by waiting in the ring for a confident owner to splurge on their dog at the very last minute, then jump in ahead of them and take the odds for himself. I'd seen them do it.

All of this was the way of the world, the back and forth of humans clawing each other, winning and losing, as though any of it mattered. None of it addresses the real victims, which were the dogs themselves. Thousands of them dead every year from accidents on the track: necks splintered in the catching pen, or injected by the vet when their legs or hamstrings snapped in collisions or falls or simply due to their desperate, uncontrollable speed. The catch-all euphemism 'broke down' makes the darlings sound like a car waiting by the side of the road for a tow truck and eventual repair instead of what it usually means, which is dead. Thousands more are killed in business decisions because they're poor breeders or too big or too small or merely surplus to requirements. 'Wastage', they call this.

Or the most common reason of all – they were too slow.

And why were they too slow? Insufficient motivation to catch the bunny. The lack of a killer instinct.

But all is not lost. A killer instinct can be developed by letting a dog kill something. Something furry, something with a bit of fight; the frenzy awakens something in them, makes a dog a better chaser. A possum or a rabbit. Or a cat, like the ones that often went missing around where we lived. Cats like Macavity, that my father said were unreliable pets that left home on a whim to find better families.

Ignorance is not only bliss. It is restful sleeps and kinder hearts and closer ties with the people around us. I wish I'd never found that tiny red disc in the bottom of one of my father's sacks. I wish I hadn't known at once what it meant. It wasn't heavy, the disc. It was cheap-looking and tinny, lighter than a coin, far too inconsequential for the object that, looking back, changed me from the person I was to the one I became.

When it fell onto my hand, I didn't scream or even jump to my feet. I couldn't. My thinking seemed to slow and become gluey, and there was a buzzing inside my ears. I was all at once so sleepy it was a struggle to keep my head from nodding. I sat there on the cold garage floor for a long time with Macavity's disc in the palm of my hand. After a while I could feel the skin around my temples tightening and my head begin to throb in time with my heart.

This was something I had never considered. It was the seventies, not the sixties, which my parents said were generally lawless times, when anyone could get away with anything. The days of trainers catching small furry animals that looked like a lure and smelled like prey and declawing them while alive with a pair of pliers so they wouldn't damage the dog in their mad panic before placing them inside a hessian sack – those days were long gone. Surely.

I knew so much less about the world then. Every night, my father tucked me in. It seemed impossible that these two actions were performed by the same person.

When I tried to list in my mind the facts that I knew about my father – I had nothing. When he was my age, did he save every penny for a waffle with ice cream at the Shingle Inn? Or did he dislike the city and never go? Did he love trains and spend hours waiting on embankments for the locomotives coming around the Norman Park bend, or did he play cricket with friends? Who were those friends? What happened to them? The truth is, I knew the same amount about his childhood as he knew about mine.

I knew nothing about his life as an adult, either – how he felt about his parents, or his favourite part of the day, or if there was any place he wanted to visit like Fraser Island or Perth, or if there was a skill he wished he had, like carpentry or fixing old cars. Who was his best man when he married my mother? He didn't watch television or go to the movies or read books or listen to music when he lived with us. He had no favourite actors or sports stars.

I'm not sure how long I sat there before I heard the bath running upstairs. I could see the night unfolding – my mother lying in the green enamel tub in water as hot as she could stand, and me going in occasionally to tempt her to eat something. She would refuse. Instead, she would tell me every terrible thing about Steve that she could think of. Things I did not want to know.

I knew all of my mother's flaws because I saw her every day, because she was the one who stayed. The truth about my father was this: we were never very close. Perhaps that's why I adored him.

I wish I could say that my mother recovered well from the loss of Steve. She got out of bed only to drag herself to work; she barely ate. At first she gave me cash from her purse and I'd ride my bike to the shop for tomatoes, cheese and luncheon meat which we'd eat with SAOs in silence, sitting on her bed. It was fine with me. I wasn't hungry either. When she pulled herself together to do the shopping, she came back with yellow no-name brand tins of boiled potatoes and of stew, and Hawaiian steaks and tins of pineapple, and fatty mince which she fried with Keen's Curry Powder and sultanas and served on toast with sliced bananas.

'This tastes like spew,' she'd say, viciously, as though I'd made it, but she ate it just the same.

I said nothing.

'What's wrong with you lately?' she said.

I didn't know how to answer. I felt caved in. Everything ached. We were both suffering from the same malady, I would come to realise when I had more experience with life and with men – a broken heart.

Soon she stopped giving me lunch money. Instead she dragged herself out of bed to spread Peck's fish paste or Vegemite on white bread, wrap it in greaseproof paper and squash it in my lunchbox with a banana and boiled egg or a few Cheerios.

'If I hear one word . . .' she'd say, standing in the kitchen in her dressing-gown and bare feet, fag dangling from her mouth.

She never did. I ate it anyway. I was never fussy, but since Steve moved out, since I found Macavity's red disc in the hessian bag, I had lost the ability to want for anything.

The house was different without Steve, more so than without my father, who'd lived lightly, on the surface. It was partly the lack of Steve's bulk and his noise and the smell of aftershave when he showered – a heady, woody cloud that floated to the ceiling with the steam. The phone in my mother's bedroom had been disconnected by a bored technician the day after Steve had left, and the lounge room gaped because, recliner gone, no one had moved our furniture back again. I found myself still walking around where it had been as though it were still there, but invisible.

It was around this time that I noticed other strange spaces in the house. Things were going missing. Not all at once, but the Shelley tea service which had sat behind glass above the divider since my parents' wedding, the various oil paintings of gum trees and swaggies, the record player, even the pottery ashtray with the swirling enamel interior, all vanished over a couple of weeks while I was at school. I treated it as one of those 'spot the differences' games designed to test powers of observation and said nothing.

One morning while my mother was taking a plastic bottle of cordial from the freezer for my lunch, I noticed her wedding and engagement rings were no longer on her finger.

'What are you looking at, nosy parker?' she said.

I didn't reply. I had learned my lesson about wanting to solve mysteries.

Then one Saturday afternoon after my shift at the TAB, I was reading a library book in my bedroom when I heard the phone ring in the lounge. I was about to get up to answer it when I heard my mother's door open.

It was a friend of hers, I thought. Or her boss at the pub, phoning to ask where she was.

About twenty minutes later when I went to the kitchen for a glass of water, she was still talking on the phone. When she saw me, she turned her back and held her hand over the receiver.

'A bit of privacy in my own bloody house, is that too much to bloody ask?' she said.

I went back to my bedroom and closed the door.

About an hour later, my door opened and my mother came in. This never happened; if she wanted me, she yelled for me to come to her. She said nothing about the dolls on my floor – not that I was spoilt or that she never had toys as a child or that I was too old to be playing with dolls – but walked straight over to my windows and closed them and then pulled the blind down.

'Go downstairs and check the backdoor is bolted and the louvres are closed and locked,' she said. 'Do it now. No noise.'

She turned on her heel and left. She was in her dressing-gown because lately she never bothered with clothes unless she was leaving the house. Everything about her was different: the movements of her limbs, which were considered and laborious, as though she was moving underwater; the shape of her face, oddly bloated and droopy. It was weeks before I discovered she was attending different doctors under different names to obtain frightening amounts of medication. Before long she began taking pills as soon as the sun set and falling asleep in her food at night. I would have to rouse her in the morning by piling pillows for support and dragging her to sit by her shoulders, tilting her head back and forming her limp fingers around a fag and her lips around a straw in a bottle of Coke.

Now I followed her to the sewing room where she began closing the windows and drawing the curtains.

'Are you deaf as well as stupid?' she said without turning around. 'Do it, I said.'

I did as she asked. In the few weeks since Steve left we hadn't spoken much. At that stage, she didn't know that Steve's leaving was my fault. I never told her, but before long, whispers and gossip would reach her, and she'd be unable to hold back the things she'd always thought about me. That I had ruined her life.

That was yet to come, though. Now, despite or perhaps because of her sadness and my resignation, we never fought. It helped that I had stopped asking after my father, where he was and if I could see him. Since I found the disc, I'd felt the heart go out of me.

When I came back upstairs, the house was dark. Every window was closed and locked. The front door also, which was never closed when we were home.

'No TV. If you must read, use a torch,' she whispered. 'And no noise whatsoever.'

She stared at me as though daring me to question her. I didn't.

We had bread and Vegemite for an early dinner, before the sun set. Just as we were finishing, I heard heavy steps and mumbling approaching the front door. Then someone banged on it, hard.

'Under the table,' my mother said.

We moved the dining chairs silently and both of us sat on the floor with her ashtray between us and our legs crossed.

I wasn't sure why. We weren't any more invisible, with all the doors and windows closed and the curtains drawn. She chain-smoked the whole time, one fag after another. She should have realised the smell of her cigarette would give us away but smokers can't smell themselves, I guess. I looped my arms around my shins and pulled them close; my mother did the same. My knees seemed to fit perfectly into my eye sockets and I wondered if this was how I'd lain before I was born, curled up tight inside my mother, listening to faint noises from the world outside, waiting for something to happen.

There was more banging on the door, then a man's deep voice called out.

'Val,' he said. 'You're making it worse for yourself, love.'

I'll never forget the shape of my mother's face, fleshy and yet at the same time hollow, as though she wasn't wearing her teeth. Even without the men outside, her face was enough to keep me quiet.

'Be smart, Val,' a different man's voice said, and then there were more thumps, as though someone was kicking the screen door. 'You know how these things work as well as we do.'

'We gotta job for you,' the first voice said. 'You'll be out from under in no time.'

The other one laughed. 'No pun intended,' he said.

We huddled beneath the table until well into the night. I don't remember falling asleep but I woke with my head on my mother's lap. Everything was quiet. I had no sense anyone was outside. When I sat up, she climbed out. She stood still for a moment. She seemed surprised. Then slowly, unsteady on her feet, she began to wander around the house, peering inside every room, as though she'd never seen it before.

'Are you looking for something?' I said.

She tilted her head when she heard me, then turned. Her face was soft, but not in the way that meant she was relaxed. Soft, as in without muscle tone, as though the essence of her was gone and all that remained was her flesh. If I'd seen her in the street, I wouldn't have recognised her.

'How did we get this house, your father and me?' she said in a strange, thready voice. 'Do you remember?'

It was as though we were already in the future. I didn't know it then, but those were the kind of questions she would ask me in those last days before I moved her to the hospice, when she couldn't remember who I was or her own name or that she and my father had divorced decades ago.

'I wasn't born then,' I said.

'Oh. Right.' She sighed and ground the cigarette she'd only just lit into the laminate of the kitchen bench. Then she gave a shiver and seemed to come back to herself. 'Those morons can't get it through their thick skulls that you can't get blood from a stone,' she said.

Only two weeks later, I left primary school for the last time. There was no graduation or fuss back in those days. I remember saying goodbye to Mrs Murphy and being shocked when, out of the blue, she hugged me.

'Don't waste yourself, Andie,' she said.

I didn't understand what she meant. Whatever happened with the rest of my life, I would always remain myself. That's what I thought then, at least.

Nothing was resolved between me and the other kids, but by then I was too sad to care. We would either make up, or we wouldn't, and besides, we would all be at high school together in six weeks. I had a feeling that this was a cycle we'd been born into and were unlikely to ever leave. I thought I'd know them forever. It's because of this that I didn't say goodbye to any of them on our last day, which has become one of the regrets of my life. We had known each other when we were all tiny and frightened. I couldn't imagine my life without them. Other than Tammy, I never saw any of them again.

By then, my mother had lost her job at the pub. It had been her habit, it turned out, whenever she closed at night, to borrow money from the till and, with tips from Steve, use the cash to punt on a night meet then use her winnings to put the money back before it was due to be banked. It was a brilliant scheme, provided she was winning. Kids don't think about money – at least I didn't – but it had been some time since we'd lived on a barmaid's wages. My mother had grown accustomed to being rich and when Steve moved out, decided she could do just as well on her own.

She quickly learned she couldn't. Soon there were no winnings to collect yet the till money still needed to be replaced. She found herself in deep, and in a blink was on the tick with another SP bookie for amounts beyond what was possible to repay on her wages. At the beginning of December, the short till was discovered by her boss. She was respected and trusted; he'd come to rely on her. He was prepared to avoid the police if she would only put the money back.

She told him she would, but of course she couldn't. I offered her the money I'd saved, but she said it was nowhere near enough and besides, only the worst kind of bludger would take money from a child. She asked Doreen for shifts at the TAB, but by then word had got around. Doreen turned her down.

'Fucking stuck-up bitch,' my mother said of Doreen one Saturday morning when I was heading to work. 'If I ever see her crossing the street, she better run.'

It wasn't Doreen's fault. At the TAB, large sums of cash changed hands in a rush. The risk was too great – both to the business and to my mother. Doreen still asked after her at the beginning of my shift, as did some of the customers, but I never told my mother this. She wouldn't have appreciated it, I knew.

'Maybe Dad could help,' I said to her once, when she was lying on her bed flicking through a *Women's Weekly*.

'The day I ask your father for anything is the day I slit my own throat,' she said, casually.

'The men who came to the house that time. They had a job for you.'

She laughed. 'On the game, for blokes like that?'

I understood then what kind of work she was talking about.

'No thank you. You don't do that kind of work when you're in debt. Working for someone else, getting the blokes they pick, paying god knows how much to the standover man – that is a recipe for a very bad life.'

'Oh,' I said.

'If you're free and clear though, it's not a bad idea.' She looked me up and down, as though she'd never seen me before. 'Your auntie Rose did that for a few years before she got sick, remember? She loved it. A smart girl could work three or four nights a week after she turns eighteen. Be careful with your clients, quit by the time you're twenty-five with a flat of your own. No mortgage. Set for life.'

'Right,' I said.

'They won't care what you look like,' she said. 'To old blokes, every young girl is beautiful.'

'Right,' I said again.

She went back to flicking through her magazine. 'Just something to think about,' she said.

My mother's eventual arrest the week before Christmas had nothing of the drama I'd imagined for Steve – no guns or sirens. She was glad of it by then, I think. I understand now there'd been a cycle of threats, of her hocking her possessions, which didn't even cover the interest, then the threats returning, then her selling more things. Steve wasn't the only SP bookie with burly debt collectors.

The day that two plain-clothed officers came to the house around 7 am while I was still in my pyjamas, she seemed almost relieved.

Although one was older and the other young, they looked so similar in their suits that they might have been related. The older one had full dark hair and a shaggy moustache; the younger one moved his jaw from side to side when he spoke, as though it clicked. She showed them in, offered them tea – which they declined, which was just as well, because we didn't have any, or any milk either. They were nothing like the cops of my imaginings, and nothing like Tammy's father. They were polite to my mother and kind to me. They recommended a lawyer she could speak to, they waited while we dressed and then offered to drop me at my grandmother's.

'Lots of people get in over their heads, Val,' one said, after they told me to pack a bag for my mother and one for myself. 'Let the courts sort it out, that's your best bet.'

'Everything was stacked against me, that's all,' my mother said as she went through the fridge, checking for perishables. 'Andie, get the carton of fags from my bedside table.'

'You'll be back home before you know it, first offence and a kid,' the other one said, while they checked the doors were locked and the gas was off.

'None of this woulda happened if I hadn't been dumped by my bloke,' my mother said, 'which wasn't my fault at all.'

Then she looked at me, dead in the eyes. *She knows,* I thought, *that I was the reason Steve no longer gave her tips, that she lost her job and got arrested and will end up in prison.*

But the next thing she said was, 'All men are bastards.' And she looked away from me, and the moment passed, and my heart started again.

The cops only laughed. 'Can't argue with you there, love,' said the first one.

'Considering the kind of blokes we deal with every day, you're spot on,' the second one said.

The police were right. We were both back at home by the weekend. Christmas was a strange day that I can barely recall. I spent it at my grandmother's, who roasted a chicken and gave me a plastic blow-up swimming pool and a new white basket for my bike. My mother, on bail, spent hours the following week watching for the mailman. Everything was calmer. The strange men had stopped coming to the door when the police became involved, but the sooner all the paperwork for her bankruptcy went through and it became obvious to everyone she had nothing, the safer we would be.

'Finally. Hoorah for the fucking public service,' she called to me one day in early January when the postie stopped on his bicycle.

When I checked inside the letterbox though, there was a different thick envelope there, addressed to my mother but without a clear window or any government identification.

She opened it. Inside was a handwritten note from someone with the title of Mother Superior welcoming my application, and an invitation for an interview at the convent school on the hill.

Chapter 23

I sometimes wonder how I would have felt if another person suggested – almost commanded – that I send my child to a particular school, one I hadn't planned or budgeted for, and a religious one at that. For my parents at least, the certainty of being told what to do might have been a relief. My father had a new life to think about, and as for my mother – quite aside from the emotional burden and stress and fear – there's an unbelievable amount of paperwork required in declaring bankruptcy, registering for the dole and being arrested and charged with fraud as a clerk or servant. She, usually so obstreperous when told what to do, filled out the school's enrolment forms as though sleepwalking, and organised copies of report cards and letters of recommendation from Mrs Murphy and Mr Swan, the headmaster.

When these letters arrived in the mail, my mother held them in her hand for a long time.

'Get a load of these,' she said eventually, before handing them to me.

I read them, then I read them again. At first I thought there'd been a mistake. It couldn't have been me that they were speaking about.

My mother shook her head. 'It's a wonder you weren't bashed up every day,' she said. She was probably right.

Even though Steve was gone, I returned to my habit of sitting on the floor of her room at night listening to her breathing, and just as well. One night the following year, the next breath I was waiting for didn't come. At first I was taken by surprise. All those months of watching, but I'd never given any thought to what happened next. She gave a throaty gurgle. Without thinking, I jumped up on her bed, sat astride her and slapped her across the face. I'm not sure why. If she'd woken, she would have killed me.

But she didn't wake. She gasped a throttled mouthful of air. I switched on her bedside lamp; her lips had turned inward and were faintly blue. I ran outside and phoned an ambulance, then ran back to her bed, where I jostled and manhandled her for the next ten minutes. She ended up having her stomach pumped but convinced the doctors it was the result of a miscalculation – a tired single mother accidentally taking her prescription medicine twice. They didn't check what she was taking or what else was happening in her life or make any other effort to see how fit she was to care for a child. They let her out after only two days.

But that was in the future. Meanwhile, my mother found a smart lawyer, who she would go on to date for a while. He was an older man with longish grey hair and a single gold earring who never stayed overnight and who I suspected was married, but he worked hard to ensure she kept the house. It was half in my father's name, which helped protect it from her creditors, and property values moved slower in those days, meaning it wouldn't clear much after the sale and would barely help her restitution. Also, the courts looked kindly on single mothers with dependent children. Things had begun to look less dire.

The following week was the interview at the convent school with the Mother Superior. I hadn't given it much thought. It seemed so unlikely, the longest of long shots, and unrelated to my real life and how I was feeling. Yet I was, and still am, task-orientated, and preferred to focus on something. I woke my mother early that morning.

'What?' she said as I dragged her to sitting.

I reminded her of our appointment. It was hard to understand what she said next, she was that groggy. Eventually I understood it to be, 'What a waste of bloody effort.'

'We don't have to go if you don't want to.'

She took a long sip of Coke and used it to swallow two pills from her bedside table. Then she put her teeth in and lit a fag while I sat on the edge of her bed, waiting.

'Certain people who shall remain nameless have put you forward, and we can't be ungrateful. So we're going,' she said. After a while, the caffeine and nicotine and pills kicked in. I helped her stand. She seemed compliant, resigned. She showered and washed her hair; she ironed our best dresses.

Still, I thought she was probably right – it was a waste of time for a lot of reasons. What if the Mother Superior asked about her job? What could she say? We would have to walk all the way there, because her car had been repossessed. What if she was asked where we parked? And what kind of people were nuns anyway? Did they speak normally, or in a kind of old-English like in *Ivanhoe*, which I was reading? I'd never been in a church. What if I was asked questions about religion, or god? I knew nothing about Christianity at all. I didn't even know Jesus's full name. What did the *H* stand for, in *Jesus H Christ*. Was it Harold?

We headed off about ten. My mother trudged beside me, scowling. I knew that every step was an affront to her, who used to zip around in her car faster than anyone. Now and then, she stumbled. She complained that her stockings were sticking to her skin.

'Keep your wits about you,' she said to me when we arrived at the iron gates. 'God-botherers always have their hand out for something.'

Now I realise it was a small school but then it seemed beyond imposing. There were many multi-storeyed brick buildings of varying ages, all of them close together, organically grown over decades. Nothing was fibro or tin. We followed the signs to the administration block; we passed fountains and gardens. There were lots of statues, many of them a woman with her arms at her sides wearing a kind of cloak and cowl, like Batgirl's but sky blue and without the mask. In one, she was standing on a snake. There was a science wing, netball courts and a home-ec building, and other things I wouldn't notice until I started there: a library that made up a whole floor, terraces with views of the river, an art studio, a rowing shed. It was the grandest place I'd ever seen; quiet and empty that day, but like something from a movie.

Inside, a receptionist ushered us to a waiting room. I was worried my mother would say something but she simply sat there, yawning, as though waiting for a bus. Finally we were shown to the Mother Superior's office. In those days of habits and starched veils, it was difficult to tell much about nuns from their plain face and hands. The Mother Superior, whose name was Sister Pudentiana, looked cross. I would learn she always looked that way.

'Mrs Tanner, Andrea. Sorry to have kept you waiting.' She was a bustling, businesslike woman with a tone that always sounded vaguely sarcastic, one of many nuns I would come to know who, had they been male, would have been CEOs or, in the past, Crusaders. 'I hope you haven't been too inconvenienced.'

We sat on old-fashioned carved chairs facing her desk. My mother gripped her handbag on her lap. I was unable to look away from the huge, gruesome crucifix hanging on the wall. I remember feeling confused about that, and about the crosses we saw everywhere, even on a chain around the Mother Superior's neck. Catholics were pro-Jesus, yes? And Jesus died from hanging on a cross? Wasn't having crosses – some of which actually included his dying body, arms stretched out, blood smeared on his side – everywhere a bit . . . insensitive? Like a taunt? I imagined Jesus would hold an anti-cross position, should anyone ask him.

I didn't bring this up, of course. I didn't have the chance anyway. At first, the Mother Superior's questions were all directed at me – my hobbies and interests (reading, riding my bike, movies), my favourite things (dogs and animals in general), and favourite subjects at school (everything). Then we heard about the history of the school since its founding, and of the order of nuns who ran it, and an explanation of their values and the charity projects the girls undertook. (I could only imagine my mother's thoughts, on hearing this. *Absolute mugs, working for nothing*, I guessed.)

'Anytime our girls are in public, they're expected to uphold the reputation of the school,' Sister Pudentiana said.

'That's to be expected, sister,' said my mother casually, as though she'd spent her life chatting with nuns. 'You won't have any problems with Andie.'

There was no way she could act demure or respectful for this long in the face of this much provocation, I thought. Any second now she would swear or say something sacrilegious.

'First semester begins in two weeks, I hope you appreciate,' Sister Pudentiana said. 'And we have a long waiting list, Mrs Tanner, of girls from our feeder schools.'

'I wouldn't doubt it,' my mother said. 'A school like this.'

'And . . . you're not actually a Catholic, are you, Andie?' Sister Pudentiana said.

I looked at my mother.

'Not technically,' my mother said, smoothly. 'She was christened but. We made sure of that. Church of England.'

Sister Pudentiana leaned forward and opened a manila folder on the desk in front of her. 'Andie's grades and references are exceptional. And the recommendation I've received from Father Paul,' – Sister Pudentiana waved a typed letter at us – 'is compelling. I've never read anything like it. He's practically pleading us to take you on. Andie has made quite the impression.'

In my whole life I had never met a priest, much less this one. I had the sudden realisation that this was the helping hand Steve had promised, and that the impressionable Father Paul, like Terry the eye doctor and who knows how many others, had found themselves on the wrong side of Steve's ledger. I refrained from looking at my mother but braced myself for her laughter. She had no patience for lies and treated hypocrites and people she called 'holier-than-thous' with particular disdain.

'Oh yes, good old Father Paul,' my mother said. 'He's always been kind to us. Noticed Andie right away.'

'I'll be frank with you, Mrs Tanner,' the sister said, closing the folder. 'Sometimes priests try to throw their weight around. The older ones usually, but not exclusively. The young ones can be just as bad. They see themselves as . . .' – she shuddered – 'groovy. As though, by virtue of being male, they think I report to them. I do not report to them. I am the head of this school.'

My mother sat motionless in her chair, frowning, as though she didn't understand.

'So you can go back and tell Father Paul that we had a lovely chat,' the sister continued, 'but our enrolments are already finalised.'

That was the end of it, I realised. I stood.

My mother stayed where she was.

'Mrs Tanner?' Sister Pudentiana said.

'Look, I get it, love,' my mother said. 'I'm absolutely jack of men myself. Quite frankly, I think you nuns have the right idea. And there are lots of good kids on your list, no doubt. I wouldn't be asking—'

My mother stopped talking. Her gaze seemed locked on the carpet at her feet, and standing beside her, I saw her mouth turn inwards and her face turn pale. She took a sudden, sharp intake of breath. Her eyes became glassy and she hunched forward, curving her shoulders as though her heart was about to burst.

'He's left us. Andie's father.' She gave a tortured sob and held one hand up to her forehead. 'The truth is, his new girlfriend's already knocked up. We're alone, just me and Andie. Just the two of us.'

A sick feeling opened up inside me when she said that, as though I were plummeting in space. The inside of my mouth turned to acid. My father was having another child. I was no longer his only, no longer special. All my plots and all my plans, all for nothing. He was never coming back to us.

'I'm afraid that's not—' the sister said.

Then I heard a strange sound and turned my head towards my mother. Her face was red and tight, her mouth and eyes squeezed shut. She was crying.

I'd never seen my mother cry. She didn't. She would never. Hers was a face that hid nothing and I'd seen her angry plenty of times, and laughing, and bored, and frustrated. But I watched as she sat in that chair in that nun's office and she sobbed like a child, with her shoulders shaking and her breath coming in wheezing gasps. I stared, horrified, and lay one hand awkwardly on her back; I didn't know what else to do. Sister Pudentiana got up from her chair and perched on her desk facing my mother, a box of tissues in her hand.

'I'm very sorry, Mrs Tanner,' she said.

My mother took two tissues and held them to her eyes. They were soon marked with her mascara. Snot bubbled from her nose. It was as though she was releasing something buried and putrid, something that caused her pain to expel.

'Mum,' I said.

'When you're pregnant, you imagine what your kid's going to be like,' she went on between strangled gasps of air. 'A bit like you, that's what you think. With some of the old man mixed in. But Andie's not like either of us, to tell you the truth.'

'I see,' the nun said.

My mother raised her head and reached out one arm. I froze as she cupped my cheek.

'She's smart,' my mother said. 'I know that. Smarter than me or her father. She's a good girl. And she tries so hard, the way she studies. She's already got a part-time job. What's going to happen to her now? No father. No one to look after either of us.' She looked at me, and I could see she was stricken. 'I want her to have a better life than me, but I'm going to fail her. I know I will.'

'You won't, Mum,' I said.

My mother ignored me and turned to Sister Pudentiana. 'The young girls who work behind the bar . . . they run around with any boy that asks them. Some of them are pregnant at eighteen with no idea of who the father is. I don't want that kind of life for Andie. But what can I do?' She covered her face with both her hands again.

'Mrs Tanner,' she said. 'I'm afraid . . .'

My mother lifted her head and gave one slow blink. 'What's your religion for, exactly?' she said.

There was a horrible pause.

'I beg your pardon?'

'I'm sorry, sister.' My mother sobbed again, and I exhaled. 'Forgive me. I never had a chance, growing up. Andie's my baby, my beautiful baby. I just want to give her a chance.'

We were all silent. I felt useless. Should I hug her? Normally she hated that, so I patted her back again. The stillness in the room was awful: the heavy furniture, the bleeding, looming Christ. After what seemed like forever, Sister Pudentiana spoke.

'All girls have to go to mass, you understand,' she said. 'Not every morning, but often.'

'Do them the world of good,' my mother said. A single tear rolled down her cheek.

'Andie would be the only non-Catholic here. Religion classes are compulsory. As is assembly, where classes take it in turns to present scenes from the Acts.'

My mother nodded. 'She's a fast learner,' she said, as though she knew what the Acts meant. She was still struggling to contain her sobs. I felt my own face growing hot, though whether from worry for my mother or a wish that I could also cry or from shame, I couldn't say.

Sister Pudentiana's mouth was tight and straight, and her eyes were narrow and as dark as her habit. She stood from her perch on the desk and extended another tissue to my mother, who took it with a shaking hand.

'There are practicalities that will need to be resolved, Mrs Tanner,' Sister Pudentiana said. 'But there is always room at the table of the Lord.'

The tears and the sobbing seemed to take the last of my mother's energy. When the interview was over, I had to support her out of the room. She seemed physically smaller, as though she'd left something behind, something that she'd never regain. I was the one who took the papers the receptionist gave us – uniform and book lists, and general requirements, like forms for choosing a language – and tucked them in my mother's handbag, which I carried over my shoulder. The receptionist offered to ring us a cab but my mother whispered that the walk would do her good. I took her arm as went out of the gate.

It wasn't until we were across the road from the school that she shook herself free from me. She stretched both arms above her head and cricked her neck from side to side. She stood taller. Her shoulders dropped, and her eyes regained their usual look. She took her handbag back from me and began hunting through it. She made a noise that I mistook for another sob, but it wasn't. It was a chuckle.

'Don't say I never do anything for you,' she said, grinning as she lit a fag. 'Christ, that was exhausting. I can't be bothered making sandwiches after all that. Tell you what, I'll shout you a pie on the way home.'

And she strode away down the street. For a long moment I watched her back as she walked and even now I remember it so well: me, aware that I was on the edge of a new beginning and knowing that no matter how long I lived, I would never understand the woman who gave birth to me.

Life at home with my mother and her boyfriends was challenging during my teenage years. I think she honestly hated me, at least some of the time. At school, though, I was happy every moment. I was the new girl; one who'd never been to church. A novelty, and often the centre of attention. The nuns and teachers were kind and encouraging, and I made friends I still treasure. The kind of childish fights to which I was accustomed never happened. We were in training to be young ladies, and young ladies did not behave that way. Somehow my father found the money for the fees, and for the uniforms and books, though not for excursions or trips, which I took it upon myself not to mention. Given my mother's bankruptcy and my father's new and undoubtedly expensive growing family, it can't have been easy. He could have just not paid the bill. They could have transferred me to a state school a dozen times.

What had happened with Steve I pieced together from different sources: my mother, mainly, as her understanding evolved over the months to come, and also my father, who was back in touch by Easter, when he was settled in his new life, and told me the gossip that floated around his circles. From what I can gather, by the time I'd picked up my bike from Tammy's front yard and was pedalling my way home, more carefree than I'd been for weeks, Mr Monaghan had picked up the phone.

I don't know for certain that he knew Steve personally. It's probable he made a number of calls, through layers of police, to find him. I don't know if they spoke, or if Mr Monaghan went through whichever officer was Steve's bagman. Either way, the message was clear: Steve was lucky this time, because Mr Monaghan was in on the joke. But next time, Steve might not be so lucky.

Next time, this nosy kid might tell the wrong person – one of the ABC journalists who were sniffing around, or a Labor politician, or one of the few clean cops. Under different circumstances, this brat might have caused Steve a lot of trouble. Perhaps he should play house with someone else's mother.

There's a greyhound . . .

. . . that I see every morning in the park near my flat. She's retired, I guess, or failed in trials or was part of a litter that didn't sell. I don't know the names of her owners, a millennial couple who own an architectural firm, but that's normal for me. People's names are difficult to remember.

The dog is called Magritte. She is black with a splash of white on her throat that extends down to her chest, and the sweetest white toes. She has a variety of outfits for the cold – my favourite is a green-striped onesie – and a Driza-Bone for rain and tiny leather booties in case of broken glass on the footpaths.

'She's a dream in the apartment,' one of her owners (James?) says to me. 'We had little dogs before, but the neighbours complained. They yap.'

I don't doubt it, of either little dogs or neighbours.

'She likes you,' the other owner (Tim?) says.

'You should get one,' James says. 'People think they're scary, but they're really not. Do you know anything about them? Greyhounds?'

'A little,' I say, as I rub my hand over Magritte's soft ear.

I'm not special. Magritte extends her head for pats from anyone as though it is her due, as though the possibility of receiving anything other than affection has never occurred to her. You can't tell the story of someone's life from the outside, neither human nor dog, but it appears she has no experience with cold, or pain, or fear or cruelty. At least, I hope she hasn't.

In 2015, a mass grave of fifty-five greyhounds was found on a property in Bundaberg. Some appeared to have been shot. Others had their skulls caved in. In 2016, hikers not far from Hawks Nest in New South Wales found the bodies of seven greyhounds scattered across a walking track. The dogs showed no serious injuries apart from the fatal ones. Also in 2015, the skeletons of ninety-nine underperforming dogs were found buried near a trial track in the Hunter Valley. Most of these had been shot in the head, or killed with a blunt instrument. I heard about another grave with more dogs in 2017 in Brisbane's south-eastern suburbs that never made the news. From the state of the skulls and evidence at the scene, it was likely the greyhounds were killed with nail guns.

I can see how this happened. At trial, the dogs were too slow. They were useless. The owners were frustrated, losing money. It wasn't worth the effort to even take them home. They weren't worth the vet fee or the cost of a bullet.

There were similar stories about the bush at the bottom of our school when it was bulldozed to make room for those new fancy houses. I knew, because over the years as both my parents aged, they went through brief stages of wanting to unburden themselves, especially my mother as her mind began to go. They gave the truth away in half-murmured asides. By that time it didn't matter anyway. It had been years since my parents had any dogs of their own, and nothing could bring those animals back or make up for the way they were treated.

Macavity was buried there in the bush, with the other cats that ended up in the hessian sacks under our house. Our dogs were there also, all of them, close to a dozen. None of them ever became stud dogs or brood bitches on farms out past Laidley. Even my beautiful Tippy went there, on the very day she disappeared from under our house. The people living in those houses have no idea what lies beneath them. There's no evidence of the dogs at all now. Only humans have proper graves.

By the time I did know where Macavity was, I had no one to tell. I could have gone to Larissa's house, of course. I could track her down even now. I will never do that. I never want Larissa to know the truth. It's bad enough that I do.

When I was a girl and loved nothing in the world so much as greyhounds, the training and racing and breeding of them was big business. We were small-timers, my parents and I. Hobbyists, by comparison. All around the country were massive puppy farms that operated like production lines, some with over a hundred brood bitches and close to a thousand cuddly, pudgy puppies a year. I've heard it said that from every ten thousand puppies whelped there is only one that stands out on the track, that wins consistently over years. I also know trainers rarely agree on the best way to make that single special pup, because breeding greyhounds is an art as much as a science.

Some say that brood bitches should be top performers themselves, and others that their racing record makes no difference if the bloodline is strong; that sires should work at stud in solid bursts because fresh sperm is better, and also that they should be spelled on alternate days because too many goes produce weak offspring. Some breeders believe that the stud dog should complement the bitch in temperament, so an aggressive bitch is best put with a sensitive dog, and vice versa.

Most people agree that there are magical combinations of bitches and studs, that sometimes unimpressive sires and dams with little to otherwise recommend them can consistently produce strong litters, but only with each other. And all that is only considering the breeding itself. Rearing and breaking in and training – each has an equal or greater effect.

But these are only theories. No one really knows how to best achieve strong, fast and smart pups. It's a mystery why some dogs and bitches consistently throw pups that love to race and win, and others, with theoretically better bloodlines or race records, do not. I am the product of parents markedly dissimilar from each other and despite, or because, of my breeding or my training and their best efforts to shape me, I turned out markedly different from both of them.

I never heard the full story behind the collapse of my parents' marriage. My father only mumbled, 'We were kids, Andie, your mother and me, and kids make shithouse decisions.' My mother had myriad answers depending on the weather. Most often she blamed me, because I wasn't a son, because I watched too much television, because I was born at all. Sometimes she blamed my father, but not often. Mostly she blamed my stepmother for stealing him away, because of course the pregnant woman whose clothes I folded on that hot Saturday afternoon would go on to marry my father and have their son Warren, the first of my half-brothers and -sisters. Against all expectations, it is them and their children, my nieces and nephews, that have turned out to be the loves of my life.

The field I ended up working in for close to four decades was protein chemistry, specifically enzymes, and I was fortunate enough to have made my own small contribution to science, to our understanding of life. It was the perfect field for someone who found joy in deciphering how things worked, yet my major wasn't an easy decision. In my undergraduate degree I felt the kind of thrill that other kids felt at a theme park – so many subjects, so little time. I loved microbiology for the thrill of realising there were many worlds embedded in our own, all of them containing forms of life that were not us. I loved zoology also, and in my final year worked on a research project evaluating the soft coral Xenia as a bioassay, observing its delicate, pale pink arms sway in the water of the tanks. I still have that paper, laboriously typed out by me in the middle of the night, the only time free in the university's computer lab, and printed on a dot-matrix.

What has been the purpose of telling my story? Reading this back, it seems I'm looking for a single, defining moment when the world of childhood fell away and I became an adult. It was when my father left perhaps or when I betrayed Steve or when I found that shiny red tag from a small collar that showed how little I understood about people and the world. Or perhaps becoming an adult does not happen in a single moment, and each of these things played a part in my coming of age.

But in reality, both of these theories are meaningless — because I am not grown-up. None of us are. Somewhere inside, buried shallow or deep, we are all still children.

Stop, for just a moment. Listen to your own heart beating and you will feel it. When you were twelve or fourteen or six, a hundred per cent of your life was childhood. Even if you live to well into your nineties, adulthood will never be all of your existence. It cannot be. After your parents are gone, you realise that inside you and everyone you know, everyone you meet, is a child — fallible and wounded, and wrong about so many things.

From where I stand in another century and look back over six decades, I think on my lucky life and those sweet times that will never come again. I remember Christmas beetles, the plain brown and the special lucky iridescent ones, bombarding us on summer nights; fruit from tins and custard from powder and beetroot in everything; dodging bindis in the front lawn; the fragile warmth of a fresh brown egg and the terror of retrieving it from under a cranky Bantam; whole days disappearing in games of canasta and chess and dolls when we had nothing to do and nowhere to be. So confident someone would feed me, wash my clothes, be there when I woke up.

I think of the people, long gone now, who did so much for me. Steve, who introduced me to a new world for reasons of his own that I will never know. I think of my father, who paid for my education and left me people to love, and my mother, alive and full of life, sharp with the world, buying me new dresses, conning a nun to ensure my future. And I think of Tippy, trotting beside me, velvet head against my leg, wide eyes full of trust.

Author's Note

I relied on several books about greyhound training in the 1970s, especially *Care and Training of the Australian Greyhound* by June Whyte, and *Going to the Dogs: A History of Greyhound Racing in New South Wales* by Max Solling and John Tracey, for which I'm grateful. All errors remain my own.

Thanks also to Christine Gordon, Silvia and Chloe Regos, Jane Novak, Ingrid Phillips-Shugg, Carrie Tiffany, and the team at Hachette Australia, especially Rebecca Saunders, Emma Rafferty, Dianne Blacklock, Libby Turner, Louise Stark, Eliza Thompson and Emily Lighezzolo.

And Robert Stanley-Turner, the reason for everything.

No generative artificial intelligence (AI) was used in the writing of this work and the author expressly prohibits the reproduction and storage of this work for the purposes of training generative AI technologies.

This work was written in Naarm, on the unceded land of the Wurundjeri People of the Kulin Nation. I pay my respects to them, and to all First Nations People.

hachette
AUSTRALIA

If you would like to find out more about Hachette Australia, our authors, upcoming events and new releases, you can visit our website or our social media channels:

hachette.com.au

HachetteAustralia

HachetteAus